Readers love
Redeeming Hope
by Shell Taylor

"…this was one of the most uplifting and sweet reads that I've read in quite a while. I highly recommend!"

—Joyfully Jay

"…this story does a really good job of staying in the land of 'possible' and really feeling authentic."

—The Blogger Girls

"I really enjoyed this story. It was so deep and pulled me in. I couldn't put it down."

—Molly Lolly

"A first for me by this author and I think she did a great job with the character development…"

—Scattered Thoughts and Rogue Words

SHELL TAYLOR

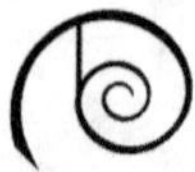

Published by
DREAMSPINNER PRESS

5032 Capital Circle SW, Suite 2, PMB# 279, Tallahassee, FL 32305-7886 USA
www.dreamspinnerpress.com

ISBN: 978-1-63476-743-9
Digital ISBN: 978-1-63476-744-6
Library of Congress Control Number: 2015950522
First Edition December 2015

Printed in the United States of America
∞
This paper meets the requirements of
ANSI/NISO Z39.48-1992 (Permanence of Paper).

To my husband—forever my biggest fan.
And to anyone who's ever felt lost. You're not alone.

ACKNOWLEDGMENTS

SPECIAL THANKS to Adele, Beth, Shelli, Viv, Meredith, and Sue. Your feedback, knowledge, and support are invaluable.

Chapter 1

As THE jurors filed into the courtroom, Adam Lancaster slipped one arm around Kollin's shoulders and gently nudged Elijah Langley to remind his partner he wasn't alone. Elijah leaned into the touch but didn't let go of Kollin's hand to reciprocate.

"Ladies and gentlemen of the jury," the judge began, nodding to the panel. "I am informed that you have reached your verdicts."

"Yes, Your Honor."

"Please hand the verdicts to the clerk, and Mr. Marshall, will you hand the verdicts to me?" The clerk handed the verdicts to the judge, who silently read the small piece of paper and handed it back. "I direct the clerk to read the verdicts."

"We, the jury, find the defendant, John L. Haverty, guilty of child abuse, class E felony offense."

Adam closed his eyes and slowly exhaled. One down. One to go. Beneath his arm, Kollin sank further into himself.

The clerk continued. "We, the jury, find the defendant, Susan S. Haverty, guilty of child abuse, class E felony offense."

Tears sprang to Adam's eyes as Kollin fell forward and buried his head in his arms. Adam gripped Kollin's shoulder and tugged him into a one-armed hug. Elijah didn't let go of Kollin's hand, but he tilted his head back to stare at the ceiling. With a heavy sigh, Elijah closed his eyes while the judge continued.

"I'd like to thank the jury for their service and diligence. Sentencing will be announced at a later date and is dependent upon the defendants' cooperation. Court is adjourned."

Kollin's parents shuffled out the side door without a spare glance in his direction, and the handful of people in the audience filed out the back, murmuring quietly to one another. Kollin didn't stand, so Adam and Elijah remained in their seats, flanking him on each side, protecting him from the worried eyes of their extended family huddled in the corner. Adam's and Elijah's parents, Adam's foster sister, Kirsten, and her husband, Derek, insisted on attending the court reading for moral support. When Kollin started to shake beneath Adam's arm, he wondered if allowing them to come was a mistake.

After several more minutes of silence, Elijah knelt in front of Kollin and Adam. Wrapping an arm around each of them, he huddled them all together.

"I'm so sorry, Kollin. I'm so fucking sorry. I'd spend every last dime I have if it meant ensuring you never had to go through this. I don't want you to ever doubt you're wanted and loved exactly the way you are in my home. It's already our home to me."

Kollin choked out a sob and threw one arm around Elijah to bury his face in Elijah's neck. "I love you," he whispered so quietly Adam barely heard him.

"I love you back, buddy," Elijah said. "Let's go home."

CHAPTER 2

"BULLSHIT, KRIS!"

Kirsten threw down her cards and glared at Adam. "How in the hell are you doing that?"

"I'll never tell," Adam sang, pitching his voice high to mimic Brittany Murphy in *Don't Say a Word.*

"Ahhh, la la la la la." Kirsten plugged her ears. "Stop it. You know that creeps me out."

"I'll never tell." He mimicked the chant again more softly.

Elijah sat back in his chair. "I will never understand how you two lived together."

Pushing himself off the couch where he'd been watching everyone play cards, Kollin said, "I think the real question is how Matthew and Amelia put up with them."

Kirsten scrunched up her face and made a sound closely resembling that of a dying seal. "You guys are so funny. Seriously, though. Adam's the worst Bullshit player ever. Like *ever*, ever in the history of time. How are you kicking my ass right now?"

"I'll—"

"Don't you dare."

Derek collected the cards and peered at Adam through the shaggy blond hair that always seemed to cover his eyes. "She's right. In the six years I've been around you two, I've never once seen you win this game."

"That doesn't mean he can't," Kollin said, leaning against the La-Z-Boy.

"Thank you, Kollin."

Kirsten flumped back against her chair. "I guess the sun really does shine on every dog's ass once in a while."

Elijah eyed Kollin and took the deck of cards from Derek. "Why're you defending him? You're usually the first one to make fun of Adam."

Kollin shrugged. "Y'all are being kinda mean."

Widening his eyes, Elijah pointed at Kollin. "You helped him. Didn't you?"

"Whaaaaat?" Kollin held his hands up and shook his head. "I would never."

Derek flickered his eyes from the couch, where Kollin had been lying, to Kirsten's seat. "You could see her cards."

"Whaaaaat?" Kollin said again.

"Oh, please. Don't even try. You're a horrible liar."

Kollin's face broke into a grin, and he clamped his hand down on Adam's shoulder. "Sorry, man. I tried. Oh, and FYI, I could see your cards in the mirror too, Derek."

"You dirty cheater," Kirsten said.

"You set this up beforehand," Elijah said and pointed at Adam.

"That's just sad, Adam," Derek said. "Involving a minor in your deceit. You're supposed to be a role model."

Unable to control his laughter any longer, Adam threw up his hands. "It feels so good to finally win, I don't even care. My losing streak started long before you came around."

"That's pretty lame," Kollin said.

"Yeah. Well, you didn't have to fold so quickly. All you had to do was deny with a modicum of believability."

"Whatever, *dude*. Can you please tell them why you asked them over so I can go to my room?"

Kirsten grinned at Kollin. "Phone date with Jase?" she asked.

Kollin narrowed his eyes at her slightly, but Adam didn't miss the way his cheeks tinged a darker shade of pink. Jase showed up at HOPE for the first time about three weeks before, and Kollin glommed onto him quickly. They bonded over their mutual love of basketball, but Adam saw the flirtatious glances the boys sent each other when they thought no one was looking. He was one of the few black kids at the center, and Adam hoped Jase's presence was the result of their efforts to reach the entire community, to let them know everyone was welcome.

"No one has phone dates anymore, Kirsten," Kollin said with all the derisiveness a sixteen-year-old boy talking to a stone-aged, out-of-the-times adult could muster. "We text or Snapchat."

Raising one eyebrow, Kirsten spoke primly. "Is that so? I'll be sure to remember for future inquiries."

"Anyway," Adam said, "we wanted to let you guys know I'm officially moving in with Elijah and Kollin—"

Kirsten shot up from the couch and threw her arms around Adam's neck. "Oh my God. You're getting married."

Adam's eyes widened, and Elijah choked on his drink and quickly pounded himself on the chest three times.

"Um, no, Kris. But thanks for that," he said, gently pushing her away.

"Shit. Sorry." Kirsten sat down and covered her face in embarrassment. "But you've basically been living here for two months. I didn't think it required a big announcement."

Having regained his breath, Elijah stepped next to Kollin and Adam. "There is a little more to it—we hope." Elijah cast a sideways glance at Kollin and continued. "Adam probably should've started by telling you that I've contacted my lawyers about formally adopting Kollin. After talking it over between the three of us, Kollin and I decided this was something we felt we needed to do, even though he's almost an adult. We're trying not to get too excited, because a lot could still go wrong—particularly Kollin's biological parents refusing to sign over rights."

Adam could count on one hand the number of times Kirsten was rendered speechless, but there she sat on the couch, hand covering her mouth, several slow tears sliding down her cheeks. She placed her hands in her lap and offered them a watery smile. "Well, that's even better news."

Kirsten stood, hugged Kollin first, and then Elijah, whispering to each of them. Derek followed behind her to offer his congratulations.

"I guess it's time we go home before I weep all over your house," Kirsten said.

Derek hugged Adam and offered a simple "Congrats, man," and then followed his wife to the foyer.

"See you guys later," Kollin said as he jogged up the steps with a wave over his shoulder.

"Thanks for coming tonight. We'll have to do it again sometime soon." Elijah one-arm hugged Derek and bent down to hug Kirsten again. "I have some stuff to do in the office before I turn in, so I'm going to head up. Be safe."

Kirsten turned to Derek. "Can I have a minute?"

"Of course. I'll be in the car."

Adam waited until the door shut behind Derek. "You okay?"

Kirsten nodded. "Are you?"

Adam shoved his hands in his pockets. "'Course I am. This is the best thing for Kollin."

"Well, duh. But what about you? Why aren't you doing this together?"

"Come on, Kris. Elijah and I have been together half a year. Adopting a teenager with me is not even close to being on his radar."

"I doubt adopting a teenager fell on his radar at all a year ago, but life happens, and things change. There's nothing you could say to make me believe Elijah and Kollin wouldn't be 100 percent on board if you wanted to adopt him as well."

Adam sighed. "Even so, it's better for everyone involved if I stay out of it. And Elijah and Kollin agree. We'll set up the legal papers so I become his guardian if something happens to Elijah. But I don't feel the need to do this the same way Elijah does. I'll always love that kid as if he were my own, but this is Elijah's thing with Kollin. This is a healing thing for them that I'm not a part of, and I'm more than okay about it. Besides, I know Kollin's different, but I'd feel weird legally adopting someone I met through the center and guilty I couldn't do it for the next one who comes through and needs a home."

Kirsten stepped forward and wrapped her arms around Adam's waist. "You're right."

Adam rested his chin on her head. "Really? That's it?"

"Yeah. That's it. I get it." She looked up to meet Adam's eyes. "I guess I always assumed if this happened, it would be all of you together. You're so damn selfless.... Are you sure this is what you really want?"

"I promise. I'm excited and happy for both of them. I can't think of two better people who deserve this more."

Kirsten pursed her lips as she pulled away. "Hmmph. I can."

"Yeah, yeah. Trust me on this one. Okay? Now get out of here. It's not nice to keep your man waiting."

"Like you know anything about keeping my man happy."

Adam laughed and then pulled Kirsten back in for a hug. "I love you."

"I love you too, brother."

ADAM'S PHONE rang, jerking him out of the haze of inputting expenditures. He checked the time and saw the "So You Want to Go to College?" course he'd signed up to teach that month had started five minutes before. He'd never remember anything without HOPE's receptionist's constant reminders.

Adam grabbed his desk phone as he locked his computer. "I'm coming now, Chloe. Thanks for the reminder."

"Wait, Adam. You have a call on line one. She wouldn't leave her name and didn't want to leave a message when I told her you were getting ready to step into a meeting. She said she'd call back, but I told her I'd check with you first."

Adam groaned. He didn't want to be late—later—for his class, but he never knew what kind of trouble the person on the other end of the line could be in.

"I'll take it, but can you let the group in the training room know I'll be a few minutes?"

"Of course. She'll be there when I hang up."

A moment later the line clicked over, and the loud background noise of the center disappeared.

"This is Adam. How can I help you?"

Silence followed his greeting, and Adam's heart sank. Calls starting out this way rarely ended well.

"Hello? Are you okay?"

Silence.

"Listen. I'll do whatever I can to help you, but you have to talk to me first. Okay? I promise whatever you tell me right now is strictly confidential."

"Adam?"

The voice sounded scared, or maybe skeptical, and made the hair on the back of his neck stand up.

"Yes. This is Adam. Is there something I can do to help you?"

"Adam… Lancaster?"

Adam's heart sped up and butterflies fluttered around his stomach as his mind searched for the owner of the somewhat familiar voice on the other end of the phone.

"Yes," he all but breathed out. "Who is this?"

"I… I can't believe I actually found you."

The butterflies danced and twisted, threatening to empty everything in his stomach as his mind led him to a door he'd not only closed but locked long ago.

"I never thought I'd hear your voice again," the woman continued.

Slowly shaking his head, Adam fell into his chair and pleaded for his brain to back away from that door.

"Adam? Are you still there?"

Adam squeezed his eyes shut and tightened his grip on the phone as he held it to his chest. The voice on the other end called his name one more time, and Adam could no longer take the sound. He slammed his phone down in the receiver and tried to take a deep breath. But it turned out choppy and short, so he drew another right behind it.

Same result.

He struggled to suck in oxygen, but once again was unable to breathe deeply. So he tried again.

And again.

And again.

True panic crept in. Adam had no control over his body. He was going to pass out.

Calm down.

Breathe slower.

But his lungs wouldn't cooperate. He struggled to remember what he needed to do to pull himself out of a downward spiral, but he hadn't had a panic attack in so many years that everything he knew felt fuzzy and out of reach.

Panic filled every nook and cranny in his body.

Adam could barely inhale before his body forced him to gasp for another breath. Lightheaded and desperate for more oxygen, Adam dropped his head between his knees. Several moments later he was able to take his first deep breath. Closing his eyes, Adam pressed his palm against his chest and began counting, slowing his breathing a little at a time.

A light tap sounded on his door, and the loud squeak of the hinges quickly followed. "Oh my God." Chloe rushed around the desk to kneel at Adam's side. "What happened? Are you okay?"

Adam took another long, slow, deep breath and nodded gently.

"What can I do? Do you need water?"

He shook his head and then rested his forehead on his knee and turned to look at Chloe. "Can you apologize to the kids in the application course and tell them I can't make it today?"

"Of course. Anything else?"

"Umm. I hate to ask, but could you call Elijah for me? I don't think I'll be able to drive for a bit, and I need to go home."

"I'm on it. Don't you move."

"Thanks. And Chloe? Please don't tell the kids why I can't be there." No need for them to worry. Chloe would do enough of that for everyone.

Chloe left, and Adam managed to raise his head enough to lay it on the desk in front of him. True to her word, Chloe returned in less than two minutes with a bottle of water.

"Elijah's on his way. He's likely to break the sound barrier getting here. I didn't know what to say that wouldn't worry him, so I told him you'd explain." She fussed with the pitiful limp throw pillow Adam kept on his couch and then kneeled next to him again. "Want to try moving to the couch?"

Adam accepted her shoulder to lean on, fumbled his way over to the couch, and then took the water she'd opened.

"Thanks. I'll be fine if you need to get back out there."

Chloe sat on the edge of the couch by Adam's feet and patted his leg. "Nope. Julie's covering the desk for me. I'm not leaving you until Elijah's here."

Adam nodded, feeling guilty for keeping Chloe in the dark, but exhaustion from his panic attack kept him from explaining. Adam hadn't heard his mother's voice in almost twenty years, and he knew, without a doubt, he could've gone twenty more without hearing it again.

CHAPTER 3

"FUCK, FUCK, fuck." Elijah swore as he swerved into HOPE's parking lot. Gravel flew up behind his tires, likely scratching his car, but he didn't give a damn. Chloe had refused to give him any details on the phone, insisting he get to the center as quickly as possible. But Elijah's perfectly-healthy-that-morning boyfriend would sooner suffer in silence than actually ask for help, so Elijah anticipated the worst.

The bell above the door jingled as he opened it, but instead of Chloe's normal smiling face, Julie sat behind the welcome desk.

"Where's Adam?"

"Well, hey, Elijah. Nice to see you too."

"Where's Adam? Is he okay?" Elijah repeated, resisting the urge to shake Julie.

"I guess he's in his office. He canceled the college application session. Chloe asked me to sit here for a few while she talked with him."

Elijah mumbled a quiet thanks and strode past the front desk to open Adam's door. He found Adam lying on the couch, hands crossed over his chest and eyes closed. His face, drained of all color, looked haggard and worn.

Perched next to Adam, Chloe patted his leg, and he slowly opened his eyes. "Elijah's here. Let me know if you need anything." She shot a pointed glare at Elijah. "Either of you."

With a squeeze of Elijah's shoulder, Chloe left the room and quietly closed the door behind her. Elijah grabbed Adam's desk chair and wheeled it next to the couch.

"Are you okay?" he asked, resting his elbows on his knees.

Adam nodded.

"Do you need anything?"

Adam shook his head.

"Do I need to call the doctor?"

Adam hesitated and shook his head again.

"Can you look at me?"

Watery eyes met his.

"You promise me you're okay?"

A single tear slid down the side of Adam's face, and he shook his head one last time. "But no doctor, for now. Just take me home?"

Thirty minutes later Elijah settled Adam into their La-Z-Boy. His cheeks had already regained a little color, and his eyes weren't quite so terrified, but he still appeared exhausted.

"Want a drink, man?" Kollin asked as he fretted from the entryway to the kitchen.

"No, thanks."

From the crease in his brow to the way he gnawed on his lip, concern was etched all over Kollin's face. Elijah couldn't blame him. Adam epitomized calm, cool, and collected through nearly every situation he encountered. The only thing that ever seemed to ruffle his feathers was… well, Elijah. Adam would work himself to the bone to help someone, but he never freaked out. And he'd never even come close to having a panic attack.

"Need anything, Eli?"

"No. Thank you. Why don't you find something to order for dinner tonight? Your choice, as long as they deliver."

"Kollin?" Adam called, surprising both of them. "Come back when you're done, and I'll fill you in before you two worry yourselves to death."

Elijah breathed a sigh of relief and smiled at Kollin. If Adam had enough clarity to be worried about their well-being, he'd be fine. He sat on the couch closest to Adam and grabbed Adam's hand.

"I'm sorry I worried you guys so much," Adam said softly. "I'm a little embarrassed right now. I think I overreacted."

Elijah shrugged and shook his head. He had no idea what to say. He'd been with Adam almost six months, but he was still just learning how to love. Adam carried most of the weight when it came to the couple stuff. He knew instinctively what Elijah needed after a bad day—when to push and when to let something go. Elijah coasted along in their relationship, allowing Adam to do all the heavy lifting, never realizing how effortless Adam made their life.

Kollin returned to the living room and plopped down next to Elijah. "I ordered a couple of pizzas. They should be here in thirty. So what's up with you?"

Elijah held back a grimace and made a mental note to give Kollin a lesson in tact.

"Like I told Elijah, I think I overreacted. The call came from so far out of left field, I never saw it coming."

"Saw what coming?" Kollin asked.

Adam met Elijah's gaze head-on for a moment—long enough for Elijah to see the panic had returned—and turned to Kollin. "My birth mom called me today."

Whatever words Elijah expected to come out of Adam's mouth, those were dead last on his list. He knew a little about Adam's childhood, but not much more than the basic story Adam shared the night they first met. It seemed obvious Adam never expected to hear from his parents again.

"Holy shit, Adam," Kollin said. "After everything she did to you? What'd she want?"

Guilt washed over Elijah as he realized Kollin knew more about Adam's history than he did. Frowning, he recalled Kirsten's suggestion that Elijah ask Adam about his past.

Six months before.

Shit. It wasn't like Elijah didn't *want* to know, but he never found a good time to ask. Ensuring Kollin coped with everyday life, stressing over Kollin's parents' trial, and the constant renovations at both of HOPE's locales always seemed more important. And when they weren't dealing with those problems, Elijah selfishly enjoyed the few peaceful moments they managed to scrounge up.

"I'm not sure. Like I said, I overreacted and hung up on her once I recognized her voice. Then I kind of.... I don't know. I thought she was out of my life for good, and hearing her again.... I started hyperventilating."

"I'm sorry," Elijah murmured, helplessly squeezing Adam's hand.

Kollin sat forward on the couch. "What're you going to do if she calls back? If she knows you work at the center, she probably knows about us too."

Adam shook his head. "I don't know. I guess I'll hear what she has to say. I have no idea why she'd reach out to me now."

"Why would you even want to know?" Kollin's voice sounded harsh.

Adam closed his eyes and sighed. "I don't know if I do, kiddo."

Kollin fell silent, and they dropped the entire conversation. All three of them remained uncharacteristically quiet throughout dinner, and for once Kollin went to bed early. Later when Elijah stripped down to his boxers and crawled under the covers of their king-size bed, uncertainty and nervousness coursed through him—two feelings he rarely experienced with Adam. The fact that his emotions mirrored Adam's heightened his anxiety tenfold. One of them had to get a grip.

Hesitantly he slipped his hand beneath the sheet and searched for Adam's. Then he linked their fingers together. Adam looked at Elijah, and though he acted surprised to see him, he still offered a tired smile. "Sorry. I was somewhere else, I guess."

Elijah nodded. "Want to talk about it?"

"No." Adam sighed. "But I guess I should."

Scooting closer to Adam, Elijah wedged one arm between Adam and the headboard. He pulled him over so he rested against Elijah's chest.

"I don't think I'll ever feel worse about anything else in my life, but I don't even know what happened between you and your birth parents. We've talked ad infinitum about your time with the Wrights, but I don't know about your beginnings or any of your time with foster families aside from a stray story or two."

Adam shrugged. "It never came up."

"I should've made sure it came up. I'm sorry for that. To never ask was incredibly selfish of me."

"Don't beat yourself up. It's not like we had a normal start to our relationship. We've both been focused on Kollin, and I wouldn't change that for the world."

"Would you tell me now?"

"Like *now* now?"

Elijah shrugged. "If you want."

Adam twisted to face Elijah. "My past… is difficult. I don't hide it from anyone at the center. Most of the kids know what I went through, but they don't know the details. I've learned to keep those close. Though I experienced and did things I'm in no way proud of, I can't be ashamed because they helped shape me into who I am today. I learned early on it's harder for others to hear and accept than it is for me to speak about."

Clenching his jaw, Elijah felt the back of his eyes tingle as he fought back tears. What the hell had happened to Adam? "I won't force you to tell me, but please know nothing you tell me would change how I feel about you."

"How about we start with just my parents tonight? It'll take forever to tell the whole story, and I'm pretty wiped."

"Whatever you want. If you're not feeling up to it, we can do it another time. I couldn't let another night go by without you knowing how much I care."

"I never thought you didn't," Adam whispered and leaned forward to kiss Elijah's lips lightly. Then he settled back into his embrace. "My dad was somewhat of a deadbeat. He wasn't the worst dad in the world. He never hit me or talked down to me or anything. He mostly went to work and kept to himself. I always thought he loved me, but now I think I only felt his love because I understood fathers are supposed to love their sons. Not because of any affection or action he ever showed me. My mom worked a lot, but when she was home, she helped me with homework and asked about my day and let me watch TV with her.

"I was one of those kids who knew early on I liked other boys. I never questioned it… never even thought much about it. I had plenty of other friends who didn't like girls, but it wasn't until I turned nine or so that I realized the other boys in my class didn't like girls in an 'I want to pull your hair and trip you on the playground' kind of way—the way I liked other boys. You know how everyone is around that age. People started asking if I had a girlfriend yet and which girls I thought were cute. One day I asked mom why no one ever asked if I had a boyfriend, because I liked boys better than girls."

Elijah closed his eyes and held his breath.

Adam chuckled. "She laughed me off and said that would all change one day, and soon I'd want to kiss girls. When I insisted if I kissed anyone, I wanted it to be a boy, she kind of shut down. She sent me to my room, and the next thing I know, my dad is standing over me, yelling about having a faggot for a son."

"What the hell? You were only nine."

Adam leaned his head into his chest and wished that was the worst part of his story. "He terrified me that night. It was the most he'd ever talked to me in one sitting, but I'd never heard the word 'faggot,' so I didn't really get it. I ended up asking my music teacher at school the next day. I'd started taking piano lessons that year through a free program the school offered. I wasn't half-bad, and I still remember how much the teacher seemed to really enjoy teaching us. I don't remember anything else about him. Not even his name."

Elijah tightened his arms around Adam.

"Anyway, I asked but I didn't tell him I heard it from my parents, and he laid it out there for me. Told me what faggot meant, and then he told me if I liked boys instead of girls or if I liked boys and girls, not to worry. I was perfectly normal. He told me to never let anyone get me down because the world is full of ignorant people who are scared of anything and anyone different from them. And then, as if my being a faggot was no big deal, he went right back to our music lesson. He acted so damn nonchalant about it, I thought I'd misunderstood my parents' reaction and everything would be fine. Later on, when things got really bad, I held on to his words like a lifeline. He helped save me.

"Of course, being a nine-year-old boy who assumed his parents loved him unconditionally, I went home and told my mom I was definitely a faggot. No doubt about it. The next weekend Mom packed up my stuff and dropped me off at her parents' house. I didn't understand why at the time. No explanation given. I missed my mom and dad, but whenever I asked about seeing them, my grandma said they couldn't take care of me anymore. After a while I stopped asking. Truthfully I loved living with my grandparents, so even though I felt a little guilty about it, I didn't want to go back home.

"My grandma died a year later—heart attack—and boom, only me and Gramps left. We did pretty good on our own for a while. He missed Grandma something fierce. I could see it plain as day, but he covered it up so I wouldn't be too sad. He always had a smile for me and always showed interest in whatever I had to say. He kept a model train village in the basement of his house. It ran from one side of the basement to the other. We'd spend hours down there, pretending we were touring the country together. But then one day, out of the blue, he had several ministrokes and ended up in the hospital. I stayed with his neighbor while he was in the hospital. After a couple of weeks, it was clear he would never fully recover, so he went into assisted living. I was devastated.

"The thought of leaving Gramps wrecked me, but I foolishly assumed my parents would take me back and thought maybe it would be different this time. I'd gotten better at taking care of myself and wouldn't be such a pest. But Mom never came to pick me up. The neighbor took me to a group home and dropped me off. She gave the woman in charge Gramps's information and told her they were trying to locate my parents. No one ever showed up for me. Gramps never got better, and I guess my parents just didn't give a damn. I haven't seen her since."

A single tear slipped down Elijah's cheek. When Kollin's parents kicked him out, Elijah questioned how anyone could abandon their own child. But at least Kollin was older, more experienced, and better prepared for life's harsh realities. Adam was just a kid who assumed his parents loved him, because that's the way the world was supposed to work. Elijah felt as though his heart had ripped in two.

"The worst part about all of it… I can't ever thank my grandparents for taking me. For nearly two years, while I lived with them, I got to be myself and not hide any part of me. I didn't have to worry about what they would say or do if I slipped up, and I learned what true, unconditional love felt like. I looked my grandfather up a few years ago and found out he's in a nursing home. He eventually developed dementia, which turned into full-blown Alzheimer's. I assume my mother eventually started coming around again because the nurse I spoke with said visitors who weren't on the approved list wouldn't be allowed in the building. I know he wouldn't have known me, but it felt like the final twist of the knife in my heart when I found out I couldn't even speak with him on the phone."

"I'm sure he knew how you felt," Elijah whispered.

"I hope so." Adam snuggled deeper into the covers, and Elijah followed until they lay flat on the bed. "That's pretty much it concerning my parents, and most of that is all stuff everyone knows. At one time the moment with my music teacher felt too personal to share. But he deserves to be honored and have his story told, even if I can't remember his name."

"Maybe I can help you find him one day."

Adam peered at Elijah. "Yeah?"

"Yeah."

"Thank you for asking," Adam said through his yawn.

Elijah hummed as he pictured a wide-eyed ten-year-old Adam watching a toy train travel across the tracks. Then he saw him a bit older, standing outside a nameless group home, wondering if his mother would ever come for him. He tightened his arms around Adam and kissed the top of his head. Sleep evaded him for hours.

CHAPTER 4

ADAM'S PHONE rang, and he eyed the thing with a sigh. After his birth mother called, he'd fallen into a funk and had yet to snap out of it. More than anything he wished he'd been cognizant enough to find out what she wanted before freaking the fuck out. After a week of silence from her, Adam assumed he'd scared her off for good. In a fit of rage or terror or Adam didn't know the hell what, he'd deleted her number from HOPE's caller ID. He no longer had any way of contacting her, even if he wasn't entirely sure he wanted to.

With a loud sigh, he picked up the phone. "This is Adam."

"Hey. We're getting ready to leave. Are you sure you don't want to go?" Adam could almost hear Kollin's grin.

"Are you calling me from the parking lot?"

"Yeah, I didn't feel like walking back inside. So you coming? Eli's being a little weird about the trip. I think he's legit scared of ghosts."

Every year around Halloween, Kirsten took a small group of kids to Asheville for the walking tour of the city's most famous haunted spots. She had an abnormal obsession with ghosts and funded the entire trip, but this year she and Derek planned to stay overnight to participate in the Ghost Hunt of the Asheville Masonic Temple. Adam couldn't think of a time he'd ever seen her so geeked out over something.

Originally Adam agreed to drive the van back to Cary after the Ghost Tour, but he'd begged Elijah to take over for him. He couldn't stand the thought of walking around in the cold, surrounded by all those people and pretending everything in his world was peachy keen. Not to mention the six-hour van ride sounded like pure torture.

Elijah agreed on the condition that Adam talk to one of HOPE's therapists. Even though Adam accepted the stipulation without hesitation, he had yet to make an appointment with Dr. Maggie. He also hadn't told Kirsten or the Wrights about Jessica's call yet. He'd probably feel better once he did, but he didn't *want* to snap out of his bad mood.

"I'll go if Elijah needs me," Adam said.

"Nah, I'm just teasing him. I better go. He's giving me the stink-eye. You'll be missed."

Adam laughed. "I doubt anyone will even notice I'm not there. Have fun and be safe. And can you let Elijah know I'm going to stay at my house tonight, since you guys won't be back until late?"

"Sure thing. See you later."

Adam hung up and rubbed his tired eyes. The center should be relatively quiet the rest of the night, with most of their regulars heading to Asheville. Since opening Home for Hope, the inn they'd purchased and renovated to function as a safe home for LGBT youth, The Center for HOPE no longer remained open all night. No other activities were scheduled for the day, and he expected his evening volunteer to arrive any minute.

As soon as Justin arrived to cover the front desk, Adam drove straight to the nearest Trader Joe's and bought three flavors of Ben & Jerry's. Then he grabbed a tub of Fluff for good measure.

He smiled as he pulled into the driveway of his old house. He hadn't been home in about three weeks. In fact, he already thought of Elijah's house as his home too, but his old place would always be special to him. It was the first house he'd ever purchased, and he sort of hated to sell it, but he didn't want it to go to ruin either. When he opened the front door, he shivered as the chill greeted him. Although the weather had been warmer that day than the past week or so, the inside of Adam's house hadn't gotten the memo.

He'd already turned off the Internet and phone service, but he was smart enough to leave the electricity on, so he turned the thermostat up to a toasty seventy degrees, stashed two cartons of ice cream in the freezer, and plopped down on the couch. Having never been one to watch much television, Adam only used an antenna to pick up local channels, so he flipped through the ten or so different stations as he stuffed his face with the world's best ice cream.

An hour later he'd tried all three flavors—with and without the extra Fluff—and thought he might puke if he ate one more bite. He walked around his house, mentally cataloguing what would go to his new home and looking at the different knickknacks displayed on his walls and shelves. A lot of it came from Kirsten, Matthew, and Amelia, but he'd kept every picture, postcard, homemade craft, and cheesy Christmas gift given to him by the kids at HOPE too.

Adam rummaged around his bedroom until he found a memory book he'd gotten two years before from one of the youth at HOPE, right before her family moved to California. He sat on his bed to look through it and smiled wistfully at the thought of the young girl who gave it to him. Kelsey would always be one of Adam's favorites. Her gentle spirit was far more resilient than Adam's and her capacity for love endless. He was sad to see her leave, and no one had touched him in quite the same way until Kollin came along.

If he didn't have the best job in the entire world, he didn't know who did. As difficult as it was to see his kids suffer, to see them get hurt over and over again by friends, by family, by strangers, it was inspiring to see them bounce right back. Each of the broken youth who walked through his door managed to teach him a thing or two.

Tears streaked down Adam's face as he lay back on his bed, clutching Kelsey's memory book to his chest. He let them fall and then curled up in a ball and ugly cried for all of the youth he couldn't help. He cried for their parents, who would never know how amazing their children were because they refused to look past what made them different, and he cried for their brothers and sisters, who might never understand why their sibling couldn't come home anymore.

Then he cried for himself—for the little boy who said good-bye to his parents too soon. For the boy who learned the hard way it wasn't always okay to be yourself. For the teenager whose heart turned cold and bitter after years of being mistreated. For the teen who turned to violence to deal with all of his pent-up rage, and finally for the young man who picked himself up, dusted himself off, and got the help he needed to live again.

That was the man he wanted to be. That was the man Elijah Langley loved and the one he deserved. That was all Adam ever needed to be.

His tears subsided slowly, and he even laughed at his theatrics. But he felt as if he'd rid himself of the dark shadow of doubt and grief that had taken up residence in his heart over the past week. Cried it right out. He considered sending Elijah a text, but before he could, he fell fast asleep, still clutching the memory book to his chest.

KOLLIN PROPPED his foot up on the dashboard of the eight-passenger van as Eli maneuvered into the light Durham traffic. He'd volunteered to ride up front with Eli to help keep him awake during the last leg of the trip. Kollin had talked Jase into going on the trip and felt guilty for abandoning him on the way back. They had a blast on the tour, but Jase passed out almost immediately against the window of the van with his jacket shoved beneath his cheek. His long, dark ringlets lay in disarray against his makeshift pillow, and his mouth hung slightly open. Kollin grinned when he saw Jase twitch in his sleep.

He'd just had his first date—and a successful one at that. He could still feel Jase's fingers threading through his when Kollin finally grew a pair and grabbed his hand. Jase had squeezed his fingers and smiled shyly at Kollin.

Handholding equaled date. Right?

"What has you smiling?" Eli asked quietly. "Or should I say who?"

"Shut. Up," Kollin answered, struggling to stifle his smile. The day before he'd done the one thing he swore he'd never ever do, and asked Eli for dating advice. Obviously he went to Adam first, but Adam vaguely shook his head and told him to ask someone else. Shocked, Kollin tried to remember a time Adam had ever turned him down—but he'd also been in a piss-ass mood ever since his mom called. Who the hell knew how long *that* would last? Patience didn't exactly rank high on Kollin's list of virtues. And since he felt like the only person at the center who'd barely even had a first kiss, he caved and asked Eli, who simply told him to man up and make a move.

"It's easy," he'd said.

Yeah, right. The damn butterflies in Kollin's stomach would've argued otherwise, but he did it, and he had to admit he owed Eli a little credit.

Eli nudged Kollin's elbow. "Looked like things were cozy between you two tonight."

"Oh my gosh. Will you shut up? You're going to wake him."

"Yeah, right. He's out like a light. Are you two going steady? Do they still call it going steady?"

Kollin buried his head in his hands and held back a laugh. "You're so old. No. They don't call it that. We're only hanging out. Okay? Can we drop it now?"

"Sure thing, buddy," Eli said, laughing. "What do you want to talk about? You're supposed to be keeping me awake."

Kollin stared out the window of the van as he picked at a stray thread on his jeans. "You think Adam's okay?"

Though subtle, Kollin saw Eli's entire body tense. No one had brought up Adam's birth mom since he told them about her call last week, but it seemed pretty obvious it remained on everyone's mind.

"I think he will be," Eli said. "He's got to be the most emotionally mature person I know. It's pretty clear he's struggling right now, but I think he'll work it out in his own time."

"It's weird. When he's at the center, it's like nothing's wrong. He's the same old Adam. But at home… I can tell he's a million miles away. I always feel like I'm bothering him when I talk to him."

Eli shook his head. "You don't bother him. Ever. If he knew that's what you thought, I'm sure he'd agree."

"Yeah. But I don't want him to be fake around me or anything. I know y'all still think of me as a kid, but I'm not as young as Adam was when his parents gave him up. I can handle shit if I need to. I'm lucky I never went into the system like Adam, but I thought we had a special connection, with our equally shitty parents and all. I swear, sometimes watching TV with him is more therapeutic than a year's worth of sessions with Dr. Will, simply because I'm with someone who knows what it's like to feel so unloved."

Eli laid a hand on Kollin's knee and squeezed. "Sometimes I think Adam is so strong we forget he's human too. He loves you, though, and I have no doubt he'll get through this."

"Yeah. I guess you're right." Kollin returned to staring out the window. "But I hope it happens sooner rather than later."

QUIET CLICKING slowly lulled Elijah out of sleep. He rolled over and cracked his eyes open to see Adam sitting at the desk in their bedroom, typing on his laptop.

"Hey," Elijah said, his voice raspy with sleep.

Adam turned, and for the first time in a week, Elijah saw him offer a genuine smile. "Morning. Did I wake you?"

"Little bit, but it's okay. I missed you last night. Here and on the trip."

Adam walked to the bed, toed off his shoes, and climbed in. "I know. I'm sorry, but I definitely needed the time alone last night. I don't know why or how, but somewhere between Chunky Monkey and The

Tonight Dough, something clicked, and all the weight bearing down on my shoulders, dragging me through the mud, fell away."

Elijah scooted over and rested his head on Adam's stomach. "I'm glad to hear that. I've been worried about you. So has Kollin."

"I didn't mean to."

Elijah shrugged off his apology. "So what clicked, exactly?"

"I don't know, really. I vegged out on ice cream for a while and then looked around my house with half my shit packed up. I thought about you guys at the ghost tour, and I thought about all the kids who have been through HOPE. I let my birth parents take enough years of happiness from me. Why should I let them take another minute? As soon as I had that thought, it was like… *whoosh.* Peace." Adam shook his head. "It's hard to explain."

Elijah smiled up at Adam. It all sounded a bit too easy for him, but then he'd never understood how Adam processed anything emotionally.

"I'm glad whatever it is worked. You're sure you're feeling okay now?"

Adam leaned down and pressed his lips to Elijah's. "Absolutely. In fact, I thought we could wake Kollin and move some of my stuff over here before we head to the inn. It's our weekend to cook lunch."

"Sounds like a plan." Elijah slid his hands under Adam's shirt and dragged his fingers along his soft, bare skin. "But first we have some making up to do."

Laughing, Adam tugged Elijah's shirt off. "Making up, huh? I wasn't aware we were fighting."

Elijah shrugged and stole a kiss. "Close enough if it gets me laid."

THREE HOURS later they pulled into the parking lot of Home for Hope. Elijah recalled the atrocious condition the inn had been in the first time he laid eyes on it. Their first priority was to make the kitchen functional and the rooms livable. Slowly but surely they ticked each room off their list until only room eighteen remained in need of repairs. That room was a complete loss, but Adam claimed it as his pet project early on, stripped the room of everything, and slowly rebuilt it himself. The one time Elijah offered to help, Adam was adamant about doing it alone, and something about his tone warned Elijah not to push. The inn boasted plenty of other projects Elijah could focus on.

They waved to two of the residents preparing the outside walls for a new paint job and walked inside to find Lucinda, Julie's mother and now full-time supervisor of H4H, at the reception desk.

"Oh, it's you guys," she said in lieu of a proper greeting.

"Thanks for the warm welcome, Lu," Adam said.

"Sorry. I thought maybe you were Kirsten. She's filling in for me over lunch."

"Oooh," Kollin sang. "Gotta hot date?"

Lucinda's cheeks tinged pink.

"Oh man," Kollin said. "You do."

"Kollin." Elijah threw his arm around Kollin's shoulder. "How many times do I have to tell you…? Tact. Find some."

Lucinda pshawed them with a flick of her wrist. "He's fine, and it's not a hot date. I'm meeting an old friend. I ran into a guy I went to high school with, and he invited me for lunch so we could catch up. I could hardly resist the temptation to eat with someone my own age. No offense."

Adam threw his arm around Lucinda's shoulders for a side hug. "I think it's awesome, and you let me know whenever you need a break. You do so much for us here—far above what we pay you. We couldn't run this place without you."

Resting her head briefly on Adam's shoulder, Lucinda smiled. "Thank you, but I don't see it that way at all. I love working here, and I'm grateful you've let me and the girls stay here for so long."

Unlike most of the child abuse victims Adam dealt with, the abuse Julie's father doled out had nothing to do with Julie's sexual orientation. Once she admitted her dad sometimes lost control and hit her, Adam helped Lucinda make her decision. After years of her husband abusing not only her, but Julie as well, Lucinda found the courage to leave him and bring her girls to safety. Home for Hope had just opened when Lucinda took the girls to safety and Adam hired her as the home's night supervisor, simultaneously providing her and her two daughters a place to stay.

"You know we're just happy we could help. Stay as long as you need."

"Actually I wanted to talk to you two about the possibility of me moving out soon. I've saved enough that I should be able to rent someplace small. It'll give the girls a little more privacy and stability, and Julie's old enough to mind her sister while I'm working nights. I plan to find somewhere close so I can pop over and help whenever you need me, though."

Grinning, Elijah whooped and scooped Lucinda up into a hug. She had worked hard for that moment, and he felt incredibly proud to be part of helping her achieve her goal. He'd be sad to see her leave. She'd been an angel for the inn when they started out. Her gratitude led her to pitch in wherever they needed her, often far above and beyond her job duties, regardless of how many times they told her it was unnecessary. Elijah also knew how important it was to her that she be able to provide for her girls.

"That's awesome. I'm so excited for you," Adam exclaimed.

Lucinda soaked in their praise and screwed up her face. "Now that I've told you guys, actually finding a place in my budget will be the hard part. Cary isn't exactly known for its cheap rent."

Elijah immediately began running through his contacts to see if he knew someone who could help Lucinda.

Adam cleared his throat. "I might be able to help you out there. I was at my old house last night, saying good-bye, I guess, and being mopey I even have to sell it. That house was the first real thing I ever bought on my own. I've been racking my brain with ways HOPE can use it but keep coming up dry. Why don't you move in? It's not very big. There are only two bedrooms, but it's better than some apartments. It's almost fully furnished, and it's close by."

"Adam," Lucinda said, her eyes wide. "I don't know what to say. I don't even know if I could afford something so nice yet."

Waving off her concerns, Adam hugged her again. "I'll stop by soon and give you a tour. And if you want it, we can iron out the details later. I'd much rather have someone I know and love use it than sell it to some stranger."

"Are you sure?" she asked again.

"Of course. Consider it a done deal."

Elijah felt like his face might split in two. Nothing sounded better to his ears than Adam officially moving out of his old house and into their home. "I can't lie and say we won't miss you here, but I'm glad you're back on your feet."

Lucinda smiled, accepting their praise with grace. "Thanks, guys. Now get in the kitchen and start the spaghetti before you make me weepy."

"How'd you know we're making spaghetti?" Adam asked.

Lucinda laughed loudly. She stopped abruptly when no one else joined her.

"Oh. You were serious?" She cleared her throat. "It's the only meal you three ever make—since the taco disaster."

"All Eli's fault," Kollin practically shouted.

"Okay, backseat cooker. You could tell me before I do stupid shit in the kitchen, you know."

"You'd already dried out fajitas for me and Adam at home. I figured you'd read the back of the packet this time."

"Cooking is not my strong suit," Elijah said.

"Yeah. I figured that out about a week after I moved in with you."

Adam bopped Kollin on the back of the head. "Feel free to cook us dinner anytime you want, kid. I'm more than happy to let you test your own cooking skills."

"Dude, you're on. I so got this."

Elijah rolled his eyes as he smiled. "All right. Get your cocky butt in the kitchen before we have eleven hungry residents hovering over us while we cook."

Kollin mock-saluted Elijah and took off toward the kitchen.

"Have a good lunch, Lucinda."

Adam followed Kollin into the kitchen, and Elijah pointed at Lucinda. "Behave," he said as he walked off.

Chapter 5

"Ooh. That's game," Adam said, setting his paddle down.

"You could go easy on him since he's the new guy," Kollin called from the couch.

Adam winked at Jase and then turned to Kollin, exasperated. "And how would he learn, then? Huh?"

"I'm just saying."

"Whatever, Koll. You're just mad Ri taught me all his tricks before he left for college."

Kollin screwed up his face and pouted. "Would it have killed him to tell me a few? Dealing with your sudden talent is cruel and unusual punishment."

Jase plopped on the couch next to Kollin and bumped their shoulders together. "It's cool. I'm gonna get him soon. He's weak on his right side."

Adam grinned as he put the paddles away. "Maybe that's what I want you to think."

"Oh yeah. I'm sure you're that clever," Jase said, laughing.

Adam pointed between the two boys as he walked out of the room. "I'm going to my office to wait for Elijah. Don't forget the rules."

Kollin rolled his eyes, but Adam knew he'd keep his distance. While they offered some leeway on field trips, everyone had to adhere to the no-touching policy at the center. Every so often the teens would complain about it, but for the most part, they understood the necessity and weren't willing to trade the security of HOPE for a quick grope.

Adam stopped by the kitchen on the way to his office to grab a bottle of water from the fridge. He eyed the box of doughnuts on the counter, plucked one out, and took a bite.

"What's the good word, Chloe?" he asked through a mouthful of food as he walked toward his office.

She looked at him the way Adam assumed mothers everywhere did the first time their child did something utterly ridiculous—with a smile as equally full of love as it was amused pity. "Well, when you finish stuffing your face, you have a visitor. She didn't want to pull you away from the kids, so she's been waiting awhile."

"Oh?"

When Adam looked toward the chairs on the far side of the room, his jaw dropped and his water bottle slipped right out of his hands and clattered to the floor. Swallowing his food, Adam raked his gaze up and down the woman sitting in the waiting area. He wouldn't have recognized his own mother if she hadn't called him a few weeks before. What he remembered as long, curly red hair was now short and straight, though Adam could see the graying roots. She seemed thinner than he remembered, and her skin hung loosely off her cheekbones. Time hadn't been kind to her, and Adam briefly wondered if the same fate awaited him.

"Adam?" Chloe asked. "Are you okay?"

Snapping his head toward Chloe, Adam closed his mouth. "Uh, yes. Sorry."

Chloe nodded uncertainly and glanced at Adam's mother, clearly unsure about what she should do. Meanwhile Adam's mother sat in the chair, looking as if she didn't know whether she should pause to open the door on her way out or simply make a hole in the window.

"Chloe," Adam began, his voice calm and even. "This is Jessica Lancaster, my birth mother."

Chloe's face paled while Adam spoke, but her Southern manners quickly kicked in and replaced her stunned expression with a smile. "Welcome to HOPE, Jessica."

"Thank you." Her voice sounded soft, shy even, and she continued to avoid Adam's eyes.

"I don't mean to be rude," Adam said, "but why are you here?"

His heart pounded, and he took a moment to close his eyes and focus on his breathing. Though surprised to see her, Adam had prepared himself for the possibility she might suddenly pop up again in his life, and had spent several restless nights practicing what he'd say so he could hold himself together. When he opened his eyes again, Jessica was still staring at the ground by his feet.

"I wanted to talk to you for a minute."

"Talk to me… for a minute," Adam repeated. Her words tasted strange on his tongue.

"Well, I tried to call, but you hung up on me." She finally looked at Adam as she defended herself, her voice rising and frustration seeping out with each word.

Adam gripped the back of his neck. "I wasn't expecting to hear from you. It took me by surprise."

Jessica nodded curtly.

"I guess we could go in my office and—"

The bell above the door cut Adam off, and for the first time in months, he was not happy to see Elijah. Adam had no idea what Elijah would do about his birth mother.

"Hey, Chloe," Elijah said as he waltzed into the foyer. He carried two trays. "I brought you a sundae."

"Oh. Thank you, Elijah," Chloe said, her wide eyes darting between Adam and Jessica. "How thoughtful."

"I try every now and then," he said as he placed both trays on her desk, wriggled one of the cups out for her, and bent down to pick up Adam's forgotten water bottle. "Did you drop this?" Elijah slid the bottle into Adam's hand and allowed his fingers to linger against Adam's. The grin he offered was solely reserved for Adam. Elijah hadn't noticed Adam's mother yet. His back had been to her since he walked in the door, but with that small smile, Elijah unknowingly bolstered Adam's confidence.

Adam smiled back. "Thank you. Maybe Chloe can call someone out here to collect those. There's someone you need to meet."

Elijah swiveled around to see Adam's birth mother sitting in the corner. He closed the distance between them and held out his hand with all the confidence of a multimillionaire CEO. "Hi, there. I'm Elijah Langley. It's a pleasure to meet you."

Terror written all over her face, Jessica stared at him for a moment and then looked toward Adam.

"This is Jessica… Lancaster." Adam spoke quietly, but he knew Elijah heard because his entire body tensed. He could imagine the look on Elijah's face, given the way Jessica quickly averted her eyes.

"Oh." Elijah dropped his hand and returned to Adam's side.

Adam ignored his piercing glare and clenched jaw so he could power through the rest of the introduction. "Elijah is my partner. My boyfriend."

Jessica's eyes flitted back and forth between them. She forced a small smile. "Of course."

Awkward silence filled the room as Adam scrambled to figure out what to do or say next. Jessica probably wanted to speak with him alone, but he could tell from Elijah's stern jaw and evil-eyed glare that he had no intention of leaving. Thankfully Jase and Julie chose that moment to enter the room, eager to collect their sundaes. Adam sent up a silent thank-you that Kollin hadn't come with them.

Neither teen paid any attention to the tension in the room as they grabbed the trays and went right back into the multipurpose room. Adam turned to Elijah and grabbed his hand.

"Would you mind waiting out here for a few minutes while I speak with her in my office?"

Adam hoped Elijah understood his silent plea. *Please don't come in, but please don't leave either.*

Elijah tilted his head and searched Adam's eyes.

"Please," Adam whispered.

With a curt nod and a quick squeeze of Adam's hand, Elijah strode to the waiting area where Jessica sat and took the seat directly next to hers. His eyes never left her as he crossed one leg over the other. Even Adam found the action intimidating, the message clear. *I'll be right here until you're gone.*

"You can come in here," Adam said, gesturing toward his door.

Jessica quickly crossed the room into Adam's small office. She took one of the hard chairs across from his desk. Adam closed the door and then sat stiffly in his desk chair.

"So what did you want to talk about?"

Holy fuck. This felt so surreal.

He'd imagined the moment so many times over the years. For a while he'd expected to be angry and to lash out at his parents if they ever showed up. Then he decided he'd tell them to leave, that he wanted nothing to do with them. Eventually he gave up hope they'd ever resurface. He felt grateful he'd grown enough to have the courage to at least hear his mother out, but his emotions were raw. He had so many questions for her, but he didn't want to give her the satisfaction of knowing he thought about her at all.

"I actually just hoped to talk, to see how you're doing," she said as she fidgeted with the zipper on her purse.

Adam stared at her, an easy feat because she still refused to meet his gaze. "You wanted to see how I'm doing?" A small spark of anger flared in his belly. Was that really her opening line? "After twenty years with no word?"

"It's not the first time I've wondered." Her voice remained small, but for some reason, that only fueled Adam's antagonism. The spark ignited and the flames of anger intensified in his chest.

"Did you bother to check on me any of those times? Did you find out none of the other foster parents wanted me either? How I ran away every chance I got in order to escape the pain?"

"Adam—"

"I'm doing fine now, no thanks to you." Adam closed his eyes and reined in his temper. Maybe he wasn't as Zen as he'd thought. "I appreciate you checking in on me after all this time, and I hope it eases your conscience or whatever the hell you're here after. Is there anything else?"

"Please, Adam. I know I don't deserve anything from you, but would you at least give me one chance? Your grandfather passed away two months ago, and I know—"

Adam's anger vanished as sadness emerged to take its place. "Gramps died?"

Jessica nodded. "I'm sorry. I know how much he loved you and how much I disappointed him when I went along with your father's plans."

Adam stared at her, dumbfounded. "My father's plans?"

His parents never actually said anything to him when they kicked him out. He remembered no remorse in his mother's eyes. He thought she would be back in a few days. Figured she forgot to hug and kiss him good-bye in her rush to leave because she must be running late for one of the important meetings she always complained about.

"Well, yes. Your father has antiquated opinions on the matter. I should've refused to take you away, and I'm sorry for that."

"You're… sorry," Adam repeated, now feeling completely hollow. He took a deep breath.

Jessica leaned forward. "Are you okay?"

Adam looked at her and their eyes met for the first time. He had her eyes.

The thought made him sick. He wanted Amelia's eyes. *She* was his real mother.

"It's a lot to process."

Jessica sat back in her chair, apparently deciding silence was the best course of action. Though Adam would never admit it, he appreciated the gesture.

"I think I'm going to need to some time."

"Of course." She opened her purse, pulled out a small slip of paper, and slid it across his desk. "This is my number. I'd love to have dinner with you, but I'd appreciate a call either way."

Adam scoffed. She'd shown him no such respect.

"If we have dinner, I'll want to bring my family. Elijah and maybe his son, Kollin."

Jessica's features tightened, but she nodded once. "Of course," she said again. "Thank you for considering this."

Adam nodded, and Jessica stood.

"I'll see myself out."

Moments later Elijah knelt by his chair. Without a word, Adam fell forward to lay his head on Elijah's shoulder. What the hell was he supposed to do?

ELIJAH FIXED dinner that evening—waffles and bacon, a weekly staple in their house—while Adam told Kollin about Jessica's visit. Kollin remained quiet, for the most part, only asking what Adam planned to do. But when Kollin barely touched his food, Adam knew he needed to talk it out with him.

He hunted Kollin down after dinner and apologized for not being more considerate of his feelings. Kollin brushed the whole thing off, and they spent the next hour bonding over shitty-birth-parent stories. By the time Adam left his room, Kollin's effervescent presence had returned. Though mentally exhausted, Adam felt better as well.

Adam flopped onto their bed and draped his arm across Elijah's bare waist. When Elijah trailed his fingers through Adam's hair, Adam leaned into the touch and practically purred in contentment.

"You okay?"

"Yeah… no…. I cannot believe this is my life right now. I'd made peace with them leaving me." Adam squeezed his eyes shut and whispered. "She wasn't supposed to come back."

"I know, but maybe it can be a good thing."

Adam looked at Elijah. "Could be, but does she deserve a second chance?"

"The real question is, do you?"

Adam grunted. "Kollin told me he sometimes still hopes his parents change their minds. He wishes they still loved him. I used to be like that, and now here I am, waffling over whether or not to let her back in."

"I think that's probably natural. Time's a funny thing. It passes so slowly, but then you wake up one day and it's twenty years later, everything's changed, and you don't remember how or when it happened."

"You think time has hardened me against my parents, or did all those years in the system do that?"

"You know, I have no clue. Maybe a little of both?" Elijah asked. "Either way you're perfectly entitled to resent her for abandoning you."

Adam sniffed, inhaling Elijah's scent. The familiar smell comforted him and bolstered his courage enough to voice his biggest fear. "I know you don't know all of the details, but do you think she still would've given me up if she'd known what waited for me in foster care?"

"I don't know, baby. I don't think anyone has the answer to that." Elijah nestled into Adam. "I'm not suggesting everyone will get a happy ending here. When I accepted that I'd fallen in love with you and wanted you in my life, I was forced to give my parents a chance to accept who I truly am. There was no way I could've been who you and Kollin needed me to be and still be part of their lives if they didn't approve. In a million years, I never would've anticipated their almost-lackadaisical response. I mean, you know how long it took until I finally believed they weren't going to drop the other shoe and bully me into giving up on you two. They changed a lot over the years, most of the time right in front of my face, and I didn't even realize it. Maybe the same has happened with your mom."

Elijah flipped onto his side and began rubbing slow lines up and down Adam's back. "Forget about her and whether or not having dinner with her will make *her* feel better or worse. Because you're right—she doesn't deserve that consideration from you. Will it make *you* feel better? Do *you* want to know what she's been doing these past twenty years? Will *you* feel better once you know why she's suddenly decided to pay you a visit?"

Adam closed his eyes briefly, then looked up at Elijah and smiled. "How'd you get to be so smart?"

Elijah scooted closer to Adam and tucked his hand beneath Adam's sleep pants. "Learned from the best."

"Mmm...." Adam tilted his head, allowing Elijah access to his neck. "Is that so?"

"Oh, absolutely," he said and squeezed Adam's ass as he kissed his way up to Adam's mouth. "Dr. Will is all kinds of amazing."

Adam groaned. His dick grew harder with Elijah's every touch. When he left Kollin's room, he wanted nothing more than to collapse in bed and sleep. But now, with Elijah pulling him closer, sliding his hands up his back, Adam knew he needed this—needed Elijah—more than sleep.

"I'll show you amazing." Adam grinned as he shimmied Elijah's pajama bottoms off, leaving him completely naked. Eyeing Elijah from head to toe, Adam said, "Fuck. I love your body."

Naturally muscular, Elijah worked out several times a week in their home gym, and Adam reaped the benefits. Elijah's body was all definition and angles. His broad shoulders boasted muscles that looked just as enticing in one of Elijah's many suits as they did bare. And his back.... Adam could spend hours watching Elijah flex the muscles of his back, and then hours more tracing the hills and valleys of said muscles—preferably with his tongue.

Smirking, Elijah grabbed Adam's arms, flipped him around, and crawled on top of him like a tiger stalking its prey.

"Oh, hell yes. I need this," Adam said while Elijah stripped him down.

Elijah ran his hand across Adam's chest and lightly traced the tattoo on Adam's pec as he lined his cock up with Adam's. Rocking back and forth, he slid against Adam just enough to torture him.

"Tease," Adam said as he arched his back.

Elijah dipped lower, providing more friction, and a small drop of cum leaked from the tip of Adam's dick.

"Please," Adam begged.

Pausing for a moment, Elijah stared into Adam's eyes and then collapsed on top of him to bury his neck into Adam's shoulder. For several long minutes, Elijah held Adam, bare skin to bare skin, and little by little, something shifted. Adam let the tension of everything shitty in his life—his birth mother, problems at the inn, worries over troubled youth—slip away. He focused on Elijah's body—the smooth skin of his chest, the way the hair on his legs prickled against his own, the weight of his body pressing him into the bed, even the hair under Elijah's arm tickling Adam's ribs. And he let go of all the other things in his life—the upcoming adoption for Kollin, the way the inn had taken off and left them happily unprepared for its success, how good it felt to see Kollin smile after their talk earlier—until all he had left was the man in his arms.

Although he claimed he didn't know how to handle emotional situations, Elijah always seemed to know when Adam needed to just… be.

Adam tightened his arms around Elijah's waist and whispered, "Make me forget?"

Elijah peppered kisses up to Adam's mouth. "Anything. Always."

Turning his body over to Elijah's more than capable hands, Adam relaxed into the bed while Elijah lavished him with attention. Elijah seemed intent on making up for every time they'd been forced to settle for a quickie. He kneaded each muscle as he worked out any remaining dregs of tension. Everywhere his hands touched, he followed with his mouth, licking and nipping at the sensitive skin and lighting Adam on fire.

Elijah made his way up Adam's thighs, and Adam grabbed his throbbing dick. He tugged on it a few times and then pulled it taut to expose his ass. Elijah didn't hesitate. He ran his tongue from Adam's thigh, up, up, up until he sucked first one ball and then the other into his mouth. Elijah swirled his tongue around and let them drop out. Adam groaned and squeezed his ass cheeks together, worried he would blow before Elijah even touched his cock. Finally Elijah swatted Adam's hand away to replace it with his mouth.

Within seconds Adam felt his orgasm start to build in his groin. He threw back his head and clenched the sheets between his fingers as he fought it off. Elijah's slippery, warm mouth on his cock felt far too good for it to end so soon. Nobody would ever be able to convince Adam touch wasn't one of the most powerful tools in the entire world. After years of being neglected by his own parents and a string of foster parents, Adam craved physical affection like a drowning man praying for a life raft. Once he finally got it, he never took it for granted, and he hugged and comforted his friends and family often. But even since day one, Elijah's touch drove Adam's body wild while still managing to soothe his soul.

Elijah slid his thumb under Adam's balls, pressed lightly against his hole while he buried his nose in Adam's pubic hair, and Adam lost the battle and shot down Elijah's throat. He grabbed Elijah's head to hold him in place as he rode out his orgasm, pumping in and out of Elijah's throat but trying his best not to choke him. After what felt like ages, he gently tugged Elijah up the bed.

"Damn. That was a huge load," Adam said, panting.

Elijah kissed Adam lightly on the lips. "I'm aware." Elijah settled on top of him, making him feel safe and secure rather than squished and stifled.

Adam wrapped his arms around Elijah. "Sorry. It's been a few days."

"Lucky me."

"Damn straight," Adam agreed. "Thank you."

"You don't have to thank me for sex, you know."

"I meant the royal treatment before the blow job," Adam said.

Elijah kissed the center of Adam's chest. "You needed a night all about you, and you seem a bit lighter. I'm glad it helped."

"You always help, even if I don't always thank you or tell you."

"I'm getting pretty good at winging this relationship thing." Elijah paused. "I love you."

Adam smiled. He knew Elijah loved him. Contrary to what Elijah believed of himself, he damn near epitomized the perfect boyfriend. He might not say the words very often, but Elijah showed Adam how he felt in nearly everything he did, from leaving their scrambled eggs a touch undercooked—exactly how Adam liked them best—to continuously supporting the HOPE center and inn with his financial gifts and his time. Adam would take action over words any day.

Adam tightened his arms around Elijah and kissed the top of his head. "I love you too."

CHAPTER 6

ADAM COULD no longer put off telling Kirsten about Jessica's sudden reappearance in his life, so he invited her to lunch at the center and wooed her with a promise of her favorite cheeseburger wrap from Etman's.

"So I had a weird visitor yesterday."

"That doesn't sound good." Kirsten dipped a home-cooked chip in Etman's ranch dressing and took a bite.

"I don't know if it is or not." Adam took a deep breath and told her about the phone call several weeks earlier and the impromptu visit from his birth mother the day before. When he finished, Kirsten set down her sandwich.

"Are you telling me you're considering meeting her for dinner?"

Adam nodded.

Narrowing her eyes, she took a deep breath. "I've always supported your decisions, no matter what, and I always will. But do you really think this is a good idea?"

Adam sighed and sat back in his chair. Kris, Amelia, and Matthew were the only people still in his life who knew him before he'd gone through years of therapy, who'd experienced how fucked up he'd been. He'd been reluctant to tell Kirsten about Jessica because he knew her first reaction would be to protect him, and he couldn't blame her.

"I don't know if it is or not," Adam said again. "But I don't think I can ignore her and live the rest of my life not knowing why she showed up."

"The same way you've lived these last ten years, give or take. Happy. Successful. Proud of yourself for everything you've overcome, in spite of the fact that some bitch who happened to push you out of her vagina sent you off to your own personal hell."

"I know what they did was horrible enough, but she couldn't have known what would happen to me in the system."

Kirsten's eyes widened. "Now you're defending her? I know you're the most forgiving person walking around on this planet, but come on, Adam. Who gives a shit if she knew or not? She knew she was your damn mother, and she knew it was her fucking responsibility to take care of you."

"Come on, Kris. Calm down. I never said I'm welcoming her with open arms, but I plan to hear her out. If I don't, I'll never forgive myself, and that's something I can't live with."

"Adam…." Kirsten sounded helpless, and Adam wished he could say something to make all of it easier for her. He knew she had only his best interest at heart. When he first moved in with the Wrights, he suffered from nightmares brought on by real-life horrors no one, let alone a child, should have to experience. His screams woke Kirsten many times, but she never mentioned them, never gave him pitying looks. Adam used to wonder if she slept through them, even though her room shared a wall with his, and he could hear every word of every phone conversation she ever had.

When Adam caved and allowed himself to feel part of their family, Kris snuck into his room whenever his dreams turned violent. At first she held his hand and silently waited for him to fall back to sleep. Eventually she climbed into bed with him so he wouldn't have to sleep alone the rest of the night.

Adam would go to hell and back for Kirsten, but he couldn't compromise for her.

"What would you tell one of the kids to do?" he asked her.

"Those kids are not my brother," she replied fiercely. "And way to be a shithead and use them to make me sound like an asshole."

"You're not even close to being an asshole," he said.

Kirsten stared at Adam again. "You better know what you're doing."

"I'm only going to find out what she has to say, and Elijah's going with me. If she has a problem with that, I'm not going."

"What about Kollin?"

Adam shook his head. "He has enough on his plate. He'd go if I asked him to, but it would drag up too much shit with his own parents, whether Jessica's legit or not. He doesn't need that."

"Are you sure about this?"

"Yeah, Kris. I am. And no matter what happens, it'll be easier having your support."

"I should kick your ass for not telling me when she called the first time."

Adam grinned. “You couldn’t if you tried, but it’s a nice thought.”

“Whatever. I could totally kick your ass.”

“Only because you know I’d never hit you.”

Kirsten made a face as she shrugged, acknowledging the truth to his statement but indicating it wouldn’t stop her. She picked up another chip. “When are you gonna call her?”

“In a few days, I guess.” Adam smiled. “Just because I’m going to see her doesn’t mean I’m above making her sweat a little. Whether she’s in this for the right reasons or not, she has them, so she must feel anxious either way. Making her wait is probably the saddest vengeance ever known to man, but it’s all I got.”

Kris shook her head. “That is pretty sad. Even for you. You don’t have any idea why she’d show up now? She didn’t mention the pathetic piece of shit who impregnated her at all?”

“Not really. And I didn’t pay enough attention to see if she had a wedding band on. Not that it would make any difference, given how long it’s been. Maybe Gramps’s death made her look at life differently, and she actually does feel remorse. Maybe she found something of mine there that reminded her of me? I can’t think of anything she could want from me. I have nothing of material worth aside from HOPE, but it’s not like the center or the inn is in my name.”

“Um… I think you’re overlooking the obvious. Elijah’s loaded.”

“Yeah. But it’s not my money. And how would she have even known Elijah and I are together? I seriously doubt she’s been following my life.”

“But think about it. Between the inn opening and Kollin’s parents’ trial, you and Elijah have been in the news quite a bit. They sure as hell made certain to point out that you two are a couple every time they got the chance. How do you know your grandfather is even dead?”

Adam narrowed his eyes at his sister. “Kris.”

“I’m just saying. You should at least look him up. Do you know where he lived?”

“South Village Nursing Home, last I checked. About four years ago,” he said.

“Can you call them and ask?”

“Fuck, Kris. No. I can’t call and ask if he’s dead.”

“You can call and inquire about his health. I’ll do it if you don’t want to.”

Adam jiggled the mouse on his computer to wake it up. "I'll search for his obituary, and if I can't find it, I'll let you call."

"Thank you. It's just… you need to be as prepared for this as you can be." Kirsten still sounded hurt, and Adam felt a small pang of guilt for being cross with her. He loved her even more for being so protective. Not many people would have the gumption to suggest Jessica might be working her way back into his life for nefarious reasons.

Kirsten picked at her food while Adam searched. Two minutes later relief washed over him—immediately followed with sorrow as he read his grandfather's obituary, dated almost three months prior. His heart twisted a little more when he saw Jessica Lancaster and her husband, Chad Lancaster, were the only survivors listed. Absolutely no mention of their son. But at least he knew his mother was still married to his birth father, or at least had been three months before.

While Adam read, Kirsten walked around his desk and slipped her arm around his shoulder to give him a tight hug. "I'm sorry. I know how much you loved him."

Shaking his head, Adam fought back a few tears. "It's fine. He was gone a long time ago for me. I can't believe he held on this long, to be honest."

"Must've been a fighter. Maybe that's where you got it from," she said.

Adam nodded and clicked the X in the top right corner of his screen. "At least I know."

"What do you need from me?"

"Same as always. Just be you," Adam said with a sad smile.

"That I can do."

ADAM WAITED three days before calling Jessica to set up dinner the following Friday. Kollin made plans with Jase, and Kirsten even agreed to drive them to a movie and pick them up afterward. Kollin had his learner's permit, but North Carolina law required him to drive supervised by an adult. Adam dreaded the day they'd have to let him out on his own.

"You okay?" Elijah asked. He covered Adam's hand with his own as he navigated through the streets of Cary.

"Yeah." Adam laughed. "I was actually thinking about Kollin driving. I'm not ready for it."

"Tell me about it. We have a while, though. Besides, he doesn't seem too eager."

"I've noticed that too. What's that all about? Matthew bought me a piece of shit car—he probably salvaged it from the junkyard, to be honest—but I didn't care. I couldn't wait to get on the road."

Elijah shrugged. "I don't know for sure, but the first time I brought up getting him a car, he seemed shocked. I think he sometimes still feels like he doesn't deserve anything I buy him."

"Maybe I should buy him a car, then, a fifteen-year-old junker."

Elijah took his hand back. "Absolutely not. He is not driving around in some heap because he feels bad about taking my money, and I will not have some monstrosity parked in our driveway. Kirsten told me what you used to drive. You better be glad you upgraded before we met."

"What?" Adam feigned surprise. "Sally was the best car ever. She had over two hundred and fifty thousand miles on her before she gave out."

Elijah side-eyed him.

Adam grinned. "You know, sometimes I forget how you grew up. And then something like this happens, and I remember how uppity you are."

"I am not uppity for wanting Kollin to have a safe and reliable car to drive around in."

Adam laughed and patted Elijah's leg. "I know, baby. You're not uppity at all. Now if you could take the next right in your car that costs more than the house I just moved out of, we'll be at the restaurant."

Elijah huffed. "You're kind of mean when you're nervous."

Adam leaned over and pecked Elijah's cheek. "Thank you," he said, confident Elijah knew what the kiss was meant for.

Several minutes later Adam found himself sitting across from his mother with Elijah's arm draped casually over his chair. Since neither of them showed much PDA, Adam couldn't tell if the gesture was a show of support or a warning to his mother, but he accepted the comfort regardless.

"Have any trouble finding the place?" Adam asked in an effort to break the ice.

"No. I've never been here before, but the GPS found it easily," she replied and took a sip of her water. She acted as nervous as Adam felt, but not quite as tense as she'd been at the center.

"I hope you like steak," Elijah said pleasantly. "It's all they serve here, but they're quite famous for it."

"I'm sure it'll be delicious."

Their waiter interrupted, and once they'd all placed their food orders, Adam took a deep breath. He was tired of wondering why his mother had reappeared in his life, and he had no interest in waiting through an awkward meal to find out.

"So… we've established you surprised me when you called after all these years. Can we get to the part where you tell me why you're here so I at least know what I'm dealing with?"

Jessica swallowed visibly and looked down at her lap. She seemed to gather herself before she looked into Adam's eyes.

"When your grandfather died, I got all of his belongings from the nursing staff at South Village. I don't know how much you knew, but he went to an assisted living home and stayed there for many years, until he couldn't take care of himself anymore. That's when we moved him to the nursing home. He was under the impression I would be able to care for you better than he would at that point."

Adam's jaw clenched. "You told him you came back for me?"

Jessica nodded. "I thought it would make it easier on him."

Adam's breath caught, and he closed his eyes. Maybe doing this in a restaurant was a bad idea. "You mean easier on you?"

Jessica fidgeted with the silverware in front of her. "I'm trying to be honest with you, Adam. Your father wouldn't have let you back in the house. I didn't have another choice."

Elijah squeezed his shoulder. He leaned into the touch and didn't bother listing the other obvious choice she had. What would be the point?

"After he died I waited a few weeks before I went through his boxes. He kept journals. He always had during my childhood too, but I suppose I thought he'd grown out of it. There were so many from his time at the assisted living home and even a few from South Village. He wrote about you often. He loved you so much. More than he loved me, I think." Jessica's eyes met his again. "I'm so sorry, Adam. Reading his words, I realized what a huge mistake I'd made. My father was the most loving person I've ever known. When we sent you to live with him, I honestly believed it was for the best. I knew he'd treat you better than your father would. I guess, after two years without you in the house, I lost perspective. It was easier to rationalize that you'd still be better off with a nice foster family than in our house."

Adam soaked in her words. He poked them around inside his head and tried to wrap his mind around what she implied and ignored the glaring truth that "nice foster families" were few and far between.

"Are you blaming this all on my father, then?"

"I'm saying if he hadn't forced me, I wouldn't have given you up."

ELIJAH RUBBED his hand up and down Adam's neck as Jessica shrugged off all responsibility for abandoning her child because of his sexual orientation. The soothing gesture kept Elijah from jumping over the table and wringing her skinny neck off her fucking shoulders. Adam's face showed no emotion, so he remained silent, immensely regretting he'd ever encouraged Adam to meet with Jessica.

Choosing a shitty man to father your children didn't mean you had to be a shitty parent too. As much as he loved Adam, Elijah would kick him out faster than he could blink an eye if he ever thought Adam might harm Kollin in any way. And he knew Adam would do the same.

They sat in silence for so long the waiter brought their food and set everything down. He asked if anyone needed anything, and Elijah quickly excused him. Uncomfortable silence filled the table until Adam picked up his fork and spread a dollop of sour cream on his potato. Following his lead, Elijah did the same.

"Is that it?" Adam asked, his tone even.

Clearly thrown off, Jessica stuttered, "I suppose so. Yes."

Adam took a bite of his potato and nodded. Though he appeared eerily calm for that conversation, particularly given how much he'd agonized over his decision to hear Jessica's side of the story, Elijah couldn't help but wonder if Adam was tiptoeing his way to the edge of a cliff.

"Does he know you're here?"

Jessica winced but nodded. "He didn't want to come, but I thought, with you being older and clearly capable of taking care of yourself, we could have some type of relationship even if your father doesn't approve."

Adam's eyes flashed as he looked at Jessica. His voice hard, he said, "Matthew Wright is my father."

Jessica's eyes grew larger, and she frowned. Elijah slipped a hand under the table to Adam's knee, and he saw some of the tension ease out of Adam's posture.

Elijah cleared his throat. "Exactly what kind of relationship with Adam are you looking for?"

"I'm not wealthy," Adam blurted out. "I don't have access to Elijah's money, and I don't ever intend to."

Adam's breathing sped up, and worry filled Elijah. He squeezed Adam's leg again.

"I… I don't want Elijah's money."

She seemed genuine, but who knew? Elijah could read a business deal better than most, but this extended far beyond his level of comprehension. Mixed with her apologies and explanations, Elijah had also heard a lot of "not my fault."

"Then what do you want with me?" Adam asked again as he took a deep breath.

"I want to get to know the boy your grandfather filled up pages and pages of journals with."

Adam took a deep breath and then another, and then he grabbed Elijah's leg.

"Elijah," he gasped.

Shit. Shit, shit, shit. Adam gasped for breath and squeezed harder, so Elijah turned Adam's chair toward him and wrapped his arms around Adam's shoulders, blocking out the rest of the restaurant. With Adam's forehead resting on his shoulder, Elijah whispered into his ear, telling him to take deep breaths, telling him to forget about everything else, telling him he was safe, telling him how much he loved him, and telling him whatever else came to mind that might comfort him.

Several moments later Adam squeezed Elijah's shoulder and said a quiet thank-you.

"You okay to sit back up?" Elijah asked.

"Is everyone watching us?"

"Not that it matters, but I don't think so. You didn't freak out or anything."

Slowly Adam lifted his head and discreetly glanced around and righted his chair. Jessica said nothing while Elijah summoned the waiter.

"Is everything okay?" he asked.

"Yes. It turns out we're short on time this evening. Can we get the rest of this to go, please?"

Jessica's eyes widened, and she laid her hand on the table. "Adam? Can I see you again?"

Adam looked at her, his face pale and his breathing still a little uneven. Elijah spoke up before he had a chance. "He's had enough for tonight. We'll be in touch."

The waiter returned with to-go boxes and emptied their nearly untouched meals one by one while everyone waited awkwardly. Once he finished, Elijah threw two hundred-dollar bills on the table and stood to pull Adam's chair out. He didn't care that he'd not only paid for Jessica's meal, but also grossly overtipped their waiter. He just wanted to get Adam home as quickly as possible.

Adam dipped his head toward Jessica and allowed Elijah to guide him through the restaurant. He didn't speak the entire ride home. As they walked into the house, Elijah asked if he wanted to talk, but Adam shook his head.

"Do you mind if I have some time to myself?"

Elijah nodded and watched Adam walk up the stairs by himself. He wished he didn't feel so helpless. When Elijah got in bed, Adam's side was empty again.

CHAPTER 7

ADAM WOKE the following morning to an empty bed—not surprising given his clock read 11:23. He'd hidden out in the guest room until nearly four in the morning. Guilt drove him to return to his own bed rather than crash in the guest room.

He knew Elijah worried about him, but he didn't know how to let him in when it came to dealing with his past. Elijah thought Adam could discover the answer to world peace, discover the cure for cancer, and still come home each night with a smile on his face. They might not always agree on everything, but Elijah respected and valued Adam's opinion. He didn't know how much of that deference Elijah based on a not-quite-accurate perception of Adam's true self. The closest he ever came to sharing the deepest, darkest parts of himself with anyone, aside from his therapist, was occasionally whispering his ugly secrets to Kirsten. Elijah deserved better than a half-present live-in boyfriend.

As much of a clusterfuck as the night before turned out to be, Jessica truly seemed to want some form of a relationship with him. Her earnestness in proclaiming she didn't want Elijah's money—almost as if she'd never even considered the idea—appeared genuine. The problem? Adam had no idea what to do next.

He shoved the blanket off, climbed out of bed, and trudged to the bathroom to freshen up for the day. Relief coursed through him as he thought of the upcoming commitment-free weekend—a rarity in their lives. Vegging in front of the TV, spending time with Elijah and Kollin, and *not* thinking about anything related to Jessica Lancaster topped his to-do list. Maybe he could even persuade Elijah to go into town and pick up some of their favorite chili cheese fries and hot wings. He wouldn't even need to change out of his pajamas if he didn't have to leave the house.

Despite his tired appearance, Adam smiled when he looked in the mirror. The day was starting to look up. He peeked into Kollin's empty room and continued downstairs to find an empty living room and kitchen as well. When he opened the door to the basement, Adam heard Elijah's and Kollin's voices traveling up the stairs.

"Morning, guys," he said as he bounded down the steps and fell onto the sofa closest to the pool table.

"Nice of you to join us," Kollin said, teasing.

"Yeah, yeah. It's usually you waking up right about now."

Kollin shrugged. "When Kirsten chauffeurs you around, you don't get to stay out too late."

"Mmmhmm…." Adam stretched his arms over his head and yawned. "How'd the date go?"

"It wasn't a date."

"Yeah, okay," Elijah said, rolling his eyes.

Kollin lined up his shot and smacked the stick into the cue ball, knocking the seven ball into the side pocket. He flashed a cocky grin at Elijah. "You better spend more time down here practicing. You're about to get schooled."

"Please. I've been playing pool longer than you've been alive."

Kollin walked around the table to eye his next shot. "That doesn't do anything but make you sound old, man."

Elijah laughed and walked by Kollin, smacking his butt with his pool stick on the way to lean down and offer Adam a quick kiss. "You okay?"

Adam smiled and nodded. "For now," he said quietly and then raised his voice to continue, "but that's gonna change if the boy doesn't tell me how his date/non-date went."

Kollin missed his next shot and huffed as he straightened up. "It was fine. There was popcorn and Cherry Coke and Goobers."

"Did you hold hands?"

Kollin rolled his eyes. "Yes, Dad, and I promise I wore a glove the whole time."

Elijah burst out laughing, but Adam stared at Kollin in shock. "How long have you been holding that one in?"

"Only since we decided to see the movie. I knew you'd annoy the hell out of me today."

Adam grinned. "Good. Then I can keep going. Did you neck in the movie theater?"

"You're so strange. I know you guys are old, but you're not old enough to call it necking."

"I know. But Matthew asked me that one time, and it embarrassed me so much I couldn't wait to use it on my own kid."

Kollin's grin could've lit up the entire room, but he quickly covered it up. "You succeeded," he said. Then he mumbled, "And we might've made out a little before we met Kirsten outside."

"Nice." Adam held his hand up for a fist bump.

"This would be so awkward if you were my real dad. You know that, right? If you two ever have a real kid, you can't be this weird."

"Hey," Elijah said, straightening up from studying his next shot. "Shut your mouth. You are my real kid."

"Yeah. I know. But not really."

"Uh… yes. Really," Elijah said. His tone brooked no argument.

Not that Kollin ever let that tone stop him. "I'm just saying, it'll be different when you have one of your own—both of you—from the beginning, without all the bullshit drama I drag to the party."

"And I'm dead serious when I promise you no other child Adam and I have, together or alone, or what-the-fuck-ever kind of way, will ever be more real to me than you are. If you're thinking I don't know what I'm talking about, I can guarantee you I do. Got it?"

Kollin nodded, and Adam waved him over to the couch, the pool game forgotten. "Same for me. Just because my name isn't going on some piece of paper doesn't mean I won't always be here for you. I'll sign in a heartbeat, if it's what you want. Doesn't change a thing for me either way."

"Okay, okay. I got it, guys. I really wasn't trying to start a big discussion."

"Then don't go around saying stupid shit," Elijah said.

Kollin scrunched up his face at Elijah, silently mocking him, and Elijah kicked at his foot.

"So how awkward was last night?" Kollin asked.

"Fine, I guess," Adam said. "She apologized, blamed my dad, told me she had no other choice, and asked if we could have some type of relationship."

"Shitballs," Kollin said. "For real?"

"For real."

"What'd you say?"

Adam laughed. "Well, after Elijah kept me from having another panic attack in the middle of the restaurant, he told her not to call us. We'd call her."

"Shit." Kollin slouched into the couch.

"You might want to spice up your vocabulary a bit," Adam said.

"Sorry, but that's some heavy stuff. She say why leaving your dickhead dad wasn't an option?"

"Ah, no. She left that part out. Gotta save some fun bits for later on, I suppose." Adam's tone dripped with sarcasm.

"What're you gonna do?"

"Koll, lay off the twenty questions," Elijah said before Adam could answer.

Adam flashed him a grateful smile and shook his head. "It's fine, but I don't know the answer to that yet. I should probably talk to Dr. Maggie before I do anything else. I never got around to it before, since I made peace with everything on my own. But considering I almost flipped out again last night, I clearly don't have everything as under control as I thought."

"I don't know what to say," Kollin said.

"Then what do you say we all agree to not talk about her the rest of the day? Let's be lazy and pretend like we have no problems today. And then tomorrow we'll talk about this together and figure out how allowing her back in my life would affect all three of us. Then, as a family, we'll figure out if we can deal with those changes."

In an uncharacteristic but still completely Kollin move, he leaned over and hugged Adam fiercely. Before Adam had a chance to reciprocate, Kollin was running up the stairs. "I call dibs on the PlayStation."

Chapter 8

Elijah climbed into bed and pressed his cold feet against Adam's calf.

"Aahh," Adam shouted, jerking his leg away. "Ice demon. Get off me."

"I gave in and turned the heat on. I think we need to accept summer is really and truly over."

"But I hate winter," Adam whined. "It's so cold."

"We could always move to Florida."

"Eww. No. I hate mosquitos more."

"Hawaii?" Elijah suggested.

"Oh my God, no. Have you seen the size of the cockroaches there? And don't even get me started on the centipedes."

"Okay, princess. Work with me here. How about Puerto Rico?"

Adam stared at Elijah in disdain. "We wouldn't be able to vote in Puerto Rico. You know how important voting is."

"Cary, North Carolina it is, then."

Adam laughed. "I couldn't leave the center, anyway. It's nice to dream, though."

Elijah's voice rose several octaves. "You couldn't even do that."

Adam shrugged and turned off the TV. "You tired or are you up to talking for a few minutes?"

"I can talk. What's up?"

Taking a deep breath, Adam flipped onto his side to look at Elijah. "I owe you an apology."

Elijah's face scrunched up. "For what?"

"The way I've been handling all of this—blocking you out every time it gets tough for me. It's not fair to you, and I'm sorry."

"Don't be ridiculous. Anyone would have a hard time dealing in this situation. That's no reason to apologize."

Adam shrugged. "Yeah. But I've known I needed to tell you about my past since we started dating. If I'd grown a set and told you in the beginning, maybe all of this would've been easier on both of us. You would've at least known what I had to deal with."

Elijah grabbed Adam's hand. "How about this? Instead of apologizing, let's agree that you'll tell me one story every day."

"I don't think I can do one a day."

Elijah ran his thumb back and forth over Adam's hand. "Then whatever you feel comfortable with. I don't want this to come between us. I'm bad enough at communicating when everything is going well."

"You're better at this than you think, you know. I'm starting to think you thrive under stress."

Elijah shrugged, but Adam knew he'd hit the proverbial nail on the head.

Adam kissed Elijah lightly on the mouth and then touched his forehead to Elijah's. "You ready now?"

Nodding, Elijah stole another kiss, and Adam scooted down farther in the bed to rest his head on Elijah's shoulder. He'd rather not see into Elijah's eyes as he talked, even if the first story was the easiest to tell.

"So you know how my parents ditched me. I stayed at the group home for about four months before CPS placed me with a foster family. The people who ran the home were, for the most part, kind and genuinely interested in making our lives better. There might've been a few only in it for the paycheck, but most of the workers tried to make the best of a shitty situation. In that aspect it wasn't too bad. But when there are that many kids living together, bad shit's bound to happen. Once the older kids got wind that I was gay, they wouldn't leave me alone.

"I suppose I was lucky they never roughed me up too badly. Mostly they just shoved me around, called me names, and made obscene gestures I didn't even understand at the time. During those four months, I learned how shameful it was to be gay, to be a faggot. I learned how unfair life could be, because they told me over and over again how I'd always be scum, always be different, and no one would ever want me—all because of something I had absolutely no control over. I tried to like girls during that stint, but even at that age, when crushes are mostly innocent hand-holding and passing notes, I just… didn't have the same feelings for girls as I did boys."

"You never told anyone in charge?"

Adam shook his head. "They said if I ever did, they'd really hurt me. I believed them. Whether they would have or if they only wanted to scare me, I never knew."

"What happened?"

"The Pearsons were the first family to take me in. And honestly I enjoyed living with them a lot. They weren't anything like Matthew and Amelia, but they cared for me, clothed me, fed me. We'd even go fishing sometimes."

Elijah snorted. "I have a hard time picturing you fishing."

"Oh, hell yeah. I was terrible. I don't think anything could be more boring than fishing, and if I happened to get lucky enough to hook a fish, it always got away. But they're good memories, at least."

"Doesn't sound too bad."

"Well, the Pearsons registered to foster because they'd been unable to have a child of their own. She got pregnant a few months after I moved in with them, and then a month after the baby was born, they sent me back. They said having an infant and a teenager was too much to handle. I just always felt like once they had their real baby, I didn't measure up anymore. Why would they want to foster a broken gay kid when they had their own perfectly healthy normal kid?" Adam shrugged. "So I went back to the home."

"I think I'm beginning to understand how you always know exactly what to say to those kids at the center. I'm sorry you had to go through that."

"You do fine with the kids too, you know. Besides, every kid, every story is different. I was sad to leave the Pearsons, but after losing my parents and my grandparents, I'd already become wary. It hurt to be rejected again, but I wasn't surprised."

Elijah pointed out the obvious. "But your grandparents didn't really have a choice."

"I know that now, but after a few months in the group home and being so young, it started to feel like they'd betrayed me just as much as my own parents had. Gramps had no control over what happened to him, but after being abandoned by my parents, I thought it was all an elaborate ruse so he could get rid of me too. You know what I mean? I thought he didn't want me for the same reason my parents didn't want me, so he faked a stroke. Of course now I know that's ridiculous. But it took quite a bit of therapy for me to really believe in him again."

Adam fell silent—not particularly eager to go start another story but not sure what else to say about the first one. He'd made peace with the Pearsons, maybe not in person, but in his heart. He held no ill will toward them and felt grateful they'd given him an entire year in a decent home.

Elijah tightened his arms around Adam and sighed. "That's some heavy shit, baby."

Adam burst into laughter and tucked his head into Elijah's chest. "I take back what I said about you being your best under pressure."

"What the hell else am I supposed to say? The place didn't sound too bad until you kept talking and told me how you became completely demoralized when they gave you up. I've never thought about foster kids constantly being rejected that way."

"Foster kids learn to be tough pretty quickly, and I'm sure all of us fall under the label 'hooligans,' at one point or another. But it's hard to be anything better when your basis in reality is so shaky."

Adam's mind traveled ahead to the foster parents whose decisions nearly cost him his life. The thought of delving into that story made his stomach queasy.

"Want to stop here?"

Adam nodded. "I want to not think about it for a while before we go to sleep."

Elijah snuggled into the covers with Adam. "I've heard I'm quite good at distracting people in bed," he said innocently.

Grinning, Adam shifted in Elijah's arms. "Is that right? Maybe you'll have to show me, then."

"MY LIFE is over," Kollin wailed as he barged into Adam's office and flopped face-first onto his sofa.

"That's no good," Adam said, saving his work.

"Adam. I'm serious."

Adam held up his hands. "I never said you weren't. Wanna tell me what happened?"

Kollin buried his head in the throw pillow. "I can't. It's too embarrassing. I can never show my face here again."

"I'm sure it's not that bad." It wasn't like Kollin to be overly dramatic, though. Not to that extent, anyway.

"Argh!" Kollin turned his head again so he faced the back of the sofa. "Jase told everyone a piece of Bubble Yum lasts longer than me."

Adam replayed Kollin's words in his head. "He said what?"

"Do *not* make me repeat that."

"Sorry. But I don't get it. Bubble Yum doesn't.... Oh," Adam said. "Wait a second. When the hell did he figure this out?"

"Seriously, Adam? Can you please not go all parental on me right now? My social life is officially ruined."

"Come on. You're sixteen. You're not supposed to last long. Besides, at that age you recover before you even finish wiping up. And I cannot believe I'm having this conversation with you."

"None of that matters when he's telling everyone I'm a one-minute man. We have to move."

"Ugh," Adam said. "Elijah and I already nixed all viable moving locations. You're stuck here for the foreseeable future."

Kollin turned to face Adam. "Then what am I supposed to do?"

"Ignore them."

Kollin stared at Adam. "That's it? Your grand advice is to ignore them?"

"Yeah. Sorry."

"You're horrible at this. I'm going to ask Elijah when we get home."

"You're more than welcome to… and to take whatever advice he gives you. But think about it first. Okay? If you go back to everyone and bad-mouth Jase, you look bad again… like you're trying to get back at him. I guarantee you there's not a guy in that room who lasted more than two minutes his first time…." Adam tilted his head. "It was the first. Right?"

"Oh God. Yes. It was the first time."

Adam sighed in relief. "Honestly the mature thing to do would be to ask Jase about it. Tell him how it made you feel and ask him why he'd tell everyone that. Explain to him that you trusted him, and he broke that trust."

"Thanks for suggesting the only thing that would be more embarrassing than what I'm currently going through," Kollin said.

"Which is why I said to ignore it. We've already established any guy with experience will know it's inevitable. The whole thing will most likely blow over in a day or two. But you really should think about talking to Jase eventually. Maybe he has a reason you don't know about yet. Did… uh… did he do the same?"

Kollin buried his head in the pillow again. "Oh my God. I was wrong. This is more embarrassing."

"Well, I'm sorry. I thought maybe if you lasted longer than he did, Jase told everyone before you had a chance to."

"I don't know. We were interrupted before we got that far."

Adam sat up straight. "Kollin Haverty, you better not tell me you two did this on HOPE property."

Eyes wide, Kollin shook his head. "No. I promise. We weren't here."

Sinking back in his seat, Adam let out a long, slow breath. Not that he approved of Kollin sneaking around where he could get caught, but if he'd been at the center, other kids could be sneaking around too. If that were the case, Adam had bigger problems on his hands than what type of candy Kollin's staying power compared to.

"Do you want me to say something to Jase?"

"No," Kollin shouted again. "Please don't. Please, Adam. Please don't."

"Chill out. I had to ask. The lines get a little blurry with you—between the dad role and the guy-who-runs-the-center role. You know HOPE has a strict no-bullying policy. It's a perfectly legitimate reason for me to have a talk with Jase."

"I know. But still, no thanks. I'll handle it."

"All right. You know where to find me. You ready for tonight?" Adam asked.

Kollin scrunched up his face. "I guess."

A few days after their disastrous dinner with Jessica, Adam called and agreed to give her a chance if—and only if—she accepted his family and career without question. She quickly agreed, and they planned another dinner—this time at their house. After everything Kollin had been through, Adam worried how well he'd handle the meeting.

He studied Kollin for signs of reluctance or stress but found none. Still Adam felt compelled to remind him, "Any time you want to bail, go ahead. And if it gets too much and you need her to leave, say the word. You come first, and I don't want this to be harder on you than it has to be."

"I think I'll be fine. Sounds like it's gonna be awkward all night, anyway."

"I won't argue with you there."

Kollin flopped down on the couch with an overly pitiful huff. "You mind if I hang out in here until it's time to go home?"

"'Course not. I can even put you to work. Want to stuff envelopes for me?"

"I'm too traumatized to work, but nice try. I'll be here wallowing until further notice." He buried his head under the flimsy throw pillow.

Adam shook his head. "Don't overexert yourself."

"STOP WORRYING. You haven't forgotten anything," Elijah said as Adam rechecked the dishes they picked up on the way home. Neither of them saw any need to cook or try to impress Jessica, so they ordered a family-style Southern meal from a local restaurant. They had enough food to feed an army.

"And who gives a shit if you did?" Kollin asked. "Let her complain about one thing…."

"Kollin," Adam said, warning him.

"I'm just saying…. She's the one who should be nervous, not you."

The doorbell rang, giving Kollin the last word. While he didn't want Kollin to be on the defensive all night, his words bolstered Adam just enough that he felt ready to see his birth mother again.

Elijah and Kollin accompanied Adam to answer the door. Pausing, Adam took a deep breath and then turned the knob. He didn't know why, but he still felt surprised to see Jessica standing on his stoop when he opened the door. He wondered if the feeling would ever go away.

She fidgeted nervously—as if she felt as unsure about the evening as the three of them did. Adam supposed that could mean any number of things—good and bad.

"Hey," Adam offered lamely. "Come on in."

Elijah stepped forward, took her coat, and laid it over the table in the foyer.

"Jessica," Adam said, "this is Kollin Haverty. He's been living with Elijah for around six months. Kollin's parents are in jail for abusing him when they found out he was gay." Adam's voice didn't waver, and he didn't take his eyes off Jessica as he spoke. He didn't want to be intentionally hurtful, but he wouldn't back down from the facts of his life to make her more comfortable either. "Elijah's in the process of adopting Kollin. He'll be our son."

Jessica's face remained neutral while Adam spoke. He'd okayed the introduction with Kollin earlier. He wanted to put all the cards on the table in the beginning in hopes of avoiding a disastrous conversation later on.

“Hello,” Kollin said politely, without offering his hand.

“It’s nice to meet you,” Jessica replied, equally polite.

“Uh… the food’s ready,” Adam said, feeling awkward again. “We usually eat in the kitchen.”

Jessica smiled stiffly. “It smells delicious.”

They shuffled into the kitchen, and Adam belatedly thought he should’ve offered a tour of the house first. Too late.

“We picked some food up at The Homeplace on the way. There’s fried chicken, roast beef, mashed potatoes, green beans, baked apples, and carrots,” Adam said, gesturing toward the counter where they’d laid the food out, buffet-style. “Help yourself.”

“Oh,” Jessica said, waving Kollin forward. “You first. Please.”

Adam resisted the urge to roll his eyes. She’d have to do better than that to win Kollin over. Several minutes later they all sat around the table. The only conversation occurred between their knives and forks as they clinked against the plates.

After several minutes of uncomfortable silence, Jessica spoke up. “Thank you for having me over. This is wonderful. I didn’t realize The Homeplace offered takeout orders like this.”

Adam shifted in his seat. “They don’t normally. The owner used to come to HOPE regularly. So whenever I’m in a pinch, she helps me out.”

“That’s lovely. What a nice perk,” Jessica said.

“I guess. I try not to take advantage of the offer. But since you say you’re making an honest effort, I figured it best not to subject you to our horrible cooking.”

“None of you can cook?”

Kollin snorted and took a bite of his chicken. Elijah nudged his elbow. Jessica looked at them with her head tilted.

“We manage well enough to stay alive,” Elijah said. “I never had a reason to cook for myself until Kollin moved in, and I’m not sure what Adam’s excuse is.”

Adam smiled at Elijah, thankful he’d made an effort. The entire situation was difficult enough without additional animosity.

“My excuse is Kris. She’s taken pity on me and fed me for years.”

“Oh?” Jessica asked, perking up. “Who’s Kris?”

Adam saw Kollin roll his eyes and shake his head as he took another bite of chicken. "Her name is Kirsten," Kollin said with his mouth full, seemingly taking his aggression out on the defenseless meat. "And she's Adam's sister."

"Your sister? I didn't realize you'd been adopted."

Kollin threw down his chicken bone. "May I be excused?"

"Of course. Do you need her to leave?" Adam asked. He'd be damned if he'd let Jessica make Kollin feel bad in his own home.

"Nope," he said as he stood. He looked at Adam. "Thank you, though."

"You wanna take your plate with you?" Elijah asked.

"No, thanks. I've had enough," he said, looking at Jessica.

"We'll be up later," Adam said as Kollin walked off.

Jessica pushed food around her plate as an uncomfortable silence filled the kitchen.

Adam cleared his throat. "No one ever formally adopted me, but the last foster family I landed with might as well have. They had one daughter, Kirsten. She's two years younger than me. We're very close, and I consider her my sister. The Wrights are heavily involved in the center and in my life. Along with Elijah and Kollin, they're my family."

Jessica perked up a bit at his story and took a bite of bacon-flavored green beans. "I'm so glad you found such a nice family."

"Yeah. It's the seven families before them you need to worry about." Elijah mumbled his sentiment loud enough for Jessica to hear.

"Seven?" she asked, setting her fork down.

Adam nodded. "I was almost sixteen when I moved in with the Wrights, but the four years before, I lived in seven different foster homes, along with the group home between each stint."

He spoke matter-of-factly, as if he were delivering the news to a large group rather than the woman who sent him off to that misery. Easier on both of them that way.

"Oh," Jessica said. "I hadn't realized. I thought you were exaggerating the other night, hoping to hurt me."

"One thing you'll learn pretty quickly, assuming you stick around," Elijah said, "is Adam doesn't lie or do things to intentionally hurt people. Like, ever." He cast Adam a quick look with a small grin. "It's almost annoying."

Adam smirked back, enjoying Elijah's underhanded way of putting Jessica in her place without sounding like a complete douchebag and still complimenting him. "I'd say you've reaped the benefits of that particular trait."

Elijah shrugged and offered another grin. Adam found the familiar gesture comforting.

Stirring the vegetables around on her plate, Jessica asked, "Did you go to college?"

Adam nodded. "Got my MBA at the University of Virginia, worked a few random jobs, and then decided to start the center."

"That's quite ambitious. I'm impressed."

Smiling, Adam thanked her, not too sure how to handle her praise. He didn't want to care so much, but his insides warmed hearing it all the same. The remainder of the meal passed in a similar fashion. Jessica asked questions here and there, but none were very intrusive, and she stayed away from any topic that could possibly delve into the bad years Adam had spent in the system. Mostly she asked about the center and the inn. By the end of the meal, Adam thought she had actually taken a genuine interest in his life. He still didn't trust her, and he didn't ask what she'd been doing the past twenty years.

Elijah spoke little, chiming in only when Adam prompted him. Jessica never asked how he and Elijah met, but Adam tried not to read into it. While their conversation was shallow, there weren't many lulls. If Adam had to guess, he'd say Jessica had prepared a list of safe topics before she arrived. Still, when she declined dessert of peach cobbler, saying she needed to head home, Adam wasn't disappointed. Though he would temporarily label the evening a success—he hadn't even come near to a panic attack—the stress and anxiety of dealing with his past had worn him out. He escorted Jessica to the door and, after a round of uncomfortable good-byes, Adam closed the door behind her with a sigh of relief.

CHAPTER 9

KOLLIN TOSSED the basketball in the air and waited for it to fall back down, directly into his hands. He'd been lying on his bed, playing catch with himself for almost forty-five minutes while he waited for Adam's birth mother to leave. He knew Adam would be disappointed in him for the way he'd acted. But he couldn't tamp down his anger while he watched her sit at their kitchen table as if she weren't the biggest bitch in the entire world. If she were anyone else, he probably would've gone off to her face, but he respected Adam too much to ruin his night.

He heard a light knock on his door.

"Come in," he called, sitting up to lean against the headboard.

Elijah walked in first, followed by Adam with two bowls of peach cobbler topped with a scoop of ice cream.

"Figured you'd want some," he said. He sat on the side of the bed and handed over one of the bowls while Elijah grabbed Kollin's desk chair.

"Thanks," he said, grabbing the bowl. "You're not eating any?"

Adam rolled his eyes as he took a bite. "Fatty gained two pounds over the weekend. No sugar for him until he's back to his normal weight."

"Maybe if my boyfriend didn't call me 'fatty,' I wouldn't be so self-conscious about those two pounds."

"Oh, please," Adam said. "I couldn't care less if you gain a hundred pounds. You're the one who's a little uptight about your weight."

"I am not uptight about my weight," Elijah defended himself.

"Two pounds, baby."

"You're the one who had us eating every piece of fried, fatty, or sugar-laden food in the tristate area this weekend. So no complaining. Besides, I'll lose them by the end of the week, and I can go back to eating sweets in moderation."

"Oh my God," Kollin yelled. "Will you two shut up? You sound like an old married couple."

"He should be so lucky," Elijah muttered.

Adam rolled his eyes but otherwise ignored Elijah's taunt. "We wanted to check on you. Doing okay?"

Kollin sighed and eyed his bowl. "Yeah. I'm sorry if I made you mad."

"Don't be, because you didn't. I already told you. You come first. Wanna talk about what happened?"

"I dunno. When we talked about it the other day, and even today before she showed up, I thought it was kinda cool. You know? Not many kids like us get a chance to see their parents again at all, and even fewer have ones who actually want something to do with them. I couldn't think of a reason why you wouldn't want to see her."

Adam nodded, but he knew all of that already. During their talk the other night, Kollin had not only encouraged Adam to meet with Jessica, but also said he wanted to meet her.

"The closer it came to time for her to arrive, the angrier I grew. What right does she have, after all this time, to just show up? You know? She abandoned you. She's not supposed to mess with you like that. And then she didn't know jack shit about your life—didn't even know who Kirsten is or what happened to you after foster care. I mean, it's not like the information isn't out there. Your whole life story is on the website. All she had to do was Google your name. It pissed me off."

"I think that's all totally normal," Adam said. "Look at me. I was a mess at first, and I'm twice your age—which means I've had twice as long to learn how to deal with my feelings."

Elijah sat back in his seat and crossed his arms over his chest. "If you don't want to see her again, you don't have to."

"I know." Kollin chopped up the rest of his cobbler and mixed it in with his ice cream. "How'd it go after I left?"

"Okay…. We didn't go anywhere deep, but she seemed interested enough in the center," Adam said.

Kollin frowned. He wished he knew why Jessica decided to turn up all of a sudden. He supposed the death of a parent could change a person's life that profoundly. As much as he wanted to support Adam's choices, he couldn't help putting himself in Adam's place. And every time he did, his own feelings got in the way. The night his dad kicked him out, he thought nothing could be worse. But suffering through his parents' trial was infinitely more difficult. He was torn between wanting them to pay the price for what they did and hoping they didn't go to jail—so one day they could maybe forgive him.

“So we’re going to keep giving her chances to come back into your life until the other shoe drops?” Kollin asked.

Elijah sat forward and rested his elbows on his knees. He dropped his head into his hands with a loud sigh. Kollin wondered if Elijah was as okay with Jessica showing up out of nowhere as he claimed.

Adam shrugged. “Or until the other shoe doesn’t drop. I’m not going into this blindly, but I’d be in a sore spot if people didn’t give me second chances from time to time.”

“Yeah. I guess.”

“Look. I know this is personal for you, but you should understand these are my choices only. Just because we have somewhat of a similar background, that doesn’t mean you have to make the same decision if one of your parents ever tries to make amends. You understand?”

Kollin nodded. “It’s hard not to imagine myself in your shoes sometime down the road.”

“I get that, and I don’t want to kill any hope you may have. But from my vast experience, things like this don’t happen very often. People don’t go from one very cruel extreme to hoping for forgiveness. I guess that’s one of the reasons I feel like I need to see this through. How could I throw away a possible opportunity to have a relationship with my birth mom when so many other people would trade places with me in a heartbeat?”

“Yeah, I guess,” Kollin said.

“You gonna be okay?” Elijah asked.

“As long as I don’t have to start being nice to her anytime soon, I’m good.”

Adam smiled. “Fair enough, kiddo.”

ELIJAH SHOVED his phone in his pocket and turned to Adam, who was sitting on their bed, diligently typing away on his laptop.

“That was my lawyer,” he said.

Adam looked up, pushed his glasses back up his nose, and scrunched up his face to help them stay put. Elijah bit back a laugh. Adam had no clue how ridiculous he looked when he did that. He probably didn’t even realize he made the face at all. “Well, what’d she say?” Adam prompted.

“Three to six months, maybe less.”

Adam's face lit up, and he shoved his computer away so he could rise up to his knees and hold his arms open. Elijah didn't hesitate. He jumped on Adam and tackled him into a huge hug while they laughed like schoolchildren. "I can't believe it."

"I'm so damn excited," Elijah said. "Can we tell him now?"

"Hell yeah. Let's go."

Elijah kissed Adam's mouth, fast and hard, and then scrambled off the bed and pulled Adam up behind him. He practically dragged Adam down the hall to tap lightly on Kollin's bedroom door.

"Yeah?" Kollin's muffled call came from inside.

Elijah pushed open the door and poked his head in. "You got a minute?"

"Sure." Kollin scooted away from his desk where he'd been working on homework while Adam and Elijah took a seat on his bed. "Am I in trouble?"

"Depends," Adam said. "Did you do something to get in trouble?"

Elijah rolled his eyes, and Kollin stared in confusion.

"Uhh… no?"

"You're not in trouble," Elijah said. "We just wanted to tell you what my lawyer said about the adoption process and make sure you still want to move forward."

Kollin perked up as he nodded.

"We have two options. We can go ahead and start the adoption process, which can take anywhere from three to six months. I'll need to get another background check since it's been a while, and they'll get background information from you too. While they're filing all of that paperwork, we'll press your parents to terminate their rights, and then all we have left is the hearing in front of the judge."

Kollin frowned. "What's the other option?"

"We wait to start the actual adoption process until your parents sign over their rights. That way we don't start anything we don't know we can finish. Might delay the process another couple of months, though. Good news is, since I have my own lawyer to prod things along, it's likely to only take three months to push everything through once we start. Maybe even less."

"Wow." Kollin looked at Adam. "I thought you said it would take way longer."

Adam shrugged. “It usually does. I’ve never seen any go this quickly. But given Elijah’s pulling the strings, I’m not that surprised.”

“Do you have a preference?” Elijah asked.

“I dunno. You think my parents will sign?”

Elijah clenched his jaw and closed his eyes. “I have no idea what they’ll do. It’s hard to say, but if I were a betting man, my gut says they sign.” Damn. What a shitty thing to have to say to a kid.

“I think so too,” Kollin said.

“You gonna be okay with that?” Adam asked. “If the side effects are too difficult, you don’t have to go through with this, you know.”

“I know. I’ll be fine. Either way.” Kollin ran his fingers through his green-striped hair, ruffling it up.

“It’s okay if you’re not,” Adam said.

Kollin picked at his jeans. “Yeah. It’s just.... It’ll suck if they sign. It’s like the surefire, no-turning-back act that they don’t want anything to do with me. But it’s gonna suck if they don’t sign too, just to be bastards.”

Oh God. Elijah hadn’t prepared himself well enough for this conversation. His excitement over getting what he wanted prevented him from seeing the situation from Kollin’s perspective. What an awesome foray into fatherhood.

“I think I’d rather wait for them to sign before we move forward. It’ll be too hard to have all of this ripped away if we start the process and then they refuse,” Kollin said.

“I think that’s a good idea.”

Elijah sighed. Should they really put Kollin through the hassle for a signed piece of paper? Kollin was ecstatic when they first mentioned formal adoption, but Elijah suspected Kollin hadn’t considered the nitty-gritty details.

Adam smiled, silently reassuring Elijah. “Whatever happens,” Adam said, “good or bad, nothing changes how we all feel about each other. So let’s just hold on to that until we know something for sure.”

“Yeah. You’re right,” Kollin said as he swiveled his chair around. “I better finish my homework, but thanks for letting me know. And for letting me choose.”

“You bet, buddy,” Adam said, standing and tugging Elijah up.

“Let me know if you have any questions or anything,” Elijah called over his shoulder as Adam pulled him out of the room.

“Thanks, Eli,” Kollin said. “Mind closing the door behind you?”

Elijah nodded, and when the door was shut, he leaned against the wall and let out a loud sigh. “That was harder than I thought it would be.”

Adam hooked his fingers into Elijah’s waistband and lined up their bodies to step into Elijah’s space. “You looked like you were on the verge of giving him everything you could, just to get him to smile. So I got you outta there quick.”

Elijah chuffed and ducked his head into Adam’s neck. “I think I might have.”

“Softie,” Adam murmured. Elijah felt Adam’s lips spread into a smile against his cheek as he planted a kiss beneath his ear.

“S’all your fault. You made me this way.”

“Mmmhmm. All my fault.” Adam ran his nose down Elijah’s neck and kissed the skin where throat met shoulder. “Maybe you should punish me.”

Laughing, Elijah pushed Adam away but kept hold of his shirt so he didn’t go too far.

“Thank you,” he said, turning serious. “I couldn’t do this without you.”

“Sure you could,” Adam said, so confidently Elijah almost believed him. “But I’m glad you don’t have to.”

CHAPTER 10

OVER THE next several weeks, Jessica visited Adam once or twice a week. Adam felt as if he'd gotten to know her pretty well, and he started to believe she truly felt remorse for her actions. They stumbled through more than one awkward conversation, but even Elijah and Kollin admitted she seemed genuinely interested in Adam's life. Adam hadn't introduced her to anyone else in his family, but he let a small spark of hope light in his chest. Jessica didn't deserve a free pass into his life. That didn't mean she should have a lifetime ban either.

As Adam tidied up his desk so he could leave for the impromptu lunch Jessica had just asked him to, he tried not to acknowledge how much the invitation had warmed him all over. The casual phone call and request for lunch would be normal coming from Amelia or Kirsten, but coming from Jessica—from his birth mother—it felt bigger. The thought both excited and terrified him.

Adam walked into Etman's five minutes early and immediately spotted Elijah waiting in the to-go line. With a grin, he snuck up behind him and discreetly pinched his delectably fine ass.

Elijah jumped and turned, and his lips formed the curve he reserved just for Adam. "Hey," he said. "What're you doing here?"

"Meeting Jessica for lunch. She called me earlier and asked. You?"

"Well, I was surprising you with lunch. Chicken salad Thursday. Point in the good boyfriend column and all that."

Adam gestured toward a booth. "Why don't you eat with us?"

"You sure?"

"Of course. I'm sure Jessica won't care."

"Perfect timing," Elijah said as they called his name. He grabbed the sandwiches and slid into the booth next to Adam. Before they even had a chance to open the bag, Jessica walked through the doors of the restaurant.

She appeared troubled, though Adam couldn't say for sure. She still greeted him with a warm smile, but she sat rigidly in the booth and refused to meet his eyes. Adam smiled back and tried to push the bad feeling aside. He didn't know her nearly well enough to jump to any conclusions, but she reminded him more of the woman who showed up at his center a month earlier than the woman he'd gotten to know the past couple of weeks.

Jessica ordered quickly, and they exchanged pleasantries. She assured Adam she was glad Elijah had joined them, but she didn't even spare him a passing glance. When she started shredding the corner of her napkin while staring at the table, Adam asked, "Is everything okay?"

Her eyes widened at Adam's question, but she nodded. "I actually spoke with your grandfather's lawyer today."

Adam's brows furrowed. "Oh?"

"Yes. He said he needs your signature on some document before I can access the contents of my father's safe-deposit box."

Adam sat up straight. "My signature? Why would he need my signature?"

Jessica waved her hand around, gave a little huff, and rolled her eyes. "Oh, it's silly. Your grandfather adjusted his will after my mom died, indicating everything should go to me. But after your grandfather entered the nursing home, he added that you should be there when we open the box, even though he'd already begun showing signs of dementia. They've been trying to find you all this time. I didn't even know the box existed before today. It's certainly thrown me for a loop."

Shock tore through Adam. *Did Gramps leave me something?* "Okay. I don't know why he'd want me there."

"I'm not sure either, to be honest. It's ridiculous. Mr. Wilt, the executor and one of your grandfather's oldest friends, claims he was quite lucid when he requested the change, but how anyone could tell at that point is beyond me. Every time I visited him, he didn't have a clue who I was." Jessica dug around in her purse, pulled out a piece of paper, and slid it across the table. "Anyway, if you could just sign this, I'll take care of everything and put this whole stressful mess behind me."

Wary of the manner in which Jessica was trying to sweep everything under the rug as not a big deal, Adam picked up the paper. He scanned the document quickly. Words like "disclaimer" and "refuses the bequest" popped out at him, but Adam couldn't tell exactly what he'd be signing away. He looked up at Jessica and then over at Elijah, who very subtly shook his head. Adam tightened his grip on the pen.

"Did he leave me something?"

Looking flustered, Jessica shook her head. "He had nothing left to leave you, Adam. Any assets he had went to pay for the cost of his health care at the nursing home, and as I said, he made this change after he'd been admitted there. He was half-loony by then. I have no idea why anyone allowed him to do such a ludicrous thing."

Elijah leaned forward. "Jessica, if I may interrupt. Why shouldn't Adam be there to open the box, if that's what the will specifies?"

"Well, why would he?" she asked, her voice high and defensive. "I've already told you he had nothing. I'm trying to save him the trouble of a trip."

"Maybe there's nothing of monetary value in there," Adam said. "But it could have sentimental value. You mentioned he kept journals. After you said something about it, I remembered him writing in them all the time. Maybe he left me one of those."

Adam's hopes started to rise. He couldn't believe Gramps had left him something, had remembered him after all those years, and that he might actually get to hold a little piece of him again.

"Of course he didn't," Jessica snapped. "I told you the man was crazy."

Eyes wide, Adam stared at Jessica. He saw the instant she recognized her blunder, and she quickly cleared her throat.

"I'm sorry. I didn't mean to sound so harsh, but this whole thing has been very difficult for me. I only meant he couldn't remember who was what. If you sign the paper, I'll take care of everything for you. I can bring whatever it is to you the next time I'm in town."

Adam set down the pen and squinted at Jessica. "Why don't you want me near this safe-deposit box?"

"What? That's ridiculous." Jessica huffed and stuttered over her words. "I told you I'm trying to be helpful. Save you a trip."

Jessica's food arrived, but no one made a move to begin eating. Everything about the moment felt off, and the shady way Jessica was handling the situation made Adam's stomach turn over. He looked at the woman he'd started to believe had come back into his life to make amends, and his heart sank. Deep in his gut, he knew whatever lay in the safe-deposit box was the real reason Jessica Lancaster had shown up at the center all those weeks before.

Adam stared down at the paper again. "I'd like to be there when the box is opened. I'm not signing this."

Elijah slid one hand onto his knee and squeezed.

"I don't know why you're being so difficult about this," Jessica said, her eyes flashing as she finally met Adam's gaze.

"I'm not being difficult. Gramps wanted me there to open the box, so I'm going to be there."

"But, Adam—"

"No," Adam said, snapping as renewed anger welled inside him. "You don't get to 'but, Adam' me. That man loved me and treated me with respect when his daughter, my own mother, didn't. He was my first example of true, unconditional love. My first example of compassion and generosity and just plain goodness, even though he didn't have to do a damn thing for me. Whatever positive qualities I managed to cling to when I escaped from what amounted to hell for me, I learned from him. And Matthew and Amelia Wright saw those qualities in me, miniscule as they may've been, and helped foster them to turn me into the man I am today. I'm damn proud of the things I've done with my life, and you had nothing to do with encouraging any part of that pride. I wanted to overlook all of our bad history and give you the benefit of the doubt, accept that you'd realized you'd made a mistake, but you will not take whatever Gramps left in that box away from me. So tell me. Why the hell should I believe anything you've said to me over the past few weeks?"

Jessica stared at Adam with her mouth wide open. He hadn't intended to go off on a rant, but once the words spewed out of his mouth, he felt damn good about it.

"You ungrateful little…." The vein on the side of Jessica's neck popped out. "How dare you speak to me like that? I've been nothing but kind and considerate of your situation since I showed up."

"My situation?" Adam asked, seething. "What the hell does that mean?"

"It doesn't even matter, because she's lying, anyway," Elijah said. "While you've in no way been rude, you also haven't shown any true regret. You've made absolutely no attempt to get to know me or Kollin, and you only speak to us when Adam is in the room."

"What?" Adam asked, gaping at Elijah. "You never told me that."

Elijah tilted his head. "I didn't want to ruin whatever was happening because of my own paranoia."

"Fuck. I can't believe this is happening." Adam took a deep breath to settle his nerves and then returned his focus to Jessica. While Elijah had silenced her with his accusation, she still looked angrier than she had any reason to. "I'm not signing this paper. After I talk with my lawyer, I'll contact the executor and schedule a time to open the box. I'll extend you a courtesy you never showed me and let you know when I go to the bank. No matter what you were to me then, or what you are or aren't to me now, he was your father, and I won't take this moment away from you. If it's all a mistake, like you're saying, you're welcome to whatever is in the box."

Jessica pursed her lips, nodded once, and stood. Leaving her untouched food on the table, she turned and walked out of the restaurant. Adam shoved his sandwich to the side, folded his arms on the table, and then buried his head in them.

"I'm so embarrassed," he whispered.

He felt Elijah run his hand up his back and then squeeze his shoulder.

"What do you have to be embarrassed about?"

Adam turned his head to look at Elijah. "Are you kidding me? I actually let myself believe she wanted to know me. Fucking hell, Elijah. I thought about including her in Christmas somehow, and the whole time she was just playing me to get at whatever's in this box."

Sighing, Elijah acknowledged the truth in Adam's statement. "There's a chance she meant what she said, I guess, but it doesn't look good. She definitely looked angry that you'd accused her of using you—rather than sad or hurt."

"I can't believe you didn't tell me she was so rude to you guys. Especially Kollin. I mean, you can take care of yourself, but I had no business inviting this shitfest into our lives with everything else he's going through. So much for putting him first."

"Stop. Right now. I don't like where you're going with this. Kollin is sixteen and more than capable of taking care of himself. He wanted you to do what was best for you. And even though this isn't turning out how we all hoped, I still think it would've driven you crazy if you'd pushed her away without seeing what she wanted."

"Following through and believing her bullshit are two totally different things."

Elijah sighed again, grabbed their wrapped sandwiches, and shoved them back in the bag. "Let's get out of here. You're not focusing on the right things, so we might as well take a break."

Anger flashed through Adam again. He looked up at Elijah and beckoned him with his fingers to stand. What the fuck else was he supposed to focus on? His mother had lied to him—again. And she'd made him think he mattered, when in reality he didn't—a-fucking-gain. Did Elijah want him to smile and pretend like none of it mattered?

Fuck that. Ignoring Elijah's outstretched hand, Adam stood. "I need to get back to the center," he said and walked out.

GENTLY PUSHING open their bedroom door, Elijah found Adam working at the computer. He walked over to the bed and sat down. It'd been a long day since Adam left him at Etman's, and the total silence from Adam had only made it longer. Doing his best to keep his frustration out of his voice, he asked, "You want to talk about this?"

"I called my lawyer. He said the box is mine. She has no claim to it unless I sign the paper, which states I don't want the contents. I called Mr. Wilt, who happens to work at the bank where the safe-deposit box is, and Amelia's covering for me tomorrow morning at the center so I can drive to Zebulon to open it. I sent Jessica a text this afternoon to let her know I'd be there around ten."

Adam never turned around, never stopped working on his computer.

Elijah pinched the bridge of his nose. He had no idea what he'd done to piss Adam off so fiercely. One second he was busy mentally rearranging the rest of his day so he could help Adam deal with the latest fallout, and the next thing he knew, Adam was out the door.

"Do you want me to come?"

"Nope."

"Are you going to tell me why you've been ignoring me all day?"

Adam still didn't turn around. "In case you didn't notice at lunch, I had a lot to deal with."

"Yeah. I got that. I also got that I was ready to jump in and do whatever you needed to help, but you left me standing in the restaurant holding your food."

"What the fuck else was I supposed to do? You told me you didn't want to talk about it. So I left to deal with the fact that my birth mother is a conniving, lying bitch who not only has no problem giving up her only child, but also has no qualms making him think she actually gives a damn in order to get her greedy little hands on the one thing I may or may not have from the one blood relative who actually loved me."

As Adam spoke, his voice gradually grew louder and his agony seeped out. Elijah felt just as furious as Adam appeared—at the entire situation, at Adam for thinking he'd blow him off so flippantly, and mostly at Jessica for making the best person Elijah knew feel so small. But the heartache in Adam's last words overpowered Elijah's anger.

Elijah's voice was resigned when he spoke again. "I don't know what I said to make you think I didn't want to talk about what happened, but it wasn't my intention. I only wanted to get out of the damn restaurant so we could go somewhere private to figure out what to do."

"Clearly I didn't need your help."

"Dammit, Adam," Elijah shouted and then lowered his voice. "Don't shut me out again. What is it about your mom that turns you against me?"

Adam finally swiveled around, but only so he could glare at Elijah. "Do not ever call that bitch my mother again."

Holding his hands up, Elijah stood slowly and crossed the room to stand before Adam. "I'm sorry. I love you, and I want to help, but I don't know how. Please tell me how."

Elijah saw the moment Adam gave in. His entire body sagged, and he stared at the ground, slowly shaking his head. "I don't know how either. I can't believe I fell for her lies. I'm so stupid."

"Hey." Elijah knelt down, rested his hands on either side of Adam's hips, and bumped his forehead against the top of Adam's head. "That's not true at all. You didn't go into this blindly. You agonized over whether or not to give her a chance, and the fact that you did only shows how incredibly selfless and forgiving you are. Most people wouldn't have given her a second shot, and that's what makes you the absolute best person I'll ever know. Never stupid."

Adam didn't say anything else, so Elijah stayed on his knees and held him while Adam cried out his pain.

CHAPTER 11

"THANKS FOR coming with me," Adam said as he peered out of the car window at the small local bank. He wasn't totally sure he wanted Elijah there. He still found the entire situation humiliating and would prefer not to have the person who thought the most of him watching. But the idea of being there with Adam seemed to make Elijah feel better, so when he asked again over breakfast, Adam agreed.

He didn't spot Jessica's car in the parking lot, but he had no doubt she'd be there. She was polite but succinct when she texted him back the day before. Part of him still hoped his suspicions were unfounded. Maybe she really had only been trying to help. Maybe she truly felt hurt Adam didn't trust her enough to handle this on his behalf. What would he do then? He'd walk away feeling either ashamed for doubting Jessica or ashamed for believing her. Neither option sounded appealing.

They found the office of Mr. John Wilt easily enough. He'd been his grandfather's best friend, though Adam didn't remember him. Mr. Wilt looked frail and several years past retirement. Yet when he spoke, his voice held vitality. Adam recognized the deep, booming sound he heard on the phone the day before, and the years seemed to melt right off him.

"Adam," he said, holding out a hand, "it's such a pleasure to see you again. I don't know if you remember me, but I visited your grandfather a few times when you were a young lad. He loved having you there, you know. Made him feel young again when not much else did."

Adam's heart twinged as he shook Mr. Wilt's hand. "Thank you, sir. That's so nice to hear. This is my boyfriend, Elijah. I hope it's okay he's here with me."

"Of course. Anyone you wish can be present. It's your box now." The man shook Elijah's hand. "Ready to get started?"

Adam shoved his hands into his pockets. "I told Jessica she could be here, so I guess we should wait."

"I see. You understand she doesn't have to be here? And everything in the box is yours. She has no legal claim to it. Your grandfather paid a lawyer and lined up witnesses to specify you had first dibs on the contents of the box. I don't mean to overstep or imply anything, but he went to a great deal of trouble to ensure *you* opened this box after he died."

Adam exhaled a long breath. He'd known that, of course, but hearing Mr. Wilt say it with such certainty felt like a thousand-pound weight lifting off his chest.

"I appreciate that, but I made a promise, so I'd like to keep it."

Mr. Wilt nodded once and invited them to sit. But before Adam's ass touched the chair, Jessica hurried into the room, looking more frazzled than Adam had ever seen her. Mr. Wilt greeted Jessica with a touch less warmth than he had Adam, and within minutes they all piled into the bank vault to pull out box 321. Mr. Wilt handed it over to Adam and escorted them into a large room with several partitions that created small cubicles.

"They're all vacant now, so choose whichever one tickles your fancy. The one on the end there is a bit larger. Might be more comfortable, since there are so many of you. The curtain draws for privacy."

"Thanks, Mr. Wilt," Adam said. Once in the cubicle, Elijah stood back to let Jessica sit in the second chair. Staring at the box for a moment, Adam took a deep breath and felt Elijah's hand on his neck.

"Are you going to open it or not?" Jessica asked, her tone hard.

Elijah squeezed his shoulder, and Adam was suddenly grateful Elijah had insisted on coming along and providing the strength he needed to ignore Jessica. With another deep breath, Adam lifted the top of the box.

Jessica leaned over, invading Adam's space to peer in the box. Her head blocked Adam's view, but he heard her swear under her breath. He nudged her shoulder a bit with his, and she took the hint, backing out of his way. Inside the box sat a smaller box without a top. It was filled with baseball cards—hundreds, maybe even thousands of baseball cards—and one envelope. Bypassing the cards, Adam grabbed the envelope with his name scribbled on the front in his grandfather's shaky handwriting. He tore it open and began to read.

Adam,

I hope this letter finds you sooner than later. I don't mean that to sound morbid, because I know you won't see it until my death, but I'm an old man and half-crazy, anyway. I don't have very many good days anymore, but when I do, I always remember you. What I have to say is going to be difficult to hear, but I suspect you're used to a difficult life by now. I hope, for the time you were with me, I made your life as joyful as possible.

I'm sorry for not being able to keep you longer. You needed more than I could offer. After your mother started visiting me again, I thought she would take you back and give you a decent life if I signed my accounts over to her. When you never came along with her during her rare visits, I stopped believing her excuses and realized I needed to take matters into my own hands. I'm far too sick to be of any value to you right now, so I asked John to do me this favor.

This box contains my baseball card collection. Most of these are probably worthless, but I know there are a few that would go for quite a bit of money. I hope you can sell these and make your life a little easier. Your mother knows about them but doesn't know where they are.

Please know saying good-bye to you was one of the hardest things I've ever done. I'm ashamed of Jessica's actions, but I hope I was able to compensate in some small way. I love you, Adam.

Love,
Gramps

Adam laid the letter to the left of the box, out of his mother's view. His mind raced, and for the first time in years, Adam had to tamp down a physical urge to lash out at everyone in the tiny room with him.

It felt so much worse than anything he'd imagined. He had undeniable proof Jessica only wanted the cards and whatever money they could bring her. Adam didn't care if they were worth ten dollars or ten million dollars. Jessica Lancaster would never see a penny of it. The only reminder he had of his gramps lay inside that box, and he'd be damned if he ever gave them up.

"I helped your grandfather build that card collection, you know. I'd get so mad because he never let me take some of them out of their plastic. When he went to the assisted living home, I searched every nook and cranny in his home for those cards. He must've taken them with him. Please, Adam. He was my father, and you said you didn't want to deny me this. At least split them with me."

Elijah spoke before Adam could. "If you want any hope of seeing Adam or any of those cards again, I'd suggest you keep your mouth shut until Adam says you can speak."

Adam grabbed his hand as he gathered his thoughts.

"Gramps left these cards to me. Legally they're mine. What's more, this letter specifically states he wanted me to have them. I wouldn't dishonor his request even if I wanted to, and certainly not for someone who lied to her own mentally ill father just to get to his money and then came back into my life for the sole purpose of manipulating me."

"This again? I told you why I showed up. It has nothing to do with these worthless baseball cards. I told you I didn't even know about this box until this week. What the hell did he say to you?" Jessica reached over Adam to grab the letter, but Adam was quicker. He grabbed her arm and held it in place until she backed off.

"That's mine too."

Elijah spoke up. "I know how we can settle this right now. Let's go."

Adam had no idea what Elijah intended to do, but he felt too numb to argue. He didn't want to stay in the cubicle with Jessica any longer than necessary, so he grabbed the box with the cards and followed him out. Jessica trailed behind them.

Elijah stopped at Mr. Wilt's office and went in. He took one of the two available seats and waved his hand for Adam to take the other, leaving Jessica standing.

"Mr. Wilt, we were hoping you could clear something up for us," Elijah said. "When did you first contact Jessica about this safe-deposit box?"

The man frowned while he thought. "I guess it took a while, because I tried to locate Adam myself first. I considered hiring someone to find him. Old man like me. I know the banking world like the back of my hand, but detective work isn't my forte. That seemed like an awfully big production, though, when I could just ask Jessica. I guess I gave up after about three weeks of thumbing through all the Adam Lancasters I could find in the white pages. So maybe two months ago?"

If there'd been a shred of hope left in Adam's heart, Mr. Wilt ripped it out with those final words. Jessica knew about the box well before she made initial contact with him. She had lied about it.

"Thank you, sir," Elijah said. "I presume we're allowed to keep the contents of the box?"

"Yes, of course. It belongs to Adam. Though, if you want to keep the contents in the safe-deposit box, your grandfather paid for it for another four years. He renewed his ownership every five years, and of course you're welcome to renew it if you wish."

"Thank you again," Elijah said as he stood and held out his hand for Adam.

Jessica mumbled something inaudible and then spun a one-eighty and marched out of the bank with Elijah hot on her heels. As soon as they were all outside, Elijah picked up his pace and rounded on Jessica, blocking her way.

"You listen to me now, and listen closely. Stay away from my family. You did enough damage to him as a child, and somehow you've managed to come back and inflict even more on him. Despite your genes, Adam managed to become kind and loving and generous. If I ever see your face or hear your name again, I will have a restraining order on you so big you won't even be allowed in the state of North Carolina. And if you think for one second I'm bluffing, I dare you to try me. I will spend every last cent I have to make sure he never has to think of you again."

"Get your hands off my wife!"

Oh no. No, no, no, no, no. No. Adam took a step backward as Elijah spun around.

"If you touch her again, I'll snap your fucking neck off," the man said as he hurtled toward Elijah.

"I haven't touched your wife, and I can guarantee every camera this bank has would verify that," Elijah said and moved a step over to block Adam's view of the man who called him a faggot with his parting words.

"You think standing in front of the fruitcake is going to protect him?"

"Chad, calm down," Jessica said. She placed her hands on his chest and forced him to take a step back.

"Fuck if I'll calm down. I will not allow some faggot to put his hands all over you," he shouted.

"For Pete's sake. He didn't touch me. You need to get back in the car," Jessica said though clenched teeth.

"Were the cards in the box?" Chad asked.

"Yes, but he left them to Adam. There's nothing we can do."

"The hell there isn't." Chad leaned around Elijah and pointed his finger at Adam. "You'll be hearing from our lawyer. We're the ones who paid for that man's lunatic ass to live in a nursing home for the past six years. That money should be ours."

Dizziness swept over Adam, and he took a step backward and tried to suck in a deep breath. The air wouldn't flow through his lungs properly, so he sucked in another one right behind it.

"Look at you," his father sneered. "You're so pathetic you can't even stand up to your old man. What a fucking waste of a son."

Elijah spun around to face Adam while his father kept spewing hatred. Elijah grabbed Adam around the waist and all but dragged him to a nearby bench, whispering calming words along the way. Adam focused on Elijah's voice, not really understanding the words coming out of his mouth but allowing the soothing tones to comfort him. When Elijah finally told him his parents had left, Adam took a slow, deep breath. He sagged against Elijah's shoulder and closed his eyes.

"You're getting good at that," he whispered.

Elijah grunted. "I wish I didn't have to."

"I'm sorry."

Elijah shook his head. "You have no reason to be. None of this is your fault."

Adam nodded and straightened up. "Can we go home now?"

"You sure you're okay to walk?"

"Yeah. It wasn't as bad this time. I used to have panic attacks all the time after the camp they sent me to. I'm remembering how to recover again," Adam said. "Plus having you here helps."

Elijah grunted again and helped Adam stand. "What camp?"

Adam's heart skipped a beat. He didn't mean to mention the camp aloud until he told Elijah the story, but he was in no condition to tell him now. Adam shook his head. "I'll tell you later. Just get me home, please."

"Of course," Elijah said and helped him into the car. Adam didn't bother to pretend he could stay awake. Closing his eyes, he slept for the short trip home.

"THAT FUCKING bitch," Kirsten screamed as she slammed several bags of Thai food on the counter. "I hope she burns in hell."

"Kirsten, watch your mouth in front of Kollin," Amelia said, scolding her as she set down two more bags.

"Please, Mom. Like he doesn't hear ten times worse at school."

"That's true," Kollin said and started opening the bags.

"Besides, it's totally appropriate in this situation," Kirsten said. She swatted Kollin's hands away and pointed to the cabinet for him to get plates.

"That's also true," Kollin said.

Adam watched as his family argued, dished out food onto their plates, and joined him at the table. Without being asked, Amelia slid a full plate in front of him, rubbed the center of his back a few times, and returned to the counter to fix her own plate.

"How you holding up, son?" Matthew asked from Adam's left.

Adam lowered his head as guilt once again raced through him. When he first told Amelia and Matthew about Jessica showing up, they were nothing but supportive. Not that Adam ever expected anything less from them, but he never wanted his family to think Jessica's return to his life meant he appreciated them any less. Now that she'd swept through and crushed him once more, Adam felt like he was putting his foster parents through the wringer again—only this time needlessly. If Adam had recognized Jessica for the malicious liar she truly was, his entire family wouldn't have dropped all of their Friday-night plans to rally around him.

Thankfully Matthew didn't push. He started talking with Kollin, so Adam returned to picking at his food. The conversation flowed freely around him. He vaguely listened as they made plans for Thanksgiving and joined in when someone—usually Kris—spoke his name. But otherwise he kept to himself. He felt too tired, too isolated, and too sad to do anything more. Before he knew it, they started cleaning off the table, and he'd barely taken two bites of his food.

"I'll pack it up for you," Amelia said quietly and whisked the plate out from in front of him as subtly as she set it there.

"Thanks," he said, hoping the single word conveyed more than it sounded like. "I appreciate you guys stopping by tonight, but I think I'm gonna head up to bed. It's been a long day."

He tried to offer a smile, but he felt it fall flat. As Adam passed, Elijah reached out to grab his hand and gave it a quick squeeze.

Adam was barely even out of the kitchen when he heard Kollin pseudo-whisper, "This isn't good. I'm worried about him."

Adam dropped his head even more. He'd lost count of the number of times he'd let Kollin down over the past few weeks by putting his own drama first, and now he'd done it again. Another tick in the selfish-bastard column for himself.

"He'll be fine," he heard Elijah say. "We'll get through this, kiddo."

Adam trudged up the stairs before he could hear anything more about how much he'd disappointed his family.

KIRSTEN GNAWED on her bottom lip, a habit she'd taken up when she stopped biting her nails. "I'm worried too."

Kollin bowed his head into his hands. "I've never seen him like this. It's creepy."

"Give him some credit," Amelia said. "He's strong."

"I know he's strong, Mom, but I haven't seen him shut people out like this since he first moved in with us."

"I'm sure her showing up again is making him relive some of the things he went through. But he moved past them once, and I know he can do it again. He just needs some time," Matthew said.

Elijah sank into a chair at the table. "If I could wrap my hands around that woman's neck, I wouldn't regret it for a second." He sounded miserable, and Kirsten's heart ached to find a way to help. The three of them had just found their slice of happiness, imperfect as it may be, and now they had to deal with this bullshit.

"Is he seeing anyone?" Kirsten asked. "He said before he thought about talking to Dr. Maggie and then decided not to."

Elijah shook his head. "Not that I know of. It'd been part of a deal we made when Jessica first showed up. But then he snapped out of his funk, so I didn't push."

Kirsten growled, and she felt Derek's hand on her arm. "Does that bitch even know what she put him through by sending him to foster care? How dare she come back into his life, knowing she would disappoint him again."

Kirsten saw Elijah's shoulders subtly droop even further. "I don't think so. I don't even know what happened to him."

"You don't?" Kirsten stared at Elijah, shocked and somewhat disappointed in both Elijah and Adam. She stayed out of their business for the most part, but how could they be planning their life together without Elijah knowing what Adam went through as a teenager?

"No. He's been telling me about it lately. I know about the Pearsons and the two couples after that who pretty much sent him back to the group home as soon as they found out he liked guys. He said the next home was bad, though, and he needed to be in the right frame of mind for it. We never got around to talking about it. Is it really awful?"

"Shit, Eli," Kollin said. "You don't know what they did to him? They sent him—"

"Kollin," Kirsten interrupted. "It's not our place."

"But it's not like it's a secret," he protested.

"Doesn't matter, son," Matthew said. "Kirsten's right. It's Adam's past to share with his partner."

"Did his biological father ever do anything to him? Adam didn't lose his shit today until Chad showed up and started running his mouth."

"Chad was there?" Matthew asked.

Elijah scratched his head. "He accused me of touching Jessica and then started insulting Adam. That's when Adam almost had his panic attack. If he hadn't, I'd probably be in jail for assault right now, which is exactly what he wanted, I'm sure. You think him being there made it worse?"

"He's never said much to me about the guy," Kirsten said. "Seemed pretty ambivalent about him. I kinda got the impression his mother's rejection hurt him more, because he never felt the same connection to Chad as he did her. Who knows, though? I can't imagine wondering whether or not my parents love me."

"It's no picnic," Kollin said sullenly, and Kirsten immediately regretted her words. Kollin wasn't always a real part of their little family, and sometimes she forgot he'd had a completely different life a year earlier.

"On that note, we should probably head out and give you guys some time alone," Amelia said. "Let us know if you need anything, Elijah. You too, Kollin."

"We'll leave too, but you better call me if something happens," Kirsten said as she hugged Elijah and then Kollin. "Sorry I was so thoughtless," she whispered in his ear.

"No big," Kollin said. "It is what it is."

Sighing, Kirsten squeezed Kollin tighter. He might be right, but she wished more than anything she could prove him wrong.

CHAPTER 12

ELIJAH LIFTED the lid of the waffle maker, stabbed the waffle with a fork to transfer it to a plate, and joined Adam and Kollin at the table.

"…and then Dedrick said Jase had the smallest package of any guy he'd ever been with."

Elijah couldn't help but laugh at Kollin's gleeful tone. He wondered if Kollin would feel this comfortable talking to them about sex if they'd raised him from the time he was an infant. Elijah would've died and dug his own grave before talking to his parents about stuff like that as a teen.

Adam, on the other hand, grunted to show he'd heard Kollin's story. Seemingly determined to pull a real reaction out of Adam, Kollin tried again. "Then Dedrick asked if I wanted to see a movie next weekend, but I don't know. I think he gets around a lot, and I don't want to go out with someone who's only interested in me because I'm one of the five out dudes in our school."

"Sounds tough," Adam mumbled.

Kollin looked at Elijah helplessly, and Elijah offered him half a smile. It'd been six days since Adam went through the safe-deposit box, seen his birth father for the first time in years, and confirmed Jessica had only wanted back in Adam's life for her own personal gain. Adam had more or less turned into a shell of himself, barely speaking to anyone, and only when prompted. He went to work, but according to Chloe, he rarely interacted with the kids on a personal level, and he barely ate anything at all. Even on Thanksgiving, when they hosted Adam's entire family and Elijah's parents for dinner, Adam remained distant and morose.

Elijah and Kollin gave him a few days of space and then treated him as if everything were normal. When Adam refused to drop the world's best impression of Eeyore, they switched tactics and actively tried to pull him out of his funk. But no matter what they said or did, Adam remained listless and apathetic. The only time Elijah managed to pull the slightest sign of life out of Adam was when he tentatively asked him to share a little more of his past. Before Elijah could even finish his sentence, Adam started yelling about how insensitive Elijah was being.

"I thought maybe we could go to the inn this weekend," Kollin said. "Eli said they're going to start painting the outside, and it's supposed to be warm. Or I can help you with room eighteen."

Adam's head snapped up, and he squinted at Kollin. "I think I'm gonna hire someone to finish that room. I've got plenty of money saved up. It'll be so much easier, and we'll finally be done with it," he said and then returned his attention to his uneaten waffle.

Elijah set down his fork. "I thought room eighteen was your baby, your pet project."

Adam shrugged. "A professional would do a better job than I ever would. Quicker too," he added as an afterthought.

"I think we've done a good job so far on our own, and there's no rush to finish the room yet. We still have some available," Elijah said.

Standing abruptly, Adam's chair almost tilted over behind him. "Maybe I don't want to finish it anymore." He grabbed his plate and scraped the waffle into the trash can, then ran some water over the dish and placed it in the dishwasher.

Stunned, Elijah and Kollin watched him stalk out of the kitchen without another word.

"Elijah," Kollin said, his voice carrying more concern than it should.

"I know," he replied, even though really, Elijah had no damn idea.

ADAM'S PHONE rang and interrupted his blindly-staring-at-the-computer-screen session. He shifted his eyes, wondering if he'd hear Jessica's voice on the other end. It had been a week and a half since the bank incident, and he hadn't heard a peep out of her. But something in his gut told him he would. Eventually. But then again, why should he trust his gut? It clearly hadn't done him any good when she popped back into his life and dangled fake love and affection in front of his face.

Adam snatched up the phone before it stopped ringing and braced himself for the sound of her voice—just as he'd done every other time the damn thing had rung over the past ten days.

"This is Adam."

"Hey, Adam." The voice on the other end of the line was hesitant, but it didn't belong to Jessica.

"Riley," Adam said, surprised. "How are you?"

"Oh, you know… busy, I guess," he said.

Adam frowned. "Something I can do for you?"

"Maybe. I don't know."

Adam ground his teeth and tried not to sigh. Couldn't Riley hurry up and spill whatever was bothering him? Guilt immediately overtook his frustration. He'd been short with all of the youth at the center lately, and none of them deserved it. He'd taken to hiding in his office most of the day to avoid biting everyone's head off. Trying to keep his frustration out of his voice, he said, "Well, I won't know either until you tell me what's going on."

"I guess I just needed to talk to someone. I haven't found anyone here who knows what I'm going through."

"Have you looked into any LGBT groups in the area? I'm sure I could find some for you."

"Not yet. It's been so hard starting over. I thought if I came to Boone for college, it'd be like a fresh start. No one would know me, and I could just be me without anyone judging me for being trans. And I guess it was great at first, but now it kind of feels like a lie. And I guess I just really miss you guys. I miss being around people who know both sides of me and love me anyway."

He could hear Riley sniffling softly behind his words, but Adam was ill-prepared to deal with him. His words hit too close to home, and anything Adam told him would reveal the weak hypocrite residing inside him.

With tears stinging at his own eyes, Adam said, "We miss you too, Ri, and I really hate to do this, but I'm going to have to call you back. Or better yet, I'll have Kirsten or Elijah give you a call. An emergency just popped up, and I need to go. I'm so sorry."

"Oh, it's no prob—"

Adam didn't wait for him to finish his sentence. He placed the phone back in its receiver and locked his computer as he stood. His head pounded and a feeling of despair traveled through his body and infiltrated his chest. He needed to get away. He grabbed his jacket and left his office. On his way out the door, he told Chloe he'd be gone the rest of the day. He had no idea where he was going, but he sure as hell couldn't stay at HOPE.

"WHAT DO you mean he left?" Elijah asked.

Chloe widened her eyes as she shrugged. "He didn't even stop on his way out. Just said he wouldn't be back. I assumed he was meeting you for something when Kollin showed up after school like normal and had no idea what happened."

Elijah slammed his fist down on Chloe's desk and made her jump.

"Sorry," he said softly.

"Do you want me to try his cell?" Chloe asked.

"No. I tried him several times this afternoon, to no avail. I figured something big was going on here."

"It's been fairly quiet today. All week, actually."

Elijah cocked his head. Adam hadn't mentioned that. "Really?"

"Yes. I suppose it could have something to do with Adam being so busy in his office." She spoke hesitantly, as if she were a teenager tattling on a friend.

Elijah balled his hand into a fist. His frustration made him want to punch a hole in the wall. "Has he left early like this any other days?"

"No. Today was the first. Is he okay?"

Wasn't that the million-dollar question? Elijah had no idea what to tell her. He didn't know anymore, but he'd sooner carve out his left eye than start telling people he didn't believe Adam would pull through. He decided to give Chloe the tried-and-true line he kept feeding Kollin. "He will be. He needs time."

"Well, you know how to reach me anytime you need me. Adam deserves better than for that pitiful excuse of a mother to force her way back into his life and tear it up again. He works so hard to improve the lives of everyone around him. I'm sure no one will mind rallying around him to do the same."

"Thanks, Chloe. I'll let you know. Let me get Kollin and see if we can find Adam."

When Elijah pulled into his driveway thirty minutes later, he was surprised to see Adam's car. He didn't know why. Adam lived there, after all, but Elijah thought Adam might go off the grid after his disappearing act. If Kollin hadn't been with him, Elijah probably would've spent the entire evening driving around Cary, searching. But he didn't want to worry the kid.

An even greater surprise came when he walked through the door and the aroma of grilled meat wafted out of the kitchen. Kollin turned to look at Elijah and raised his eyebrows, a small smile on his face. He dropped his book bag in the middle of the foyer and took off for the kitchen. Elijah was right behind him.

Adam stood next to the counter, cutting up vegetables and tossing them into a large bowl for a salad. He wore an apron with the words COULD YOU SEARCH MY POCKET FOR MY SPATULA? in bold letters splashed across the front.

"Hey, guys," Adam said with a smile on his face. "Hungry?"

"You cooked." Surprise laced Kollin's voice as he walked around the island and gave Adam a quick, one-armed hug.

"Yeah. We've been eating a lot of takeout lately, so I figured it was time we had some real food. I left work a little early today and ended up going to Trader Joe's. I got stuff to make homemade pizzas, but they didn't have the sausage you like, so I went to Fresh Market too." He pointed to the steaks on the inside grill. "But then I saw these and couldn't resist. So we can have pizza tomorrow night, I guess."

"This looks great," Elijah said and gave Adam a quick kiss on the cheek. "Need any help?"

"You can probably take the steaks off. I need to finish cutting this cucumber and pull the potatoes out of the oven. Then everything will be ready."

Kollin flashed Elijah another smile, bigger this time. He was clearly excited about the sudden change in Adam's temperament. Not quite as fast to pick up whatever act Adam was trying to lay down, Elijah warily returned Kollin's smile. Though Adam seemed involved and animated, something still felt off. Adam smiled, but the corners of his eyes didn't crinkle up. His voice sounded cheery but a little too high-pitched. And though Adam did his best to avoid Elijah's gaze, he couldn't miss the panic in his eyes.

"So I heard from Riley today," Adam said as they all sat down.

"Really?" Kollin asked. "How's he doing? When's he coming to visit?"

Adam frowned then but quickly slid his false smile back into place. "Sounds like he needs a friend, to be honest. Seems a little lonely up there. Maybe you could give him a call?"

"Yeah. The only reason I haven't is I figured he wouldn't want anything to do with me now that he has all those college friends." Kollin cut a piece of his steak and bit it off his fork.

"You know that's not true," Elijah said. "Riley was closer to you than anyone else at the center."

"Only because he was so great when everything with my parents happened. I always felt more like a burden to him than anything else."

Elijah shook his head. "Being in your life is a blessing, never a burden." His voice sounded hard, harsher than he'd intended, but he felt tired. Too tired. Couldn't he have one day when the two most important people in his life saw themselves as everyone else did? One day when they saw how much joy and goodness their footprints left on the world?

Judging by the way Adam and Kollin were both staring into their plates, Elijah guessed that day wouldn't come any time soon.

The rest of dinner passed quickly enough. Adam remained falsely cheery and even surprised Elijah when he asked about Dedrick, the random guy Kollin had brought up earlier in the week. Before long Kollin asked to be excused, leaving Adam and Elijah alone to clean up dinner.

"You cooked," Elijah said. "I can get this mess."

"I'll help. You've been carrying most of the load lately. It's time I got back to normal before you guys get tired of me and kick me out."

He attempted an air of levity in his voice but failed miserably, and the joke fell flat.

Elijah ignored it. "I can think of a few reasons to keep you around besides your handiness in the kitchen."

"Oh yeah, I know how to wield a vacuum too." Adam rolled his eyes but grinned.

This time Elijah laughed but cut it short when he spotted a brown envelope addressed to Adam on the counter. "What's this?"

"Hmm?" Adam asked, turning from where he'd been loading the dishwasher to eye what Elijah held. "Oh, that. Legal papers. Jessica's suing me for those cards. They got here right before you guys got home." Adam rinsed another dish and placed it in the dishwasher.

"What? Why didn't you tell me earlier?"

Adam shrugged and kept loading the dishes. "I don't know. Didn't see a reason to. There's no way to prove the cards are hers. I'll call my lawyer tomorrow."

"That's what she's saying? He bought them for her?"

"Yep. Said he gave them to her every year for her birthday, but she left them at his house because he loved them so much. Said the Alzheimer's must've made him confused, made him think they were his. She's also saying he was lost to the disease by the time he added the rider to his will. According to her, even if the cards weren't already hers, I have no legal claim to them because he was not of sound mind."

"Shit."

Elijah felt like he'd been punched in the gut, but Adam smiled and pecked his lips. "Want to watch some TV?"

"Watch TV? Don't you want to talk about this? Figure out what we're going to do?"

Adam picked at his thumbnail. "I already told you what I'm going to do. I'll call my lawyer tomorrow and deal with it then. There's no point in worrying about it now and nothing either of us can do."

"We could start working on a plan to take her down!"

Adam's face hardened, and his eyes flashed. "Look. I've been in a pissy-ass mood for almost two weeks. All I wanted to do tonight was fix a nice dinner to apologize for being a giant asshole and to pretend like my fucking nutjob of a mother doesn't exist. Can you just fucking leave it alone and do that one thing for me? Or is it too difficult to stay out of my damn business for once?"

Elijah stared at Adam, his eyes wide. "Uh, sure. Whatever you want."

He walked into the living room and sat in his recliner while Adam took the couch, fake smile plastered back on as if he hadn't just snapped at Elijah. Adam had never spoken to him like that before. Even when Elijah deserved to be put in his place, Adam always treated him with respect. The rare times Adam blew up when he shouldn't have, he always recanted immediately and apologized almost before he even finished his tirade. Adam might not have raised his voice, but everything about the exchange, from his words to the cold tone of his voice to the poor attempt at cheerfulness afterward, felt like Adam had just given him a giant middle finger.

Elijah had no idea what to think of this Adam.

CHAPTER 13

ADAM STARED at the clock as it flipped from 5:59 to six o'clock, and turned off the alarm before it had a chance to wake Elijah. What he really wanted to do was pull the covers over his head and stay in bed all day. Since that would never be an option for him, he needed to pull his shit together. Shoving all his dark thoughts and feelings aside seemed to be the last option he had left, but he found the charade to be exhausting. Adam watched the clock for another three full minutes and then took a deep breath and rolled over to slip his arm over Elijah's.

Elijah immediately relaxed into his embrace, a small sound of sleepy contentment escaping his lips. Adam clenched his jaw together, angry he couldn't make the same sound. He quickly locked the feeling away and smiled before Elijah rolled over.

"Mmm… miss waking up like this," Elijah said as he rubbed his eyes.

"Sorry. Like I said last night, I'm trying to get back to myself."

His voice sounded clipped even to his own ears, so Adam leaned down and kissed Elijah's chin.

Elijah remained quiet for so long that Adam shifted away. He was ready to start his morning rituals when Elijah said, "I'd rather you get some help."

Nope. Nope. And nope. He didn't need help. He'd gone through years of therapy. He knew what they'd say, and when he needed it most, all of their words had failed.

"I don't need therapy. I told you last night I'm starting to feel better. Once I get this bullshit lawsuit done and out of the way, I can put her behind me for good. Out of sight, out of mind."

"Uh. Not exactly. I tried that approach. With Brian. Remember? You were the one who suggested I talk to someone, and I feel pretty confident you wouldn't tell Kollin to shove all of his feelings about his parents down until he forgot about them."

Adam pulled away from Elijah, flung the covers off, and got out of bed. "What-the-fuck-ever, Elijah. You're using my own words against me now? In case you haven't noticed, I'm not some sixteen-year-old kid, nor am I a closeted thirty-four-year-old man who's scared to talk to his daddy. I already dealt with all of my mommy issues when I was a teenager. I needed a few weeks to process it all. Now that I have, I'm fine."

"You're obviously not *fine*, or you wouldn't be speaking to me like this. Do you even hear yourself? This isn't you."

Adam rifled through his drawers and ripped his clothes out to take to the bathroom with him. "What exactly is it you're looking for from me? You and Kollin walked around on eggshells for weeks while I worked through my shit, and I appreciate the space you gave me and the concern you showed. But this is me being okay now, so you two need to back the fuck off. Damn it, it's like you want me to be depressed."

"Of course I don't fucking want you to be depressed. I want you to be happy. But baby, this is not happy. This is some plastic version of happiness that wouldn't even fool a stranger on the street, much less me."

Tamping down his urge to scream "fuck you," Adam clenched his clothes in his hands and turned toward the door. "I'll shower in the guest bedroom." He grabbed the handle to the door and jerked it open, but pulled up short when he saw Kollin standing in the hallway. Regret for everything he'd said flooded him instantly.

He opened his mouth to say… to say what? The look on Kollin's face told Adam everything he needed to know. He heard everything, and Adam's words hurt him deeply. Shame replaced regret, and as Kollin took a step backward, Adam heard Elijah get out of bed. Adam's flight response took over, and he lowered his head as he shoved past Kollin without a word.

"YOU OKAY?" Eli asked Kollin for the fiftieth time as they neared his school.

"I told you I'm fine. It's not a big deal."

"You know he didn't mean any of what he said. Right?"

Kollin sighed. Of course he knew that. Sorta. Maybe. But didn't most people say what they really meant when they got all worked up and let their guard down? They might regret it later, because who wanted to let those shameful feelings out. But at the time, they really and truly meant it. "Doesn't matter. It's not like he even said anything bad about me."

"Implying your therapy isn't important is not okay. Nor is putting us down for how we've tried to support him. He knows that. I need to make sure you do too."

"I get it. Okay, Eli? I'm not going to suddenly flounce therapy because Adam's having a midlife crisis."

"Is there anything you want to talk to me about?"

Kollin groaned. He loved Eli. He really did. And most of the time, when Adam wasn't bogged down with all the parental shit he had to deal with, living with Eli and Adam was the best thing ever. They included him in everything. They never judged him and always told him how proud they were of him and how much they loved him. They gave him enough freedom to feel like he was getting away with shit, but not enough that he actually did get away with shit, and he always knew, without a doubt, he could go to them with any problem he had.

But Eli could be relentless when he thought Kollin might be having trouble dealing with something. Like he thought if he asked enough times, Kollin might change his answer.

Sometimes he was right…. Not that he'd ever admit it to Eli.

"Can I please go to school without the third degree? I'll process my feelings while I'm there, and we can do our nails and talk about it tonight."

"You're not getting near my nails again," Eli muttered.

"You're no fun," Kollin said, relieved he'd dropped it. "Besides, you rocked that black polish… for the two seconds you wore it."

Eli rolled his eyes, but Kollin saw the smile on his face. "Get to class, kid. Love you."

"Love you too." Kollin opened his door but stopped before getting out. "I promise I'll let you know if and when I need to talk. Okay?"

He stood quickly and slammed the door before Eli had a chance to pull him into another conversation. He hadn't lied to Eli, but he worried about Adam. He'd been so relieved to see Adam smile the night before that he hadn't stopped to really look at him. Thinking back on it, he saw the missed signs. He didn't know what to do with this Adam, who seemed far more broken than Eli ever had.

Eli had been one hell of a hot mess, but at least he had a grasp on what bothered him. He just constantly fought it. Adam looked like a feral cat who'd just been locked in a cage for the first time in fifteen years—trying his best to figure out what to be mad about and lashing out at everything that passed by in the process.

Kollin knew those feeling too well, but thankfully Dr. Will helped him recognize them and put them into perspective. He still felt that way from time to time. The key was to not take it out on anyone else.

He'd just grabbed the door handle to the school when he heard someone shout his name.

Surprised, Kollin turned to the voice he'd recognize anywhere.

"Riley." Kollin let go of the door and jogged toward the corner entrance to engulf Riley in a huge hug. Students milled around them on either side, but neither of them paid them any mind. Riley looked a little different. His hair was much shorter, almost a buzz cut, and Kollin thought he'd bound his chest, something his parents had never let him do.

Man, it was good to see him. Riley was the one person from the center who'd really stepped up and been there for Kollin after his father abused him. They talked every day back then, sometimes for hours. Riley provided Kollin with the outlet he needed to bitch about his parents without having to worry about Adam or Eli overreacting. They'd grown so close, Kollin considered Riley to be his soul mate. When Riley left for college, Kollin promised himself he wouldn't drag Ri down with his issues during that exciting time in his life. But Kollin missed him more than words could say.

"What're you doing here? Don't you have class?"

Riley shrugged. "Fall break. A guy on my hall lives in Raleigh. Said he'd drop me off."

"So you're in for the whole weekend?"

"Yep. Want to ditch school today and do something?"

Kollin cocked his head back. "You know I can't ditch. It's against center rules."

"Well, yeah. But now that you're the owner's kid, I don't think they'd kick you out."

"Come on, man. It's not like that and you know it. I'd be the last person Adam would give a second chance to at this point. Besides, I don't want to let Eli down after everything he's done for me."

Riley nodded. "I get it. Don't want to mess up a good thing. I guess I can catch you later, then."

"I'll be at HOPE after school. Want to meet me there, or do you have plans with your parents?"

"Nah. I didn't even tell them I was in town." Riley gestured up and down his body. "They wouldn't approve, and I didn't feel like dealing with it."

Kollin frowned. "Where are you staying?"

Shrugging, Riley shook his head, and Kollin recognized Riley's short hair and taped-down chest were the only changes in his friend. The same weariness that haunted Riley's eyes whenever he spoke of his parents, the same droop to his shoulders, the same defeated look in Riley's gaze… they all remained.

"Why don't you stay with us? I'm sure Eli won't care, and you're over eighteen now. Adam can't say shit about it."

"I don't know…."

The bell rang, signaling Kollin had five minutes to get to his locker and then to class. "Look. I gotta go. Just be at the center after school, at least. Hell. Spend the whole day, but promise you'll be there?"

"Yeah. Sure. I'll be there."

Kollin gave Riley one final hug and took off, his excitement at seeing Riley again only slightly outweighing his concern for Adam and Elijah.

ADAM SAT in the waiting room of his lawyer's office, absently tapping his foot on the floor. He wasn't normally a fidgeter, but all the nervous energy had to escape somehow, and it beat having a panic attack every day. The outside door opened, and Elijah walked in. He offered Adam a small smile as he crossed the room and sat down.

Adam had sent Elijah a text right after he scheduled the meeting—mainly in an effort to keep Elijah off his back, but partially as an apology for blowing up earlier that morning. He knew Elijah wanted to be part of the process, but Adam didn't want anyone else there. He thought a text would convey "I'm keeping you in the loop but not asking you to be there." Apparently he thought wrong.

"What're you doing here?" Adam asked in lieu of a greeting.

"Didn't want you to do this alone."

Guilt flooded through Adam, but he ignored it. "I didn't ask for company."

"I know. I'll sit out here if you don't want me in there."

Adam's anger deflated a little, but he didn't apologize. "It's not like you won't find out anyway."

Elijah's sigh was barely audible. "I'm not here to argue, but I want to be here in case you need me. Regardless of whatever you're feeling toward me, you're my partner in every sense of the word—business, life, boyfriend, parenting. If you walk out of that office and blow by me without a word, fine. Nothing I can do about it. But if you need me, I'll be damned if I'm in my office instead of here."

Tears welled up behind Adam's eyes, but he willed them back. He wasn't worthy of Elijah's love or kindness, and the fact he'd received both without asking only made him angrier. Adam stared down at his hands and remained silent. After Elijah's little speech, nothing but a genuine apology would fit, and Adam was in no condition to apologize. He didn't want to hurt Elijah or Kollin, but he knew Elijah wouldn't stop until Adam put the crumbled pieces of his life back together. So he continued to jiggle his leg and tap his thumb against the armrest until his lawyer, Mr. Beuford, called him back.

Adam hesitated at the door to glance back at Elijah, still sitting in his seat, bent over with his elbows on his knees. "You coming?" he asked quietly.

When Elijah looked up, his smile was tentative, but his eyes were lit with hope. They broke Adam's heart. Before long he'd snuff that light right back out again. Adam was too damaged. Too broken. He didn't deserve Elijah Langley.

"WHAT DO you mean she actually has a chance?" Kirsten asked.

Adam shrugged. "Beuford said if she's got anything proving the cards are hers, I'm most likely out of luck. It's called a will contest, apparently. Gramps can't give something away that wasn't his to begin with. If Jessica has a birthday note or something like that mentioning one of them, it might be enough."

"But what about the letter? It specifically states he wants you to have them. Isn't that and the will enough?"

"I don't know, Kris. If the cards weren't his to give away in the first place, I guess it's not enough."

"When will you know?"

Adam shrugged again. "I'm thinking about giving her whatever money they're worth. I have some in savings, and if that's not enough, I can get a second mortgage on the house."

"Adam, no. You better not give that woman one damn cent. What the hell is wrong with you?"

Adam snorted. "A lot, in case you haven't noticed. Besides, I want it to be over with. I'm tired of dealing with her. I'm tired of being disappointed by her. I'm tired of disappointing Elijah. I'm tired of disappointing Kollin. And I'm tired of disappointing myself and moping around all the damn time, but I can't snap out of it. She's like a huge storm cloud over my head, except instead of a storm cloud, she's the fucking superstorm in *The Day After Tomorrow*, and I'm one of the extras on the streets of New York, buried under eighty feet of snow. Nixing her from my life permanently is worth whatever amount of money I have in my bank account."

"Oh, Adam." Kirsten sighed, and Adam knew he'd let her down too. "Do you really think if you pay her off, she'll just disappear? Maybe if she knew she'd bled you dry with this one transaction, but she's seen where you live and who you've chosen to spend your life with. Elijah's pockets will never run dry, and anyone with half a good eye can see he would do anything for you."

"It's not like we're married. His money isn't mine. Even if we were married, I'd never let him pay her off for me."

"Oh, believe me, *I* know that. But she doesn't. And even if she did, your fucking sperm donor doesn't, and it seems like she does whatever he wants."

Adam's stomach turned over. He'd managed not to think about the fact that his biological father had shown up at the bank. He had enough trouble dealing with the emotions that Jessica's betrayal had brought up. Chad looked old and haggard, but Adam had seen bits and pieces of himself in his face, and it made him sick. Adam rubbed his face with his hands in a useless attempt to rid himself of those features.

"What do I do, Kris?" Adam asked, his voice cracking. "I can't keep doing this. I can barely function at work. I feel like an imposter. Those kids have it together more than I do right now. I hate being home and seeing the concern in Elijah's and Kollin's eyes. I hate the pity in their voices. I hate how understanding they are and that I'm putting them through this."

Kirsten rounded the corner of Adam's desk and knelt down on the floor next to his chair. "You need to talk to someone—"

"I've been through all the therapy before—"

"So do it again. You say you hate feeling like this, and you hate what you're putting your family through? Do something about it. You've beaten this once before. You can do it again."

"It took me years to move past everything that happened to me, and it all came rushing back the second I heard her voice. I don't have that much time. Kollin needs me now. And Elijah doesn't need me at all. He's got the entire world at his fingertips, and all I'm doing now is dragging him down with me." Adam choked back a sob as he spilled his deepest, darkest fear to his sister. He hoped like hell she'd tell him how wrong he was, but he knew he wouldn't believe her. He'd fallen into an endless downward spiral, and aside from feeling bad for hurting his family, he had no desire to pull himself out of it. He'd make whatever excuses he had to until there was no one left to give them to.

Kirsten shoved his chair to the side so she could stand in front of his computer. "Do you know what cards he left you? Let's see what they're worth so we know what we're dealing with. If you don't have enough to cover it in savings, Derek and I will make up the rest. We'll get them off your back for a while, and then you'll go to therapy and get the help you need—the help you give everyone else who walks through those doors."

Adam shook his head. "I can't let you do that."

"Bullshit you can't. I love you, and I will not lose you to some heinous bitch who doesn't know how to stay the hell out of your life. She doesn't deserve a single penny of your money, but I'll be damned if I let her take you from me or Mom and Dad or Elijah and Kollin. Now where are the damn cards?"

Adam knew by the cock of Kirsten's hip she wouldn't give an inch on the subject, so he opened his bottom desk drawer and pulled out the old box. He'd been carrying them with him everywhere he went, too scared to leave them anywhere. He had no intention of letting Kirsten and Derek pay for anything, but he did need to know what the cards were worth. It would be easier to play along.

"Most of them are probably worthless, but there are a few in plastic cases in the front. Maybe I could only give her those."

Kirsten glared at him. "What's the first one?"

Adam picked up the small stack separate from the rest of the cards. "Year 1955 Bowman, Mickey Mantle," Adam read. "Card number two hundred two."

Kirsten clicked away until finally she turned to Adam, her eyebrows raised. "This one went for over three thousand dollars at an auction two years ago."

Adam sat up straight. "Really? I figured they'd be a couple hundred, tops."

"Says here it depends on the condition of the card, but all of these look as if they've never even been touched."

Adam frowned and grabbed the next card. "Check this one. Year 1948 Leaf, Jackie Robinson. Card number seventy-nine."

"Anywhere from two grand to twenty-five hundred," Kirsten said a few minutes later.

Adam set the card down and took another one. "Looks like this one came out of a Cracker Jack box. There's even a small stain in the upper corner."

"Who's on it?"

"Ty Cobb. Year 1914. Shit. This is old. Gramps wouldn't have even been born when this card came out."

"Maybe his dad passed it down to him," Kirsten said as she typed. "Or maybe he bought it when he started collecting. I can't believe he never told you about these."

Adam shrugged. "I kinda remember him showing them to me one day. At the time they just looked like a bunch of old cards. I was way more interested in the train set in the basement."

"Adam," Kirsten whispered. "This card last sold for over sixty grand."

"What?"

Kirsten pointed to the screen. "Says right here it's rare to find one in good condition. How bad is that stain?"

Adam handed her the card. The mark, maybe half the size of his thumbprint, covered the bottom right corner of the card, but it didn't mar any of the words. Someone probably held the card with greasy fingers, maybe after eating some of the caramel-flavored treat the card came with.

"How much does Jessica know about these cards?"

"I have no idea. There's no way of knowing what information she's told me over the past couple of months is true and what she lied about so she could get her hands on these. She never mentioned them to me, but she never mentioned being hard up for money either."

"Are there any more wrapped ones?"

"One. A 1955 Willie Mays. Topps. Card number one ninety-four."

"A little under three grand."

Adam stared at Kirsten. He had no idea the cards would be so valuable. Even if the Ty Cobb card only garnered a fraction of what they found listed because of the small smudge, several thousand dollars' worth of baseball memorabilia currently lay on his desk. Cards his gramps obviously cherished and cared for. Cards Gramps had specifically wanted Adam to have to ensure he had a little help in life.

Cards his birth mother wanted to hock to the highest bidder to get her piece of the pie.

In that moment Adam wanted nothing more than to grab the cards and crumple them in his hands, marring their perfection forever, destroying them and any chance Jessica had at gaining anything from them—just like she'd destroyed him. But then Kirsten wrapped her arms around him. Adam buried his head in the hollow between her neck and shoulder, and he wept.

CHAPTER 14

ELIJAH TOOK a deep breath and tapped lightly on Adam's office door. After the meeting with Mr. Beuford, he and Adam had parted awkwardly—Elijah trying not to push and Adam clearly wanting to be left alone. Kirsten called him after lunch to fill him in on the value of the cards. She also divulged that Adam had opened up to her about everything he'd been feeling.

Elijah tried his best not to be hurt that Adam was honest with her instead of him. Kirsten had been in his life a lot longer than Elijah, and they'd been through so much together. He didn't ask what Adam said, and she didn't offer up the information. Elijah would wait until Adam felt ready to tell him.

"Yeah?" Adam's muffled voice called.

He opened the door and walked in slowly, trying to get a feel for Adam's mood. "Hey," he said, taking a seat in one of the chairs.

"Hey." His voice sounded scratchy. Elijah could tell he'd been crying, but one look at the set of his jaw, and Elijah knew better than to ask.

"Riley's in town for the weekend and needs a place to stay. Kollin offered our spare room. That okay with you?"

"Sure. Whatever. He's always welcome."

Elijah nodded. "Figured. But I wanted to check, anyway. I talked to Kirsten today. She told me about the cards."

Adam's eyes never left his computer screen. "Something else, isn't it?"

"It really is. Have you gone through the rest to make sure there are no hidden gems?"

"No. I didn't want to think about it anymore, so I put them away."

Of course he didn't. Elijah tried again. "Okay. Want me to take a look?"

Adam's jaw twitched as he considered Elijah's question. His face didn't give away any hint as to what was rolling through his mind. When he finally spoke, his voice sounded strained. "If you want to, I guess that would be fine. We'll have to get them appraised somewhere so it's official. I have a feeling Jessica could give a shit about the rest of them, though. She wants the Ty Cobb card."

Elijah shifted in his seat and took a deep breath. He was 99 percent certain Adam would balk at his next suggestion, but on the 1 percent chance it got this woman out of their lives any sooner, he'd risk it.

"What if we gave her replacement cards? She'd get what she wanted, and you'd get to keep what your grandfather left you."

Adam cut his eyes toward Elijah.

"And where would you suggest I get these replacement cards?"

Elijah didn't miss how Adam changed his "we" statement to an "I" statement, but he ignored it for now. "Anywhere online. There are auctions going on all the time."

"I could probably swing a few of the cards with my savings account, but I'd have to sell my house to buy the big one. And before you even suggest it, I'm not taking your money. This is my problem, not yours."

"In case you've forgotten, your problems are my problems."

"Only because you make them yours," Adam shouted. "I've told you a million times I can handle this on my own."

"Dammit, Adam." Elijah stood abruptly, shoving his chair back. "Why are you trying so hard to push me away? What the hell did I do to earn this wrath from you?"

Adam stared at him, openmouthed. "Un-fucking-believable. You think this is about you? Of course you do, because the entire world revolves around Elijah fucking Langley. So when my entire fucking failure of a childhood gets thrown back in my face, it's gotta be all about you too. Well, right now I'm a little busy, but I'll pencil in some time tomorrow to make sure you're feeling okay about everything. Will that work for you?"

"Fuck you. That's not what I meant, and you damn well know it. You don't want to tell me about your past? Fine. You don't want to tell me how you're feeling? Fine. You'd rather share with Kirsten. I. Get. It. But don't fucking act like you're not doing your damnedest to piss me off with every word that comes out of your mouth. I've been patient and supportive, and all you've done is throw it back in my face. All I'm asking for is a little respect."

"Umm, guys," Chloe said from behind Elijah, making him jump. He turned and saw her head poking in the door. "I'm sorry, but you need to keep it down. The kids can hear you out here."

Chloe's face flushed tomato red, and Elijah had to give her props for interrupting their shouting match.

"Sorry, Chloe," he apologized. Adam remained silent, so Elijah gave her a small smile. "I'm heading out in a minute, anyway. We'll keep it down in here."

"Thanks, and sorry again."

The door clicked behind her, and Elijah turned back to Adam. "I'll take Kollin and Riley home with me and pick up dinner for all of us. Anything you want?"

Adam didn't look up from his computer screen, even though Elijah knew he wasn't actually seeing it. "I'll get something on my own and stay in my old place tonight."

Elijah gaped at Adam, eyes wide. "You don't have any furniture there anymore. Besides, Lucinda is moving her stuff in this weekend."

"I've got some blankets in my car. I'll be fine."

"Adam." Elijah pinched the bridge of his nose as panic crept inside his heart. "Don't do this. Please? We can work this out."

Adam swallowed but kept his gaze on his computer screen as he closed his eyes. "Tell Kollin I'm sorry."

"YOU EVER look at your life and wonder just how in the fuck it's *your* life?"

Kollin looked to his left where Riley lay on the opposite of the bed, almost mirroring Kollin's position as they stared at the ceiling and listened to music.

"You mean like how did I go from being kicked out of my house to living with the richest man in town?"

Riley snorted. "Your life is the gay, twinkified version of *Annie*."

"Dude. I'd rock the shit outta that role. I'd have all the cute boys lining up for my…." Kollin waggled his eyebrows and laughed at himself. No one would be lining up for his scrawny ass any time soon.

"You sure about that? You'd have to dye your hair bright orange. Might not go too well with pink suspenders."

"Meh. I'll figure something out." Kollin nudged Riley's elbow. "What would your movie be?"

"Shit. I dunno." Riley ran both hands over his face and scratched the top of his head. He tucked one hand beneath his head and rested the other on his stomach, seemingly in thought. "Probably *Fight Club*."

"The fuck is *Fight Club*?"

Riley closed his eyes and shook his head. "It's an old movie, probably came out before you were born. The main guy goes schizo, I guess, and starts a fighting club. He thinks it's with his best friend, but really his best friend is him. He ends up fighting his friend without even realizing he's fighting himself. He has no idea who he really is."

Riley sounded so vulnerable as he described the movie that Kollin understood it was his way of telling Kollin everything wasn't okay. But Kollin had no idea how to deal with that. He rolled onto his side and propped his head on his hand. Linking his fingers through Riley's, Kollin waited for Ri to open his eyes and look at him. "I think you're more suited for a remake of *The Incredible Hulk*."

Riley shook his hand free and tucked it under his head with the other one. "So I'm a monster that kills other people instead of one who beats up himself? Thanks, Koll. Love you too."

"Hear me out. Okay?" Kollin jiggled Riley's elbow. "Hulk spends the whole movie trying to deny who he is because he has all of these people in his life telling him it's not possible for him to be the Hulk and be in control at the same time. But in the end, when he accepts who he is, he figures out how to control himself."

Riley cut his eyes toward Kollin and let out a long slow breath. "I think that analogy might be a bit of a stretch. The Hulk came back in *The Avengers* and tried to kill Black Widow. Remember?"

Kollin flopped back on the bed. "We all make mistakes. Doesn't mean we have to wallow in guilt for the rest of our lives."

"What in the world do you have to feel guilty about?"

Kollin glanced at Riley and then covered his eyes with his elbows. Kollin had plenty of guilt, and most of it centered around Riley. Compassionate, caring Riley, who never once mentioned how lonely he was or how hard it was to be trans.

"Mostly for all the times I bitched to you about stupid shit without even once asking about you."

The bed shuffled as Riley rolled to his side. "You don't need to worry about that. You had a lot going on, and I was glad I could be there for you."

"I don't mean all the stuff about my parents. After that, when I went on and on about wanting a boyfriend or complaining about one of Eli's dumbass rules. It's all a little childish compared to you thinking your life relates to some dude who's batshit crazy and somehow kicks his own ass. The fuck, Ri? Who the hell would watch that shit?"

Riley laughed. "My mom watches it every so often. She likes Brad Pitt."

Kollin raised his arm to look at Riley. "Can't say I blame her for that. He's pretty hot for an old guy." Riley's lip turned up in a grimace, and Kollin gasped. "You don't think he's hot?"

"He's all right. I mean, he has all the perfectly symmetrical features that most people like, but I guess I go more for the Louis Tomlinson type."

Kollin cocked his eyebrow up. Riley was just trying to make Kollin feel better. He knew Kollin was a huge Louis fan and often imitated the singer's clothing and hairstyles.

"I'd've pegged you more for Liam."

Riley pulled one of Kollin's suspenders and let it snap back to his chest. "What can I say? I guess somebody's managed to change my mind."

"You're so full of shit." Kollin laughed and pushed himself up. "You wanna get outta here and find something to do?"

The way Riley's face fell made Kollin wonder what he'd said wrong, but just as quickly as it had disappeared, Riley's smile was back. "Wanna go see a movie? I haven't been to one since school started."

Kollin hesitated and considered pushing Riley for more information. He had a way of always distracting Kollin from digging too deep into Riley's life. It didn't help that Kollin would chase a rabbit at the drop of a hat, but Kollin desperately wanted to be as good a friend to Riley as Riley had been to him.

But Riley had already shrugged his jacket on and stood at the doorway. "Change your mind?"

Riley's eyes were bright. Kollin bit his bottom lip and promised himself he'd press Riley another time. He didn't get to see his friend often, and he sure as hell didn't want to spend their time together moping over all of their troubles. Once Ri was back in school, Kollin would find out why he seemed to be struggling so much and then lying to cover it up. Tonight… they'd veg out on popcorn, hot tamales, and Cherry Coke.

"Nope. Let's roll."

"THANKS FOR coming over," Elijah said as he closed the door behind Kirsten.

"Of course. I'm worried too," Kirsten said, shedding her coat. "Where's Kollin?"

"He and Ri went to a movie. Riley couldn't have timed his impromptu visit better. He's kept Kollin distracted the past two days. Both of them looked better today."

"That's a relief." They walked through the sitting room and into the living room.

Elijah took his place behind the bar while Kirsten grabbed a stool. "What's your pleasure?"

"Whatever you're having is fine."

"The usual, then." Elijah grabbed two tumblers.

Kirsten grinned and scratched at the top of the bar. "Adam really hasn't been home since Thursday?"

Elijah shook his head and added two ice cubes to Kirsten's glass. "Not while I was here. He stopped by yesterday for a change of clothes. Left a note saying he didn't know when he'd be back."

"I can't even believe this is happening. I never thought he'd regress to this point, especially after he met you."

Elijah poured two fingers of espresso tequila into their glasses and pushed one in Kirsten's direction. Kirsten had visited Elijah a handful of times over the past months to lend a friendly ear over a drink. Though the conversation they were preparing to have terrified him, the familiarity of their routine helped settle his frazzled nerves.

"Was it this bad the first time?"

"Oh, it was worse. Way worse. He came into our house this little shithead, pissed off at the world. But Mom and Dad had warned me he'd had a tough time in foster care. They said he would probably try to push us away, but he needed someone to love him. So I kept smiling and let whatever he said roll right off. Looking at him was painful sometimes…. The constant agony he lived with was tangible." Kirsten looked up at

Elijah, a sad smile on her face. "But for some reason, one day out of the blue, he started trying. The pain stayed in his eyes, in his voice, but he treated all of us with respect. He went to class and did his homework and did the chores. My parents were hopeful, but they couldn't hear him scream at night."

"He's told me about the nightmares."

"I know." Kirsten stared into her drink. "Anyway, he couldn't hold the charade together too long. He started acting out again, calling me names and then apologizing almost immediately after. He couldn't skip class anymore or he'd be sent back to the home, but he'd disappear after school and not come home until late. Once he stayed out all night. Walked in the next morning while we were eating breakfast as if he'd done nothing wrong. Mom and Dad tried their best to discipline him, but he didn't care. It was as if he wanted them to send him back. He wasn't going to run away, but he gave them every reason not to keep him."

"What changed?"

Kirsten shrugged. "Adam changed. First he came out to us, as if we didn't already know. He wore some ridiculously twink outfit he wouldn't be caught dead in now, which I gotta say is a damn shame. He rocked some of those clothes, back in the day. He told me later that when Dad called him son while speaking to one of our family friends, even after he knew Adam was gay… that was the moment he became determined to start healing. It was a long, tough road. He didn't change overnight, but we could see how hard he tried to deal with everything life had given him, even on the days he disappeared."

"Then this disappearing act he's pulling now isn't new?"

"Oh no. I mean, he hasn't done it in years, but his first instinct back then was to run."

Elijah let out a long, slow breath.

"He'll come back," Kirsten said, laying her hand on Elijah's wrist.

"What if he doesn't? I can't make him stay with me, but I can't lose him either. He holds our family together. What am I supposed to do?"

"You pick yourself up and start over again. But I know he'll come back. Have some faith."

"Faith in what? I don't even know what happened to him. Everything I've heard so far is shitty. Yeah. And I don't blame him for falling apart after everything his mom has done. But how am I supposed to believe he'll come back when all he's done is run from me, and I have no tools in my arsenal to help him deal with everything he's going through?"

"Don't make this about you, Elijah."

Kirsten's tone was fierce, protective, and Elijah looked at her, stunned. *What the hell?*

"About me? All I'm trying to do is help him! Did he tell you I was trying to make it about me?"

"No. I would've told you that, but have you been listening to anything I just said?"

Elijah stared at Kirsten, not bothering to answer the rhetorical question.

"Then you should know," she said pointedly, "I never knew what was wrong with Adam back then. I saw his pain, and I loved him anyway. I saw his anger and his agony and his abuse in the way he avoided me and the way he tried his best to hurt me, and I loved him anyway. He pushed me away and called me names, and I loved him anyway. I'm not saying it's easy or even fair, but because of the two vile people who brought him into this world, Adam is at a critical point in his life. You have to make a decision. What are you willing to do to be with my brother?"

"Anything."

"All you have to do is love him. He'll come around eventually."

"Kirsten—"

She held up her hand. "I know it's different for you than it was for me. I was a stranger, bound and determined to love another stranger because it felt like the right thing to do. If it didn't work out, I didn't have anything to lose but some punk I had to share a bathroom with. You two already not only love each other, but share a life. I know it's harder, and if you choose to walk away, I won't blame you. It's not an easy road, but make no mistake. Adam will move past this and have to deal with everyone he's hurting right now. Deep down he already knows that, and it only makes it harder for him to move past all of this shit. He's just not able to see himself very clearly right now. All we have to do is love him until he can love himself again."

Elijah closed his eyes and soaked in Kirsten's promises. He still didn't buy that he was making it all about him, but he understood her point. He didn't need to know what happened to Adam in foster care to be able to stand with his arms wide open and wait for Adam to return.

"I'm not used to not being able to fix things. Since Adam and Kollin came into my life, it feels like I have no control over anything anymore."

"Relationships are messy—even the best ones. But they're kind of worth it too. Right?"

Elijah laughed humorlessly. "I just want him home again. I could deal with the rest of it if I knew he was coming back to me."

"What's Kollin say about it?"

"Nothing since Adam left. Riley's been here, and for the most part they've stayed off together." Elijah paused. "Something's up with Riley too, and as much as I love the kid, it makes me worry more for Kollin. He's been doing pretty well lately, but then this thing with Adam weighs on him. And now Ri's in town, probably dumping his problems all over Kollin too."

"He's a tough kid. Levelheaded. The three of you will get through this. I can take Kollin anytime if you want to have a night alone with Adam."

Elijah shook his head. "I'd rather keep Kollin with me for now, but thank you. Once this blows over, I'll take you up on that offer."

"That's the positive attitude I'm looking for." Kirsten threw back the rest of her drink. "How's the adoption coming along?"

"Better than expected, which is the one bright spot here. His parents agreed to sign over their rights."

"That easy?"

Elijah shrugged. "Not really, but sort of. They tried to make a deal to reduce their jail time, and when my lawyer basically laughed in their faces and pointed out they didn't just abandon their child, but beat him to a pulp, they caved."

"That's amazing. Have you told Kollin yet?"

"No. I found out yesterday. Figured I'd wait at least until Riley's gone, but I'm hoping Adam will be home first too. Wouldn't hurt for him to have some good news."

"He's going to be so happy for you two."

Elijah titled his head. "Hope so."

Kirsten slid off her barstool and grabbed Elijah's hand to pull him down the length of the bar until they stood in front of each other. She was so tiny she barely reached Elijah's shoulders, but when she wrapped her arms around his waist and buried her head in his chest, she managed to comfort him anyway. "My brother loves you. He'll get past this. I promise."

He rested his chin on top of her head and squeezed her tight. "If you say so."

THE COLD December air whipped around, making Adam pull his jacket closer as he sat on the wooden dock and dangled his feet over the still water. Paddleboats lined each side of the dock, but no one dared bring them out this late in the year. In fact, the park seemed to be completely deserted, even though it boasted a gorgeous sunset over the lake.

Adam twisted open the scrap bread he'd brought with him. The ducks had already left for the year, but he thought the fish might bite. He sat in silence for a while, watching the sun creep closer and closer to the horizon, doing his best not to think about anything. Occasionally he saw someone running on the trail on the opposite side of the lake, but for the most part, he was alone.

Exactly how he wanted to be.

He'd been sitting on the dock for about thirty minutes when an older woman walked down the rickety planks and sat on one of the benches behind him. Manners forced Adam to turn his head and acknowledge her with a small nod, but he put his back to her again as quickly as possible.

"Haven't seen you here before," she said.

Adam rolled his eyes, since she couldn't see him. "Needed a change of scenery tonight."

"Mmm," she agreed. "As scenery goes, this is hard to beat."

"It's beautiful."

They watched the sun drop below the horizon, and the woman stood and slowly walked to the railing next to Adam. She tore up her own slice of bread and tossed the bits in. Adam had watched his soggy pieces sink to the bottom long before and thought about telling her the effort was futile, but he didn't want to engage in further conversation.

"I know it probably seems silly to you, but my husband and I fed the ducks here every day this past summer. He passed in late September, and I haven't been able to miss a day since, even though the ducks are long gone for the winter. Old woman like me… you'd think I'd be able to accept death, accept change by now."

Adam peered up at her, but she was focused on the lake, lost in her memories. "I'm sorry for your loss."

"Thank you," she said. She paused for a minute, as if gathering her thoughts. "You sound like you're carrying a burden as well."

He had no idea how she made that presumption from the handful of words they'd exchanged, but given he'd never see her again, Adam didn't see the harm in confirming. "Yes, ma'am. Been having some family struggles lately."

"Ah. You need to work it out, then. Family's important."

"It is," Adam agreed. "It can also be challenging sometimes."

"Indeed it can," she said. "But nothing of value in this world is easy."

"That's an understatement."

The woman glanced at him, a small frown on her face. "Telling you how to live your life is none of my business, but I've found forgiving a loved one, even if they haven't asked for forgiveness, is far more rewarding than hanging on to the anguish caused by the treason they've committed."

Adam barked out a laugh. "If only it were that easy." Adam heard the bitterness in his voice and lowered his tone. "I'm sorry. There's this whole complicated mess with my birth parents, and my partner's been great about the whole thing, but apparently I'm on a mission to ruin us too."

The woman remained silent for several moments, and Adam wondered why he'd told a stranger something so personal and painful. Ready to apologize again and leave her to grieve her husband alone, Adam was surprised when she spoke again.

"Take it from someone who's been around a long time. You don't have to carry the weight of the world on your shoulders alone, and you don't get a do-over. You may get a second chance to right your wrongs, but whatever time you lose before you make that step is gone. Don't waste it."

"Yes, ma'am. Thank you," Adam said politely but succinctly. He didn't have the heart to tell her he wasn't strong enough to forgive Jessica. He knew he'd never be strong enough. How could he ask Elijah for forgiveness when his actions were unforgivable? He heard the old woman's words. He just didn't believe them.

ELIJAH HEARD the door open and a set of keys land on the foyer table. He'd just finished cleaning up from his dinner with Kollin and planned to tie up some loose ends with work before Monday rolled around. Kollin was in his room, catching up on homework since he'd entertained Riley all weekend. Thankfully conversation over dinner centered around Riley, and they avoided discussing why Adam hadn't been home. Maybe now he wouldn't have to.

Elijah said a quick prayer and went into the foyer to see Adam walking up the stairs.

"Hey," Elijah said, following him. Kirsten told him to love Adam, so that's what he'd do. Even though he wanted to throttle Adam for disappearing for so long, or even give him the same cold shoulder he'd been getting. But Adam needed to know Elijah loved him.

"Hey," Adam replied. His entire body stiffened, but he didn't stop walking.

"You hungry? I can bring up some leftovers if you want to shower and eat in here."

Adam cast him a sideways glance as he walked into their room. "No thanks."

"You okay?"

Adam nodded.

Elijah ground his teeth and tried not to feel resentful for Adam's attitude. He tried again. "Want to talk about it?"

Adam shook his head no. Apparently his return did not mean things were going to improve. It was time to go downstairs and leave Adam to his misery. Elijah had shown his love. He had nothing left to give. Except….

"I love you," Elijah whispered. He knew Adam heard because he froze as he kicked off his shoes.

A slight slump of Adam's shoulders was the only response Elijah received as Adam took his sock off. He remained silent while he took off his other sock and tossed both of them toward the hamper.

Elijah's carefully controlled emotions snapped. All of the times he was patient and understanding when he wanted to shout at Adam or shake him or even just walk away from him piled up in front of him. He wondered how much more he'd have to endure before Adam finally decided to own up and take care of himself again.

Besides, he deserved more than to be shut out by Adam when all he'd ever done was love him the only way he knew how.

"For fuck's sake, Adam" Elijah shouted, gripping his hair. "Will you say something? I feel like giving up right now. I'm in way over my head with this entire mess, and I don't know what to do anymore."

Adam snapped his head around. His glare looked almost triumphant. "Is that what you want? To give up on me?"

Elijah threw his hands up in the air. *That he responds to.* "Of course not. You're my fucking happily ever after. I would follow you to the ends of the earth and back if you asked. I feel like I've pretty much proven that over the past few weeks. But until you tell me what's going on, I'm going to keep messing this up because that's who I am. I fix things, and I can't fix this. I tried waiting you out. I tried pushing you to talk to me, to talk to anyone. I tried acting like everything's normal, but nothing about this situation is normal. And the fucking worst part about it is everyone at the damn center knows what happened to you. Everyone except me. How can I help you when I don't even know what the hell I'm fighting against?"

Elijah wanted to bite the words back into his mouth the moment they escaped. Not only had Adam made it clear he wasn't ready to talk yet, Kirsten had warned him about pushing Adam too far, too fast. But the words were out there, and Adam looked so enraged Elijah couldn't regret letting his anger take over. At least Adam still had some fight left in him. Elijah just needed to make him direct all of that rage toward Jessica.

"You want to know what you're fighting against? Is that it?" Adam asked. "Hell, I can tell you right now. You're fighting against me and my demons. I've had some sick shit done to me, and in return, I did some sick shit to other people."

"Damn it, Adam. Can you stop with the fucking vague confessions? I know you—the real you—and you would never intentionally hurt someone."

"That's what you think. Huh? What if I told you I put someone in the hospital? Attacked him and beat him mercilessly until three guys pulled me off of him."

Elijah blanched. "I… I'm sure you had a good reason."

"A good reason? What exactly constitutes a good reason for treating someone with less respect than I would a dog? What would've happened to him—to me—if those guys hadn't pulled me off of him? The only reason I didn't get juvie after that was because of all the shit

I'd gone through at my previous foster care. But none of that means I had a good reason."

Adam's voice, so full of despair and defeat, brought Elijah up short. He squeezed his eyes shut and stopped himself from screaming right back. Elijah took a deep breath and opened his eyes. "What happened to you?"

"It doesn't matter."

"The hell it doesn't. This thing that happened.... It's standing between us. The longer we don't talk about it, the bigger it gets. I already feel like we're on opposite ends of fucking Mt. Everest."

Adam turned away from Elijah. "You'll think less of me."

Elijah strode forward, wrapped his arms around Adam's waist from behind, and tucked his head into Adam's shoulder. He wanted to cry. It felt so good to touch Adam again. "When are you going to believe me? That'll never happen. All you've done for weeks is push me away, and all I want to do is love you. Today. Tomorrow. And the day after."

Adam didn't say anything right away. His breathing sounded labored but controlled. And when Elijah felt a single wet drop land on his hand, he realized Adam was crying. Several long minutes passed as Adam laid his arms over Elijah's.

"My fourth foster family was extremely religious. They didn't just want to return me when they found out about my sexuality. They wanted to cure me. So they sent me to camp."

Elijah's stomach plummeted. He didn't think he could open his mouth to speak without vomiting, so he stayed quiet and waited for Adam to continue.

"I don't know if they knew what actually went on there, and I've never told anyone the details beyond my therapist, but it was horrible. To call it a 'pray the gay away' camp is entirely misleading. More like a concentration camp. They tortured me. Made me watch gay porn but punished me if I became aroused. They made me recite prayers they wrote for me, and if I refused, I didn't eat that day." Adam took a deep breath. "I still have a couple of the scars on my body. They're small, though. You can't see them through the hair on my thigh unless you're looking. I don't tell people how bad it was. I've heard some camps aren't as bad, so I downplay the whole thing as if I hated the camp, so I eventually ran away."

Tears fell freely now from Adam's eyes as well as Elijah's. He tightened his grip on Adam's waist, and all of the words running through his mind—to say how sorry he felt and how no one deserved to experience such atrocities—fell short of conveying how he actually felt inside.

"I ran away one night when one of the counselors snuck in to mess around with my bunkmate, and I lived on the streets, eating out of garbage bins for three weeks, before the cops picked me up and took me back to the group home. I spent one night in the hospital for malnourishment and dehydration.

"I told one of the nurses there about the camp. She said she talked to the cops, but since I'd confessed to running away three weeks prior, they didn't press charges against the camp. I couldn't prove where I'd gotten my injuries, and back then, that type of camp wasn't illegal anywhere. Besides, I was just a faggot, bastard kid. It's not like they actually gave a damn about me, anyway.

"The kid I beat up… he was in the group home with me. Made some snide remark my first night back about making the faggot boy suck his dick. Fuck. I… I lost it. I guess I lucked out that they didn't send me away. I don't know. Maybe they actually felt guilty for sending me to that shithole foster home, but I got mandated therapy instead. I ran away from the next three foster homes practically before they'd even learned my first name. But one of the leaders at the group home sat me down before they placed me with Matthew and Amelia and told me I'd better make an effort with this family because I wouldn't be getting another one."

Adam laughed, but there was no humor in the sound.

"I told her that was fine with me." Adam tightened his grip on Elijah's arms. "But then I met Kirsten, and it felt like she stared right into my soul when she smiled at me. She held so much kindness in her eyes it made me want to cry. I tried to fight it, treated her like shit, and it never even fazed her. A week in I decided to play the straight guy again." Adam paused. "I guess you know the rest."

Elijah didn't speak for a while, allowing Adam's story to settle between them. He couldn't believe Adam had endured all of that as a child, and Elijah never even had an inkling about it. He felt as if he'd failed Adam on the most basic of levels by never asking about his past.

"All I can think about is how worried you were that I'd see you differently after you told me. And you know what? I do." Elijah kept his arms tight around Adam as he spoke. “You’re even stronger than I ever knew. Most people would’ve let something like that consume them, turn them hard and angry, but you used your pain to enrich the lives of everyone around you. Do you have any idea how special that is?”

Shaking his head, Adam squirmed out of Elijah’s embrace. “I’m not a hero because I did the right thing.”

“But you did so much more than the right thing, baby. You went far above and beyond what most people would do, and you overcame a nightmare of a past to get there.”

Adam barked out a laugh. “You call this overcoming my past?”

Elijah closed his eyes. He was walking a very thin rope. Depending on how he chose his words, he’d either reel Adam in or send him barreling away.

“I’m saying you did it once. You can do it again. You have so many people in your life who love you and would do anything for you.”

Adam narrowed his eyes. “How is it heroic to drag the people who love me most through the mud while I work on my most recent mommy issues?”

“Damn it, Adam. Stop twisting my words around. I’m trying to help.”

Adam shook his head slowly and turned to their dresser to yank open a drawer. “Maybe I’m beyond help. Either way, I don’t want it. From you or anyone else. Feel free to pass that message on to whomever you’d like.”

“So you want me to keep watching you fall more and more into yourself?”

Adam walked to the closet, grabbed a duffel bag out of the bottom corner, threw it on the bed, and shoved clothes inside. “Not at all. You don’t have to watch me do a damn thing anymore.”

Horror gripped Elijah’s chest. Adam couldn’t actually leave. “What? Don’t be ridiculous. We were finally getting somewhere, and now you’re leaving me?”

“We didn’t get anywhere,” Adam spat out. “You might’ve heard all of my dirty little secrets, but that doesn’t make this *our* fight. It’s always been mine, and it always will be mine.”

“Who are you?” Elijah asked. “I don’t even recognize you anymore. What happened to the man I fell in love with?”

Adam looked at Elijah, and every ounce of pain, regret, and rejection shone through his tortured brown eyes. “He’s gone, and to be honest, I don't know if I have the courage to bring him back. What if she comes back again? How many times am I going to have to pick myself up off the ground because of the disgusting and shameful feelings the thought of her—or him, for that matter—bring to the forefront of my mind? You say I'm strong? What if I just got lucky the first time?"

Elijah stepped forward, instinct driving him to envelop Adam in his arms, but Adam flinched away.

"I know it's hard to see right now, but I do love you and I refuse to drag you down with me."

Adam grabbed his bag and walked past Elijah. "If Kollin asks, tell him it's better this way." The conviction in Adam's voice made it clear Adam believed his words with every fiber of his being. How had they ended up this way?

Without another word Adam left their room. Elijah stayed rooted to his spot, listening to Adam's footsteps pounding down the steps and then their front door opening and closing. Tears pooled in his eyes as he sank down on his bed, wondering how everything in his life had gone to shit in a heartbeat.

CHAPTER 15

"HEY, KOLL," Elijah shouted up the steps. "Can you come down here for a minute?"

He'd managed to avoid talking about Adam before Kollin left for school. But when Adam called in sick and asked Kirsten to handle his responsibilities until further notice, Elijah knew he needed to man up.

It seemed Adam wouldn't be snapping out of his downward spiral anytime soon.

Kirsten was shocked when Elijah told her Adam left him the night before, not only because Adam left Elijah and Kollin, but also because he didn't mention a word of it to her when they spoke.

That small detail fueled Elijah's hope Adam's actions weren't permanent.

"What's up?" Kollin asked as he jogged down the steps.

"We gotta talk. Let's go in the living room."

Kollin groaned. "What'd Adam do now?"

Elijah sighed and ignored Kollin's question until they sat down.

"Okay. I have good news and bad news. Which do you want first?"

"Oh God. What now?"

Taking that as bad news first, Elijah took a deep breath. He'd spent the afternoon mulling over what he would tell Kollin and how he could soften the blow. He finally decided Kollin deserved—and could handle—the unvarnished truth.

"Adam's moved out for a while."

"What? What do you mean, 'for a while'?"

"I don't know, buddy. He came home last night, and we talked. He finished telling me about his years in foster care, and then we argued about how he's handling all of this. He keeps pushing me away, and I don't know how to deal with that. I probably pushed him too much."

"So he just left?" Kollin asked, clearly still in a state of disbelief. "I mean, I knew he hadn't been here over the weekend, but everyone kept saying he needed time. I thought he'd be back."

Elijah shrugged, unable to deliver an answer that made sense.

"Wait. Does this mean you two broke up?"

The words might as well have formed a sword and stabbed Elijah in the heart. He'd avoided thinking of what Adam's actions actually meant to their relationship. It was too much for him to wrap his brain around what Adam's problems meant for the two of them… the three of them.

With a confidence he didn't feel, Elijah offered a wan smile. "Not if I have anything to say about it."

"I can't even believe this. Adam is so… Adam. He would never abandon anyone. How did this happen?"

"I don't know. He's spiraling downward so fast I can't keep up. I thought we'd made progress last night, but then he shut down."

Kollin shook his head. "That's some bullshit, Eli."

Elijah nodded.

"Dammit, part of me wants to be really angry at him. Like super pissed." Kollin sighed. "But part of me gets it. There've been so many times I've wanted to run away, and he went through way more shit than I ever did."

"Oh, I'm pissed as hell at him. If he'd accept help from us, he could focus on healing and let us worry about sorting out the legalities."

Kollin spoke his next words so quietly Elijah almost didn't hear them, but the undeniably sad truth of them nearly broke him in two. "He promised me he'd never leave me like they did."

Elijah pulled Kollin into a hug. "You know he's not thinking straight. Yeah? No matter what else is going on inside him, he truly believes that not being here is what's best for us, not for him."

"Can't we do something to make him understand he's wrong about that? Do you think he'd come back?"

"I've tried, Kollin. So many times. But I can't get through to him. I don't know what else to do."

Kollin sat on the couch and stared at his hands for a while. "What the hell is the good news, then?"

Elijah forced out a laugh, but it felt foreign. "I heard from my lawyer, and your parents agreed to sign the papers needed to relinquish parental rights to me. As long as you're still on board, we can move forward with the adoption process."

Kollin's face lit up, and Elijah wished Adam were there to see it. "Are you shitting me? That's awesome." Kollin threw his arms around Elijah's neck and squeezed him in a tight hug. "I'll have to call you Dad for real soon, huh?"

Elijah laughed again, this time more genuinely. "Only if you want to."

The smile on Kollin's face stretched even wider, but then his shoulders drooped and he frowned. "Did they even care?"

Elijah didn't need to ask whom Kollin was asking about, but he had no idea how to answer. Kollin's parents were nothing more than worthless piles of shit in Elijah's eyes, but he couldn't say anything like that to Kollin.

"You know, I think maybe they did. Not signing is the only way they had left to hurt you. Signing over their rights is the only decent thing they could've done for you at this point. Maybe they felt some remorse."

Elijah overlooked the other obvious truth—Kollin's parents truly didn't want him anymore. He only needed one glance at Kollin's face to see all of the possibilities his future held, and Elijah couldn't imagine anyone not wanting to be part of Kollin's life.

Kollin's face clouded over, but he quickly swept it away with a sullen smile. "Yeah. I guess."

"We'll probably never know. So I say think whatever makes each day easier."

"What're we gonna do about Adam?" Recognizing he'd reached Kollin's limit for discussing his parents without breaking down, Elijah dropped the subject.

"We have plenty of time to figure that out. It'll be a few months before everything is official. I'm hoping he'll come around soon, and if he doesn't, we'll figure something out then."

"I guess. I kinda wanna shake him. You know? Like yell at him and then shake him some and then give him a big hug."

"Trust me, kiddo. I know. But we gotta have faith in him. He'd have faith in us."

Kollin pressed again. "And if he doesn't come back…?"

The question hung heavy in the air, and Elijah honestly didn't know the answer, so he said the only thing he could be certain of. "At least we'll have each other."

ADAM LOOKED out the window as he drove down the Outer Banks coastline. Every so often he could see the coast, but on that particular stretch, houses lined both sides of the road. With Christmas only a couple of weeks away, some were even decked out with full-blown nativity scenes or huge, inflatable snowmen. Normally a great fan of Christmas, Adam couldn't even bother to get excited about the homes with elaborate light displays. He should be busy buying gifts for his family, preparing for his first Christmas with Elijah, and helping Kollin cope during his first Christmas without his parents. Instead Adam was running away from anyone and everyone who cared about him.

His parents saw the ugliness inside him early on. If the two people who brought him into the world couldn't even stand to raise him, how could he expect anyone else to be part of his life? He had to push Elijah away, and now he hated himself even more for letting Kollin down too. Disgusted, Adam shook his head as he thought of how disappointed Kollin must be—further proof his father was right. Adam was weak, and everything he touched eventually turned to shit.

When he ended it with Elijah, Adam swore his heart ripped in two. He felt like his entire body split in half, but he knew how close he was to pounding the final nail into his coffin. He should've walked out then, but he knew what would happen if he told Elijah about his past. He knew he'd receive nothing less than unconditional acceptance, and selfishly he wanted that feeling one more time.

Elijah's arms felt like a soothing balm to his jagged and incomplete soul. He'd held on as if he were being tossed around in an angry ocean and Elijah was the only life raft in sight. When he finished his story, he took a deep breath, faced the murky, unknown waters, and jumped—letting go of Elijah for good. Something he never would've imagined happening in a million years.

He hated his mother for turning him into that person.

He hated himself more for allowing her that much power over him.

The houses on either side of him slowly began to disappear, and within a few minutes, Adam had an unobstructed view of the ocean. He always loved driving along the Outer Banks and had discovered some of the quaintest restaurants and shops during his trips. But the expanse of highway with nothing but trees and ocean topped his list of favorites when he needed somewhere to escape and be alone.

He could barely make out the Cape Hatteras Lighthouse in the distance and knew he'd soon be forced to follow the road over the sound and back to the mainland. Just as well given the late hour. He needed to find a place to stay for the night, and he should probably find some food. He hadn't eaten since the half pack of nabs and Dr Pepper he had for breakfast on the drive to the coast, but food held very little appeal. He only ate because he knew he should.

As he approached the bend in the road that would lead him away from the beach, Adam made an impromptu decision to pull over. The night air was too frigid for him to walk down to the water, but he rolled his window down a bit so he could hear the waves crashing against the shore. The salty air filled his nostrils as he wrapped his arms around the steering wheel, rested his temple on them, and stared out the window. He thought about how happy he was a few months before—how his life felt complete with Elijah and Kollin. He wished they'd taken the time to go on a family vacation to the beach, even if only for a few days. But between work at the inn and Kollin's parents' trial, they'd pushed it off until next summer.

He thought about the first time Jessica called him and sent him into a panic—how the mere sound of her voice brought a tidal wave of long-forgotten self-loathing and shame slamming right back into the center of his chest. All the years of therapy had disappeared in an instant. All because he was too pathetic to fight for himself.

He remembered how hopeful he was—even when he refused to admit it aloud—when Jessica said she wanted to get to know him again, that she regretted sending him away. He thought about the time they spent together, how he not only told her things about his life, things that mattered like Elijah and Kirsten and Kollin, but also how he asked about hers and became invested in everything she did. He wanted happiness for her. They didn't have another conversation about her giving him up. They never brought up Chad and they didn't speak of Gramps, but Adam enjoyed getting to know the woman who gave birth to him and raised him the first nine years of his life. He assumed the rest—wading through the muddy waters of their painful past—would come later.

But Jessica never had any intention of getting to know him, not really, and Adam had no way of knowing if anything she told him was true. He hated himself for caring, and even though part of him wanted to fight for Elijah and Kollin, a larger part of him wanted to stay isolated, with nothing but his aching heart and tormented thoughts to keep him company. It was better for him and better for those who loved him. If he wasn't strong enough to fight for himself, how could he ever hope to help everyone else who relied on him? The weight of their problems stacked on top of his weighed Adam down so much he could barely breathe.

No. He'd made the right decision. Leaving was best for everyone.

Adam turned his head, resting his forehead on his hands to stare down into the darkness of his car. He realized Jessica had already won. She'd beaten the life out of him not once, but twice—and this time for keeps. So much for all of the people who had ever believed in him, who praised him for his accomplishments. They didn't mean a damn thing once he abandoned everyone and everything in his life.

A single tear slid down his cheek, immediately followed by another. Within moments they fell freely from his eyes.

Jessica had won, and Adam had no fight left in him.

He might as well give her everything she wanted.

KOLLIN BARELY noticed when Julie joined him at one of the tables reserved for homework. He'd been reading *Les Misérables* for his English class. He had two days to finish the damn book before the quiz on Friday, but over the past thirty minutes, he'd barely even read one page. His mind kept wandering to Adam, wondering where he was and when he'd be home. Hell. *If* he'd be home.

He played it cool when Eli told him about Adam leaving. Elijah sounded rough, and Kollin didn't want to make him feel worse, but Kollin started to feel like he was reaching the end of his rope too. He'd gotten to a place where he could think of his parents without falling into a deep pit of despair, and he knew he owed it all to Eli, Adam, and Dr. Will. But between the pressure of Riley's surprise visit and Adam's midlife crisis, Kollin felt as if he were struggling to cope.

Though he tried to play off whatever troubled him, Riley slipped a few times. He'd yet to come out as trans at college, and apparently his parents refused to pay his tuition after that year. He blew off both problems when he blurted them out, but the listless attitude he had about college and the damaged way in which he viewed himself worried Kollin.

And Adam…. Well, he had no idea what the hell to think there. Adam was literally the best damn person Kollin knew—or he was before all this shit happened. Kollin didn't know if he could still make that claim. He had fallen into a constant state of agony over Adam, fluctuating between intense anger and complete acceptance of his struggles to cope.

Kollin didn't dare voice his thoughts, though. Even when Eli pushed and told Kollin it was okay to be mad, Kollin didn't take the bait. How selfish did it make him if he stayed mad at a guy for taking some time for himself when his entire world imploded? Kollin would have done the same thing if Eli and Adam let him, but they forced him to talk not only to Dr. Will, but also to them. He'd resented the hell out of both of them at the time. But in hindsight he understood they were simply pushing him to heal.

"Kollin," Julie said, tapping his arm. "You okay? I've been talking to you."

"Sorry, Jules. I'm kinda tired."

"That's okay. I just asked where Adam's been this week. Is everything okay?"

"Uhhhh… yes. No. I guess." Kollin had no idea what to tell Julie, so he squirmed in his seat. He didn't want to bad-mouth Adam. Aside from being his caregiver, he ran the inn. If he wasn't living with Adam, he'd be just as curious as Julie. But he didn't think he needed to tell everyone Adam had flipped out and left them all high and dry.

"Oh… kay," she said. "Well, can you tell him we boxed up the rest of his stuff and stacked it in the garage for him? He said he would do it before we moved into his old house, but I guess he got busy or forgot."

Kollin looked at her. He forgot Julie and her family had moved into Adam's old house. If Julie lived there, that meant Adam must be somewhere else. But where? Had he really left everyone?

"I'll be sure to tell him when I see him," Kollin said as he grabbed his book and stood. He shoved his chair under the desk with a loud clatter, just in time to see Kirsten walk into the room.

"Kollin," she said immediately, her eyes wide. She narrowed her eyes and motioned him toward her. "Come with me to Adam's office for a minute, please."

Without waiting for a yes or no, she turned and walked out of the room.

"Fucking chalupa," Kollin murmured as he stalked after her and left a bewildered Julie alone at the table. A heart-to-heart with Adam's sister was the absolute last thing he needed.

As soon as the door closed behind him, Kirsten rounded on him and stared him down.

"I am so damn livid at Adam right now. I mean, what the hell?"

Shocked, Kollin stared at her. "Uh… what?"

"How could he just up and leave like that? Without so much as a note or a phone call or even a damn text."

Kirsten had a point. Kollin had thought the exact same thing over the past couple of days, but he pushed it away every time.

"Yeah. It really sucks," he said lamely as Kirsten paced around the office.

"Like I have time to just drop my job on a whim and take over here. I have clients relying on me too."

Right? God. She was so right. Come the fuck on. He couldn't bad-mouth Adam too much in front of his sister, so he chose his next words delicately. "That's totally shitty of him, Kirsten. You have every right to be pissed."

"Thank you," she huffed, flopped down on the couch, and looked up at Kollin. "And you. I mean, if I were you, I'd be even more pissed. Leaving you like that, after everything you've been through."

Kirsten's voice softened as she spoke, and her words hit Kollin right in the heart. Still, guilt and obligation toward Adam kept him from voicing his own anger. "Yeah. But, I mean, he couldn't help the timing, and it's not like I'm his real kid."

She stayed silent for a while and then quietly said, "You and I both know that's not true. Adam would be gone right now even if he'd been your biological dad. His feelings toward you have nothing to do with blood."

Tears welled up in Kollin's eyes, and the tinges of anger he'd felt all week turned fierce. With a shaky voice, he shouted his fury to Kirsten. "Then why the hell did he leave me? I thought if anyone left, it would be Eli, but he's been a damn rock through this entire disaster. Adam is supposed to be the rock. Adam is supposed to be consistent and reliable and trustworthy. He's supposed to know how to handle everything. And dammit, he's not supposed to leave!"

"You're right. He's not," she said. "But as much as we want to believe Adam is a superhero, even Batman was afraid of bats. That doesn't excuse Adam's behavior, particularly his up and leaving without a word to any of us, but it tells us that, once Jessica came into the picture and poured her own special brand of poison all over Adam's life again, this was bound to happen—no matter what any of us did. He'll come back to us in time, but until he does, and even after he does, remember it's okay to be mad at him. It's okay to yell at me or Elijah or Dr. Will. No one expects you to have it all together right now, so stop trying to carry the entire world on your shoulders."

"What am I supposed to tell everyone?"

"Whatever you want. I get that, in some way, they're all Adam's kids. I feel the same way. You're all mine too. But you actually *are* his kid, and kids will always, until the end of time, fight with their fathers and then vent to their friends about how they have the world's worst dad in the entire world."

Kollin shook his head. "I don't want people to think less of him. Besides, it's not my business to share. Is it?"

Kirsten patted the couch next to her, and Kollin fell into the spot with a *humph*. "That's very admirable and mature of you. What I would suggest is to choose one person you really trust to talk with about all of this stuff. Make it a friend, not me or Dr. Will or Elijah's parents, but someone your age who you would normally vent to if one of your parents grounded you. Do you have anyone like that?"

Kollin nodded. "I guess I could call Riley. That way it's still separate from the center too. You know?"

"That sounds perfect. How's he doing lately? I'd hoped to see him more when he visited."

"I dunno." Kollin scrubbed his face with his hands. "Doesn't sound like college is everything he expected. I kind of hate to drop more shit on him with this, now that I think about it."

Kirsten shook her head. "Riley loves you. He'd want to know what's going on in your life. Besides, sometimes helping others helps us help ourselves. Maybe that's exactly what Riley needs."

Kollin laid his head on Kirsten's shoulder. "Thanks, Kirsten. I feel a little better."

"Thanks for listening to me vent too," Kirsten said.

Kollin flushed, knowing she started the whole charade to get him wound up enough to express his own anger and frustration. She would sooner wear a crushed-velvet dress with platform shoes than complain to him about Adam. His chest already felt lighter, though, so he was grateful she'd worked her magic on him. He hoped Kirsten was right and Adam would come around. She knew him better than anyone—even better than Eli. Someone just needed to find him so they could all sit him down and knock some sense into him. Literally.

ADAM PULLED into the parking lot of Newton & Brown and quickly glanced in the rearview mirror to make sure he looked halfway presentable. Not that he cared to impress Chad or Jessica, but he wanted to appear somewhat professional.

When Adam walked into his lawyer's waiting room, he avoided looking in his birth parents' direction. He walked through to the main office and took a seat next to Mr. Beuford.

"You sure you want to do this?"

Adam nodded. "I want them out of my life, and this is the quickest way to do it."

His lawyer remained silent for a moment and then cleared his throat. "I don't mean to overstep my boundaries, but this seems like a rash decision you may later regret, Adam. This is not like you at all."

Directing his focus on his lawyer, Adam bit back a smartass comment. Mr. Beuford had been his lawyer since he opened the center, and Adam considered him smart, reliable, and trustworthy. In fact, he'd often called him Rafiki—when Mr. Beuford calmly tendered his wisdom in a manner that made Adam see a different side to an issue. Adam respected him immensely, but he was in no mood to hear him out.

"There are no other options, if I ever hope to be 'like me' again."

Mr. Beuford tilted his head to one side and scrunched up his face. "Don't be such a dumbass, son. You know that's not true."

Adam's mouth dropped open, and he stared at his lawyer. He had never spoken to him so harshly. "What do you know about it?" Adam asked, his voice hushed.

"Over the years I've watched you give and give and give to people who needed it. Not only children and youth, but adults as well. People from all walks of life. Most of them deserved it, but even the ones who spit everything back at you… you handled them with a rare grace and compassion we don't see much anymore. That's not a quality you learn. That's something you're born with, and you either polish it until it shines, or you piss it away and waste your God-given gift. Those two people"—he jutted his finger toward Jessica and Chad—"they don't deserve a damn iota of any good part of you. That's what I know about it."

Mr. Beuford huffed, and Adam thought he'd finished his rant. But he kept right on going. "Your damn pinky has more integrity and compassion than the two of them combined, and if you don't believe me, you should listen to the other people in your life who love you and are worried about you. And if you don't believe them, there are hundreds—think about that now—literally hundreds of youth alive today because of you, because you overcame your past and found who you were born to be. Don't let lowlifes like these two take that away from you." Mr. Beuford had become worked up and was leaning forward as he spoke. He settled back into his seat and straightened his jacket. "Elijah said to tell you he loves you, and he'll be waiting whenever you decide you're ready. Kollin too." Then he completely avoided Adam's gaze.

Adam's head swam as he soaked in Mr. Beuford's words. The final ones felt like a warm ray of sunshine lighting up his darkened heart.

Elijah still loved him. He knew that. Of course he did. Elijah was so compassionate. So faithful. So damn *good.*

But Adam still wasn't good enough for Elijah. Or was he? He'd helped all of those youth, but it all felt tainted. Jessica's black mark tinged each and every one.

But Elijah still loved him.

Elijah still loves me.

Kollin would never forgive him. He'd abandoned him after promising he never would—after promising he'd be better than Kollin's own parents.

But Mr. Beuford had said Kollin too.

Before he could work out anything else, his birth parents' lawyer opened the side door and called everyone into a large conference room. Adam sat on one side with Mr. Beuford, and Chad and Jessica sat on the other with their lawyer, a man whose name Adam couldn't remember. It reminded him of all the mediations he'd ever seen on TV.

After offering everyone a drink, their lawyer said, "So, you indicated your client is willing to make a compromise?"

"It seems so," Mr. Beuford said. He cast a long, side-eye stare to Adam and continued. "Adam is under the impression Mr. and Mrs. Lancaster are much more interested in obtaining the select few high-dollar cards than the entire set. He's willing to part with those four if we keep this out of court, and he's able to keep possession of the remaining cards."

"How do we know there's not a stack of cards in there worth more than what he's giving us? Huh?" Chad asked. "Stupid little queer sure did cave fast. He probably got them all appraised and kept the good ones for himself."

Adam sank down in his seat. The other lawyer made a lackluster attempt to settle Chad while Mr. Beuford calmly replied, "He's willing to submit the cards to an impartial third-party appraiser to verify that the cards he keeps are not valuable."

"Even so. Jess says there's thousands of them," Chad continued. "At a dollar a pop, that's still a grand. I didn't pay for that old bag of bones to sit in some shit-hole home all them years for nothing."

Adam raised his eyes to meet Chad's. His face looked rough. Too many years of smoke and alcohol had taken their toll, and the seemingly permanent frown Adam remembered from his childhood morphed into a sneer as Adam held his gaze.

"See you finally grew some balls to look your old dad in the face. Huh?"

"You are not my father," Adam said. His jaw clenched tight as he spoke, but even as the breath left his lungs, he felt a little lighter.

"You're damn right about that. Your mom probably whored around on me to get a faggoty little shit like you."

As much as Jessica had hurt him over the past weeks, Adam still felt a twinge of sadness that she had to share her life with a man who would speak about her so horribly. But Jessica only rolled her eyes and slapped his arm.

Adam shook his head. "Amelia Wright is my mother, and Matthew Wright is my father. I may have your DNA, but that does not make you my parents. And Gramps is one of the few reasons I'm still alive. I never would've survived my years in foster care if it hadn't been for him and the kindness of one other person, practically a stranger, who accepted me exactly as I was. I'll be damned if I'll sit here and listen to you put that man down and then let you see one fucking cent from those cards."

Adam felt as if a ten-pound chain had loosened around his heart, and it fell away with a loud thud as he stood. "You want those cards? You better bring more impressive legal representation than this guy, who didn't even have the common sense to tell you to keep your fucking trap shut. Because I will hire the best damn team of lawyers in the country to back up Mr. Beuford. They will find Jimmy Hoffa's cold, dead body before you ever lay a finger on a single one of those cards."

Dizzy with adrenaline, Adam turned on his heel and walked out of the room. Before the door slammed shut, he heard Jessica screech, "What the hell were you thinking?"

Adam stormed out of the lawyer's office, Mr. Beuford hot on his heels, and stumbled to a nearby bench to collapse in an embarrassed heap. He took a deep breath and looked at Mr. Beuford, who had a huge smile on his face.

"Did Elijah really say he missed me, or were you just trying to get me to tell them off?"

"Oh no. I never expected that. I only hoped you'd let me tell them no deal."

Adam's heart sank. He hadn't told Chad off because of Elijah—not really, anyway. Adam might very well be all of the things Chad claimed, but he refused to let anyone bad-mouth his gramps. Adam squeezed his eyes shut. The adrenaline rush of telling off his birth parents still coursed through his veins. If he'd found the strength to stand up to the two people who had hurt him the most, maybe he could find it again to accept the help he needed and be worthy of Elijah's love.

Adam offered Mr. Beuford a sad smile. "Glad I can still surprise you."

Mr. Beuford laid a hand on Adam's shoulder. "What say we go call Elijah and set up a meeting with one of his fancy lawyers? Jessica may want to pull out after the show you put on in there, but that man is a piece of work. So I want us to be ready no matter what."

"I can't ask Elijah for help. Besides, I trust you to handle it. You haven't let me down yet."

"Why the hell can't you ask Elijah for help? He's damn near driven me crazy this week, trying to get information out of me. Attorney-client privilege means nothing to that man."

Adam scrunched up his face and studied his lawyer. "He has?"

"I told you what he said." Mr. Beuford flushed. "He filled me in on everything going on. I hope you don't mind, but he thought it best I know the full situation. And, well, he's quite persistent. I didn't have much choice other than to listen to him."

"How'd he even know we've been in contact?"

Mr. Beuford shrugged. "He didn't. He wanted me to be prepared, in case. He wanted the best possible outcome for you, so you wouldn't live with regrets."

Tears welled in Adam's eyes, and he tugged at his ear to distract himself. Even when Adam was being a world-class asshole and running away from everyone, Elijah's only concern was ensuring Adam didn't walk away with remorse.

God. He'd been such a fool.

He wanted to cry, to spill all of his problems and feelings at Mr. Beuford's feet, to ask him if he thought Elijah and Kollin would forgive him and if he deserved their love. But Elijah needed to hear all of those words first.

"Thanks, Mr. Beuford. I have something I have to do, but if you happen to speak to Elijah today, can you let him know I'm okay and I'll see him soon?"

Smiling, Mr. Beuford held out his hand for Adam to shake. "It'd be my pleasure."

THE MOMENT his watch ticked over to 1:00 p.m., Adam opened the door to Phoenix Tattoo, drawing the attention of the receptionist.

"Adam," Sara greeted him with a smile. "I didn't know you were coming in today. How are you? It's been so long."

He returned her smile, and the motion came easier to him than it had in weeks. He might be acting on impulse, but he knew, without a doubt, he wanted the tattoo. Taking time to think about it would do nothing to change his decision. "I guess I can't complain, and I don't have an appointment. I was hoping someone could squeeze me in. I can wait however long you need me to."

Sara clicked away at her computer as another client walked in. She greeted the new girl with the same warmth she had Adam and said she'd be with her in a moment. "You're in luck, Adam. Richard doesn't have anyone scheduled until two thirty. Do you know what you want?"

"Yes, and it's fairly basic. Shouldn't take him long at all."

Several minutes later Richard sauntered up front. His long, bushy beard suited his heavy frame, and the baseball cap he always wore to cover his balding head faced forward. Adam knew he'd turn it around before he started his work.

"How's it going, Adam?" he asked, waving him back.

"Eh. It's been better. I'm thinking some new ink will help me get back to a good place."

Richard grunted. "Usually does, man. Whatcha got in mind today?"

Adam pulled a piece of paper out of his back pocket and unfolded it to set it in front of Richard.

"Nice. You adopting?"

Adam shrugged. "In a manner. Good as."

"I hear ya. I can do this now easy. Want it jazzed up any?"

Adam scratched the back of his head and nodded. "Yeah. These points normally represent the birth mom and adoptive mom, but that doesn't work for me. I was hoping you could somehow work these in?" Adam flipped the paper over.

Richard studied Adam's sloppy drawings for a moment as he smoothed his hand over his beard. "You just Google this shit or something?"

"Caught me. I was in a bit of a hurry."

"Give me a few minutes, and I'll see what I can come up with… unless you'd rather think on it awhile and come back later?"

Adam bit his lip. He really wanted a complete tattoo that day, but Richard had a point. It would be on his body forever, and permanently marking his skin with Chinese symbols hastily scrawled on the back of a piece of paper wasn't his finest idea.

"It's important to me to have it done today, but if you have something better in mind, I'm all for it. I appreciate it, man."

"You know I look out for you. Grab a seat and let me stencil this out real quick. Any particular color you looking for? Want some more of that rainbow shit?"

Adam laughed, full-bellied and loud. "Whatever floats your boat. I trust you."

An hour and a half later, Adam walked out of the shop, feeling more carefree than he had in months. He could still feel the lingering sting from the needle, but Richard's variation of his idea had been simple and perfect. Adam couldn't be more pleased with his new ink.

He got in his car and stared at the clock, trying to figure out where he should go next. Flowers were probably in order, but Adam didn't want Elijah to think he was trying to sweep everything under the rug with a few roses. He also knew his euphoric feeling of triumph over Jessica and Chad would eventually pass, and it would take him several months of therapy to move past his latest parental disappointments. He held on to the fact that he actually wanted to get better instead of wanting to constantly swim around in the sea of murky depression he'd plunged into weeks before.

Deciding roses were a bit too cliché, Adam swung by the closest Trader Joe's and picked up a bag of Cookie Butter cookies and a single tulip. Nerves fluttered around his heart as he parked next to Elijah's car at Langley L&C. If Elijah's stern secretary, Sherri, was surprised to see him, she didn't show it—not that Adam ever expected her to display even one iota of emotion. Elijah had praised her work ethic on countless occasions, but no one would ever say that schmoozing the public was her strong suit.

Sherri reached for her phone as soon as Adam walked through the doors, but Adam held up his hand. "Do you think I could surprise him today?"

Sherri's frown deepened. "Mr. Langley does not like surprises at work."

Adam sighed internally even as he widened his smile and swept the tulip out from behind his back. "Maybe just this once? Please, Sherri?"

Adam thought he would keel over in shock when the corners of Sherri's mouth twitched up into a not-quite-really-but-almost smile. She took the flower primly and laid it delicately on her desk. "Just this once."

"Thank you. You're the absolute best."

Adam tapped lightly on Elijah's office door and waited for Elijah to call him in. Opening the door a crack, Adam slid his hand inside first, dangling the bag of cookies for Elijah to see.

"Kollin? What're you doing here? You're supposed to be in school."

He heard Elijah scoot his chair back, so he quickly stepped in front of the doorway before Elijah could join him in the hall. Though Elijah's message gave Adam enough hope to believe a reconciliation lay in their future, he knew he deserved to be put through the wringer for his actions over the past few weeks. Adam had no delusions they would have a quick forgive-and-forget conversation.

"Adam," Elijah breathed, widening his eyes. He took two giant steps forward, but right before Adam could curve his lips up in a smile, Elijah's feet faltered, and he stopped in the middle of his office, clearly unsure how he would be received. "What're you doing here?"

Taking a step forward, Adam kept his eyes on Elijah. He could beat around the bush or he could suck it up and be a man. He didn't have time for the former. "I came to apologize for how I've been acting, for pushing you away and being a shitty boyfriend and business partner and co-dad and basically every other shitty thing I've done lately. I'm sorry for hiding parts of me that I should've told you about a long time ago. And I'm sorry for running when things got hard for me.

"It was never you. Or Kollin. It was always me and how being deceived by Jessica and Chad made me feel like less than a person all over again. Even during the times I could remember the good things I've done, I just as quickly remembered I have parts of him and her in me. And when I think about that, I feel like I'll never be worthy of anyone—and definitely no one as good as you."

Running out of steam under Elijah's scrutinizing stare, Adam held up his bag of cookies. "I thought these would be a good icebreaker. I had to give your flower to Sherri so she'd let me in here without buzzing you. She almost smiled at me," he said, finishing his heartfelt speech somewhat lamely.

Adam forced himself to stop talking, even though Elijah made no move to respond. Most people would've shrunk under Elijah's stone-cold glare. Adam had told him more than once he hoped he'd never be on the receiving end of that look. He felt a sense of pride for not backing away, but if Elijah didn't speak soon, Adam would start rambling again.

"Your peace offering is cookies?" Elijah finally asked. "Do you have any idea how much I've eaten while you were gone? I put on seven pounds."

Adam released a long, slow breath, and tears welled up in his eyes. But for the first time in a long while, they were happy tears. He and Elijah had a long way to go, but Elijah wouldn't make it more difficult on him than he had to.

He was so damn lucky Elijah chose him.

"S'probably better if you don't take them. I didn't pick anything up for Kollin. Don't tell him. 'Kay?" Adam's voice sounded weak, but Elijah didn't seem to care. He closed the distance between them and pulled Adam into a hug.

Adam winced as Elijah pressed against his sore skin, but he clung to Elijah all the same.

"Please don't ever leave me again," Elijah whispered. "I was so lost."

"I'm so sorry. I hated hurting you."

Elijah raised his hand to swat the back of Adam's head. "Then don't do it again, jackass."

Adam laughed, but a sob of overwhelming relief drowned it out. "I thought it was asshole, not jackass."

"Nah. That one's reserved for when I do dumb shit."

Neither of them seemed to be willing to let go of the other, so Adam held on until Elijah pulled back to look at him. Elijah's puffy eyes and red nose did nothing to diminish his wide smile or the twinkle in his blue eyes. Adam had never seen Elijah more beautiful than in that perfectly imperfect moment.

"I love you," he said.

"Marry me," Elijah replied.

Fear sliced through Adam. He'd just created a tattoo on his chest for Elijah, a permanent declaration for the world to see that he and Kollin would always be in his heart. But he was still too broken to take that step.

"Um…."

"I don't mean now," Elijah said. "I mean, I totally will if you want to, though by the look on your face, I'm guessing that's a no. But we've never really talked about it, so I want you to know that's what I want with you. These past few days—weeks, even—have made me realize I don't *just* want to spend the rest of my life with you, I want to be tied to you in every way possible." Elijah closed his eyes and took a deep breath. "Marriage was never really something I saw for myself. I always thought people did it because that's what they're supposed to do. But loving you, I understand why people want to make that commitment. I know neither of us is very religious, but I can't think of any vow I'd rather make in front of God or any other higher power than to promise to love you and Kollin until my last breath."

A single tear trailed down Adam's cheek, and Elijah cupped the side of his face to brush it away with his thumb. "I promise I'm not pressuring you. I just want you to know. Okay?"

Nodding, Adam took a step back. "I actually have something to show you. I think it will answer you better than any words I could ever say, but I was hoping to show you and Kollin at the same time. Can you get out of work early so we can pick him up together?"

Though Elijah tried to cover it up, Adam didn't miss the way his face clouded over.

"Oh fuck. How pissed is he?"

Elijah hesitated, and Adam knew him well enough to know he was choosing his words carefully. "I don't think he's going to welcome you with open arms."

"I get that. I didn't expect *you* to, to be honest."

Elijah smiled, though he looked sad. "I'm angrier at you for what you did to Kollin than what you did to me."

"I don't think the two of you combined could possibly be madder at me than I am at myself. He didn't deserve any of this."

"Nope," Elijah agreed. "But then, neither did you. He'll come around, and so will I. But he's pretty hurt. Not that he bothers to tell me, but he talked a little to Kirsten about it. She may start charging us for all of these therapy sessions soon."

Adam snorted. He couldn't disagree. She'd been his favorite therapist over the years.

"Just give me a few minutes to wrap some stuff up, and we'll head out."

Adam smiled and stepped closer to Elijah. He tilted his face up and pressed a soft but firm kiss against Elijah's lips. Elijah wrapped his arms around Adam's waist to pull him closer, and Adam smiled through the kiss. He could still feel the darkness Jessica's betrayal had brought back into his heart, but in Elijah's arms, he felt strong enough to fight it.

CHAPTER 16

"WHAT'S WRONG now?" Kollin asked as he slid into the passenger seat of Elijah's car.

"Nothing's wrong," Elijah assured him as he backed out of his spot and turned the car toward home.

"Then why're you picking me up early and being all secretive?"

Elijah took a deep breath and glanced at Kollin. They'd decided Adam should go straight home so he could see Kollin without all the commotion of suddenly showing up at the center after nearly a week away. But that left Elijah in charge of preparing Kollin and delivering the news.

"Adam's home."

Kollin's head swiveled around to glare at Elijah. "Just like that?"

Elijah tilted his head to the side. "Might want to hear him out."

"He left us, Eli. He promised he wouldn't."

"I know."

"You just let him right back in. Didn't you? No questions asked."

Pretty much, and Elijah didn't regret it for a moment. "This is what we both wanted. Remember?"

"Hmmph," Kollin said, looking out the window.

He remained silent the rest of the way home, so Elijah left him alone with his thoughts. Forcing Kollin to accept anyone's opinion never ended well. When he pulled into the driveway, Kollin didn't move to open his door, so Elijah waited.

"I'm scared as soon as I see him, I won't be mad at him anymore."

"What's wrong with that?"

"Why should he get off so easy?"

"Come on, Koll. You know better than that. No matter what you say when you walk inside, Adam's not getting off easy. You know he hates himself for letting you down. You'll probably forgive him long before he forgives himself." Elijah shook Kollin's knee. "Besides, it's okay to be angry with him and still be glad he's home. He understands mixed feelings better than anyone."

"I guess."

Kollin didn't look too pleased, but he grabbed his book bag and got out of the car. Elijah was surprised he'd expressed that much anger after days of keeping it all locked in, but he supposed with Adam home, Kollin didn't feel as if he needed to hold back any longer.

When Kollin opened the front door, Adam stood in the foyer, shifting from one foot to the other. The uncertainty in his stance made him look more like someone Kollin's age than his own.

"Kollin," Adam said, shoving his hands in his pockets. "I'm so sor—"

Kollin cut off Adam's apology by crashing into him and engulfing him in a huge hug. With Adam's arms pinned to his side, Kollin said, "Just so you know, I'm still mad at you. Eli and Kirsten both said it's okay to be glad you're home and still be mad at you for leaving. So that's how I feel."

Adam nodded as he struggled to return Kollin's hug. "I'm still mad at me too."

Kollin let go and took a step back. "Maybe you shouldn't be. You got enough to deal with, and you can't run off again."

"I won't. I promise."

Elijah briefly closed his eyes as Kollin sized up Adam. "That's what you said last time."

"I did," Adam acknowledged. "I guess I can't promise it won't happen again because I don't know what the future holds. My past…. It kinda fucked me up, you know? I thought I'd dealt with it a long time ago, but then Jessica showed up and manipulated me again…. I wasn't as over it as I thought. What I can promise is to try my hardest to move past this and heal again. What I can promise is to never stop loving you. I didn't this time. I fell too far inside my own head, my own pain, to behave as I should, but I never stopped loving you. Either of you."

Kollin nodded. "I get that. You're really okay if I'm mad at you?"

"As long as you guys take me back, I'm more than okay with that."

Kollin glanced back at Elijah, so he smiled and nodded. "I dunno about this guy, but I vote yes."

"I already voted yes," Elijah said. "Guess it's up to you, Adam."

Adam sucked in a deep breath, and he momentarily looked as if he were saying a quiet prayer while he pulled himself together. "I definitely vote yes," he said.

Kollin grinned. "So, are we gonna celebrate, or what?" he asked, breaking the seriousness of the moment.

Adam laughed, and Elijah threw his arm over Kollin's shoulder. "I imagine we could scrounge up some food."

"Uh, actually," Adam said, "I have something to show you first."

Adam grabbed the bottom of his shirt and lifted it over his head to reveal a large bandage over his chest.

"Holy shit. What happened to you?" Elijah stepped forward to get a closer look. "Are you okay?"

Adam began peeling off the tape on the side of the bandage. "I'm fine. This is what I wanted to show you guys, to prove to you how serious I am." Ever so slowly—it felt like ages to Elijah—Adam tugged the bandage off and revealed a new tattoo on his almost-bare chest. "I don't take getting ink lightly. Just because I'm covered in it doesn't mean they don't all mean something.

"I've told Elijah, but this date," he said, addressing Kollin as he pointed at the date that had previously been the only ink he'd allowed on his chest, "is the first day Matthew called me 'son' after I came out to them. It was something so insignificant to him, he probably didn't even realize it, but that moment was another turning point in my life, and I swore I'd never put anything else so close to my heart.

"But both of you deserve a place as close to my heart as I can get you, so I had this done today. The triangle and the heart woven together like this is used as a symbol for adoption. The heart, of course, is obvious, and the triangle's three points represent the birth mother, the adoptive parent, and the baby. I know I'm not the one legally adopting you, but I've told you, in my heart, I might as well be. I hope this is proof."

Elijah's mouth dropped open. Even with the irritated red skin around the tattoo, Elijah could see its beauty. "I had the guy change it up a bit to fit us better, so instead of drawing a normal triangle, he made each line represent one of us. So the bottom line spells out 'hope' and represents Kollin. This line here says 'strength' and represents Elijah, and I'm this one. It says 'compassion.'"

Kollin and Elijah stared at Adam while he fidgeted nervously in front of them. Kollin finally spoke up. "Well, you really know how to apologize to someone, don't you?" He altered his voice to sound eerily similar to Adam's. "Oh, I'll just permanently mark my body to show you how much I love you. No big deal."

Adam laughed, but Elijah stepped closer to him, and with a feather-light touch, ran his fingers over the word "strength." Tears glistened in his eyes when his gaze met Adam's.

"Strength, huh?"

Adam nodded. "Strongest person I know."

Elijah smiled. "Wait until I fall off my A game. You'll be singing a different tune eventually."

"Never."

"It's perfect," Elijah whispered. "I love how you see each of us, especially yourself."

Adam looked at the ground and tugged on his ear. "S'not the easiest time in my life for me to choose a positive quality about myself, so I channeled my inner Elijah."

A slow smile spread across Elijah's face, and he flicked his eyes over Adam's bare chest. "And your inner me said your best quality is compassion? Surely he could've thought of *something* else," he teased.

"Ugh… you two aren't going to get gross, are you?"

"Probably," Elijah said as he took a step closer to Adam and wrapped his arms around him, careful to avoid rubbing against Adam's new ink.

"I'm outta here, then," Kollin said. He started toward the kitchen, but Adam grabbed him by the back of his shirt and tugged him back.

"No way. Family time first," Adam said. "I feel pretty great right now, but I'm not stupid enough to think this feeling will last forever. Let's go out. You guys can fill me in on whatever I've missed. And if you want to know, I can tell you where I've been and what happened at the mediation."

"Food first," Kollin shouted.

"Shocking," Adam said, rolling his eyes.

Elijah shrugged. "Some things never change, man."

Threading his fingers through Elijah's, Adam grinned. "I will forever be grateful for that."

ELIJAH WALKED into his bedroom, feeling almost shy. After their mini family reunion, Kollin bailed to his room almost immediately. Though he participated during most of dinner, Elijah didn't miss how Kollin also held back—not quite meeting Adam's eyes and not joking nearly as often as he normally would.

He knew Adam didn't miss Kollin's reticence either. Elijah saw the pain in Adam's eyes as Kollin walked up the steps, but he offered no platitudes. Adam wouldn't have appreciated them if he had. He may have some damn good reasons to bail on everyone, but he made his bed and now he had to lie in it. Elijah suspected Kollin would come around sooner rather than later, anyway. Aside from being the type of person to forgive easily, Kollin was in the unique position of understanding what Adam had gone through. But then again, teenage boys were prone to holding on to anger just because they felt like it.

As for Elijah, no matter what he told Adam earlier, he'd forgiven Adam long before he even walked into his office. Elijah had lived almost a week without Adam, and he didn't need to live another one without him. Screw "too fast." Who cared that they hadn't even been together a year or if Elijah was in the closet until earlier that year? He didn't need to mark off eight of ten boxes in some arbitrary checklist to know his life was immeasurably better with Adam. He saw no reason to make either one of them suffer by holding Adam's actions against him. Especially when Adam wasn't capable of thinking clearly at the time.

Adam smiled at Elijah from beneath the covers as Elijah crossed the room for the bathroom and started his nightly ritual.

"You know what I missed most besides the two of you?" Adam called out.

"What z'at?" Elijah asked as he brushed his teeth.

"This bed. It's amazing. Did angels handcraft it?"

"Uh… no. That would be Tempur-Pedic." Elijah turned the water back on to rinse his mouth. He spit, and then he peeled off his shirt and tossed it into the hamper. "Mind if I take a quick shower?"

"'Course not. I'll try not to fall asleep waiting for you."

Elijah rolled his eyes but took the hint and hurried through cleansing his body, hoping Adam would be up for some makeup sex. He finished in less than five minutes, but in another moment of uncertainty, Elijah pulled on a pair of boxers and climbed into bed.

"Hmm…," Adam sighed, his eyes closed. "Maybe angels own Tempur-Pedic."

"Still going on about the bed? I'm starting to think you didn't come back for us, but for the comfortable sleeping conditions."

"Obviously. That sounds exactly like what I said," Adam said without missing a beat.

"Ass," Elijah mumbled.

"That's my line." Adam opened his eyes and rolled onto his side to look at Elijah. "You know nothing hurt more than being away from you. Right?"

Elijah thought for a moment. He didn't want to get into a deep conversation about everything right then, but he didn't want to lie either. "I want to know that, and I think maybe after some time, I'll believe it again."

Adam placed his palm on Elijah's chest. "I didn't realize how much I'd come to rely on you being part of my day, until suddenly you weren't. And not seeing you, not being with you every day… made it harder to get back to a place where I wanted to be here. It's so fucked up. I can't even explain it because right now even I'm yelling at myself, saying 'then you never should've left them, idiot!' But when I was running, it felt like the only option. It's so strange to look back and see my actions and my thought process because I know how flawed it all was. But at the time… I was 100 percent positive you two were better off without me. If I'm being honest, a tiny part of me didn't care even if that wasn't the case. I truly wanted to drown in my own sorrows, but I never believed I deserved you either."

Elijah covered the hand Adam had on his chest. "The scariest part for me was feeling like you didn't need me anymore, particularly knowing how much I desperately need you. I felt like I didn't offer you enough of an anchor to root you to the ground. It may take me some time to believe that you're not going to slip through my fingers one day, and there'd be nothing I could do about it."

"You know, maybe—and I'm not justifying my actions—but maybe in the long run this can be a good thing for us. We never know what could happen to either one of us. A car accident could take one or both of us out in the blink of an eye. I'm sure you've pissed off plenty of people in your line of work. Who knows when one of them will come after you. Not to mention your string of blonde exes are bound to hunt me down one day."

Elijah laughed, and Adam leaned over to kiss under his chin. "I'm serious, though. I know a guy, healthy as a horse, ate well, exercised regularly and everything. Dropped dead one day at work. Massive heart attack. No reasonable explanation. I hope I never forget how this past week felt without you because I never want to take you for granted—or the things you do for me and for Kollin and the people around us."

Elijah tightened his grip on Adam's hand and tugged, moving Adam over to lie on top of him. Adam's arms framed Elijah's face. Their chests, groins, and ankles touched. Elijah had never been more excited that Adam wore no underwear.

Running his foot up Adam's calf and back down again, Elijah said, "Wanna know what I missed?"

Adam threw his head back and laughed. "Nice segue."

"Can't help it. It's been forever, and you're saying all kinds of sweet shit to me now." Elijah rose up and nipped Adam's lip. "And I'm practically aching to have you in me."

Adam didn't need any more persuading. Thrusting his hips, Adam rubbed his cock against the fabric covering Elijah's and then shimmied the underwear down his legs. Eager, Elijah wrapped his legs around Adam's waist and pulled him down for a kiss. The rough bandage covering Adam's new tattoo irritated his skin somewhat—Elijah didn't want anything between them—but he figured it was a small price to pay for what the ink beneath it symbolized.

Adam slinked a hand between them to grab both of their cocks and slowly jack them off together. The feeling of Adam's dick rubbing against his own made Elijah's eyes roll back in his head, and he tore his mouth away from Adam's.

"S'too much. Get me ready."

Adam nodded and kissed his way down Elijah's neck and chest. He released their cocks and offered two fingers to Elijah's mouth. Elijah sucked them in gladly, running his tongue around and in between them. Adam trailed his tongue over the ridges of Elijah's taut abs, and the heavy, shameless moans escaping from Elijah's lips told Adam the teasing touches were akin to torture. When Adam decided his fingers were good and wet, he slid both into Elijah, slowly pumping in and out while he continued to lavish Elijah's body with his mouth and tongue.

Elijah threw his head back on his pillow and groaned in relief. This was exactly what he needed. Not just sex. Not just Adam topping. But Adam showing how much he still craved Elijah, how completely he owned Elijah. He missed feeling tethered to Adam, but with each stroke of Adam's fingers and each caress of his tongue, Elijah felt the rope tying them together weave back into place.

Elijah tugged on Adam, trying to get him back up his body, but Adam shook his head and continued his journey down. He tortured Elijah with every casual brush against his prostate. Adam never gave him enough, purposefully avoiding it on one stroke, giving it a light brush on the next, and then several nice hard rubs when he pulled away again.

"Dammit, Adam," Elijah whined. "I need more."

He tugged again and could've wept when Adam slowly pulled his fingers out. Instead of lining his cock up to replace his fingers, Adam gripped the base of Elijah's shaft and his balls and raised them up. While he squeezed his hand tight enough to act as a cock ring, Adam spread his tongue out and licked a flat stroke over Elijah's hole. He slid his tongue right in on his second pass, and Elijah saw stars by the time Adam buried his face between his ass cheeks. He rubbed his stubble around while his tongue did some sort of magical samba inside him.

Even Adam's vice grip on his dick wouldn't be enough to keep Elijah from blowing his load all over the place if Adam kept it up much longer. Finally Adam pulled back and crawled up Elijah's body. With one swift motion, he breached Elijah's body.

Elijah groaned. He anticipated more pain, but Adam had somehow ninja'd lube onto his cock. Between that and the generous stretching he'd given Elijah, Adam slid right in with no resistance. It felt like heaven and home all at once.

He felt complete.

Adam didn't waste any time. He grabbed Elijah's dick with a slicked-up hand and stroked as he thrust in and out of Elijah. Foreplay was over. Adam chased his own orgasm and worked like hell to give Elijah one first.

"Oh fuck. Touch yourself," Adam said. He leaned down and hooked Elijah's legs over his arms to provide a deeper angle. His hair was wet, and a lone drop of sweat rolled down Adam's nose and sat on the tip as he worked to bring both of them release. Elijah had never seen anything more damn beautiful in his entire life.

Elijah's orgasm crashed into him out of nowhere. There was no warning, no tingling in his balls, no churning in his belly. One second he was stroking himself and admiring his sexy-assed boyfriend, and the next he had cum splattered all over his face.

"Oh fuck," Adam grunted and thrust jerkily into Elijah's ass several more times. He held still after the final push and collapsed on top of Elijah. His dick slowly slid out, a warm gush of cum hot on its trail.

Immediately Adam winced and rolled off Elijah, gingerly covering the bandage on his chest. "That probably wasn't the best idea, considering I can't take a shower for a day or two."

Elijah shook his head. "There's nothing you could say to me to convince me that was a bad idea."

Adam laughed breathlessly. "Touché."

They lay in silence for several minutes, catching their breath until Elijah threw the covers off and headed toward the bathroom.

Adam whined. "I think I'll clean up tomorrow."

"You're not the one with cum all over your face and ass."

Elijah made quick work with his washcloth and hurried back into bed. He didn't want to miss a moment of Adam's good mood. Rough days lay ahead, so he wanted to soak up every second of the good ones. Encouraging Adam to roll over, Elijah slid his arm over Adam's waist and turned him into the little spoon. Then he pressed his face against Adam's back and sighed.

"I know I sound like a broken record, but I missed this." He kissed Adam's spine. "And this." He trailed his tongue along the bottom of the tattoo that covered the expanse of Adam's upper back. "I definitely missed this tattoo."

"Mmm…," Adam sighed. "I missed that too. I love it when you trace that one."

Elijah studied the tattoo. "I don't think you've ever told me what this stands for."

"Haven't I?"

"Not that I recall." He nuzzled his nose along Adam's back.

"Makes sense, I guess. It was my second tat. Right after the date on my chest. It's part of the yoga sutra, and it means 'Prevent the suffering that is yet to come.'"

Surprised, Elijah pulled away. "I didn't know you were into yoga."

Adam laughed. "I wasn't. I mean, I tried to be after I found this saying, but it only took two classes to realize it's so not for me."

"So you got this to remind yourself not to suffer?"

"Not exactly." Adam's voice lost some of its spark. "I guess I lost focus on the saying these last few months. Maybe I should've gotten the damn thing on my forehead instead. In a nutshell it means all humans suffer, and all suffering is real and valid. Just because I experience something horrible doesn't mean Joe Blow on the street cares. Nor do I particularly care if his cat died that morning, which means at the end of the day, there's no universal hierarchy of suffering. And since no one is immune to it, we should always be prepared for and understand what causes our individual pain in order to prevent further unnecessary misery."

"Sounds… complicated," Elijah said. "That's a lot to get out of these three words."

Adam raised one shoulder and then twisted his head around to kiss the side of Elijah's mouth. Elijah went back to tracing the lines on Adam's back—something he'd done a hundred times before, without realizing the true meaning behind the words. The script swirled and flowed in gorgeous curls across Adam's shoulders, and now that Elijah knew all of Adam's past, he understood how perfectly the tattoo suited his life. He dropped a kiss in the very center of Adam's back.

"I hate how hard life has been on you, but I love that you've let beauty come from your pain," he said. He snuggled against Adam, happy to have him back. "And I'm not only talking about this ink."

Adam didn't respond right away, and if he did at all, Elijah never knew. Within minutes he fell into the most peaceful sleep he'd had in months.

CHAPTER 17

THE NEXT couple of weeks passed quickly for Adam. Returning to the center was easier than he anticipated. Kirsten had told everyone Adam had some personal issues to deal with and he'd taken a last-minute vacation. She assured them he'd be back soon, so everyone welcomed him with open arms. No questions asked. Kirsten had faith he'd claw his way back into the light. It humbled him, and Adam wondered for the umpteenth time how he found such an amazing group of people to love—and who loved him.

His new therapist worked him in quickly, and Adam suspected Elijah had played a part in that. He was a little too eager to recommend her when Adam decided not to see someone he already thought as of a friend. Adam considered asking Elijah how many favors he had to trade to work him in with one of the best therapists in the tristate area, but he was used to Elijah's endless list of high-powered contacts. Though the process was slow and painful, Adam respected his new therapist immensely. After only five sessions, he might not be as quick to smile or joke around as he once was, but he could find joy in most activities and still wanted to heal his wounds.

After his first session, with thoughts of Jessica's betrayal fresh in his mind, he wanted nothing more than to drive until he had nowhere else to go. Instead he thought of Kollin and Elijah and turned his car toward home. As soon as he walked through the door, he asked for space and trudged up to the spare bedroom to sit alone in his pain. That quickly became his routine. His guys knew that after a therapy session, he needed time alone, and he hoped they knew he would always come back.

Two weeks to the day after Adam's first therapy session marked his first Christmas with Elijah, and of course Kollin's first with them—his first without his parents. They spent Christmas Eve with Elijah's parents, who spoiled Kollin so much Adam wondered if they'd need a second car to tote his haul home.

Christmas Day would be spent opening presents between the three of them and then having a big family breakfast together. Kirsten was fixing dinner for all of them, along with Matthew, Amelia, and Derek's parents. As long as Adam refrained from thinking about how he'd hoped to spend at least part of the day with Jessica, and Kollin didn't think about his parents too much, it might shape up to be a pretty good Christmas.

Elijah snaked his arm around Adam's waist from behind and tugged their bodies close together. With his soft lips mixed with rough stubble, he kissed across Adam's shoulder. "Morning, baby. Merry Christmas."

Adam sank into Elijah's embrace and tilted his head to give him better access. Elijah grazed his hand up Adam's stomach to his chest, and he palmed Adam's pec and rubbed his morning wood into the crack of Adam's ass.

"Merry Christmas indeed," Adam replied.

"I can't believe we don't have to go anywhere, and we're still up before seven," Elijah said. He bit Adam's shoulder. Adam squirmed and his cock plumped. Elijah took the movement as encouragement to continue. He grabbed Adam's dick and stroked in time with his thrusts, hardening Adam's cock more.

Adam arched his back. "What time do you think Kollin's gonna get up?"

"As long as it's not in the next three to five minutes, I don't really care."

Adam reached back to grab Elijah's thigh and chuckled. "Three to five minutes, huh? Quite the lofty goal."

"You know me," Elijah said, quickening his hand and his hips. "I like to aim… fuck… high." Burying his forehead into the center of Adam's back, Elijah grunted. Adam knew the sound well. Elijah was already close. Realizing this simple act—a sweet, slow, sexy morning snuggle—had brought Elijah so quickly to the edge, ratcheted up Adam's desire. Moments later he felt the warmth of Elijah's release slick up his back and slide between his ass cheeks. And Adam's eyes rolled back, his own orgasm rolling through him just as slow and sure as their lovemaking.

Elijah kissed his way back up to Adam's neck and pulled him close again. Content to fall into another slumber, Adam settled into Elijah's arms. They'd worry about the mess later. He'd barely closed his eyes when a knock came from their bedroom door.

"Hey," Kollin shouted. "You guys up yet? Merry Christmas."

Adam sighed, but Elijah sprang up. "He's up."

"I think you're more excited than he is," Adam said. He laughed as he threw off the covers and shouted to Kollin, "We'll be out in a minute. Don't you dare head downstairs without us."

"Wouldn't dream of it," Kollin shouted back. "Just so you know, I'm gonna sit here right outside your door. So don't take your time or anything."

Elijah finished cleaning up and waved Adam into the bathroom with a washcloth. "Lemme get your back real quick. We can shower after breakfast."

Adam grinned. "Yeah. You're definitely more excited than he is."

Elijah looked over Adam's shoulder to meet his eyes in the bathroom mirror. His smile was nothing short of radiant. "This is the first Christmas I've actually cared about in… forever. Plus it doesn't hurt we got him a fuck-awesome present."

Adam's smile slid slowly off his face. Sometimes he forgot how far Elijah had come in the past year. He so naturally fell into the caregiver role in their little family it often felt like he'd been part of Adam's life for longer. Yet they hadn't even known each other last year at Christmas, and Elijah had been still firmly locked in his closet, completely unaware of how unfulfilled his life was. Some people might look at Elijah and think he'd become an entirely different person over the past year, but Adam was more inclined to believe Elijah was always a strong, caring man. He'd just buried that man beneath pain and denial.

"I'm sorry I almost ruined it for you."

Elijah shook his head. "Nope. Not going to hear that today. We've talked ad nauseam about it, and we probably will for a while. Today is for making happy memories. Our first Christmas as a family together."

Adam nodded and smiled. "I think I can handle that."

ELIJAH BOUNDED down the steps ahead of Adam and Kollin, already pulling out his phone to take pictures and videos. Kollin rolled his eyes when they told him they heard Santa's sleigh on the roof overnight, but he also ducked his head and grinned. His parents stopped doing the whole Santa charade years before, when Kollin found out the truth about the jolly, rosy-cheeked fat man. But Elijah was determined to give Kollin the best Christmas possible. That included a visit from Santa, dammit. He didn't give a shit whether Kollin believed in him or not.

The gift from Santa sat unwrapped in the center of the room, small and inconspicuous. Kollin walked right past it and sat down on the couch. Looking over at the tree in the corner, he asked, "How're we gonna do this? One gift at a time? Free-for-all? What's the deal?"

"I always checked out my gift from Santa first," Elijah said innocently.

Adam shrugged. "Matthew and Amelia didn't do Santa by the time I got there, so that's fine by me."

"Oookay. That'd be awesome, but Santa didn't actually come here," Kollin said, using finger quotes around Santa.

"You sure?" Elijah asked. He gestured toward the center of the rug, barely able to contain his excitement.

Confusion swept over Kollin's face when he saw the keys, but Elijah could tell the moment it clicked. "You got me a car?"

"No way. I was in bed all night. Adam can vouch for me. Looks like Santa got you a car, though. Or at least something that needs keys."

Adam snorted. "Maybe we should go look in the driveway," he said, inflecting his voice to sound melodramatically curious. Elijah waved a quick middle finger at him.

Kollin grabbed the keys off the floor and ran toward the foyer to pull the door open.

"Holy shit," Kollin shouted. "Is that a Mazda3?"

"According to Santa, the Mazda3 is safe, fuel efficient, and sporty enough for the younger generation," Adam said. "And who can argue with Santa?"

Kollin turned, jumped up, and hugged Elijah around the neck, his feet dangling inches above the ground. "Thank you," he said and then dropped to grab Adam. "And thank you for keeping him from going overboard."

"You never know with Santa. He's pretty stubborn."

Elijah snorted. "I've heard Santa's elves can be pretty damn stubborn themselves."

"This is insane," Kollin said, his eyes wide and bright. "If I were still at home—"

Kollin's face fell immediately, and his shoulders slumped. Elijah felt like someone had taken a baseball bat and beaned him in the back, knocking the breath right out of him.

"I mean…. I didn't mean," Kollin whispered as he stepped back.

Tears filled his eyes, and when he hit the glass front door, Kollin sank to the floor slowly. He buried his face in his knees and covered his head with his arms. Elijah watched helplessly while Adam kneeled beside Kollin. He told himself Kollin didn't mean it, willed himself not to be disappointed that Kollin still didn't think of their home as his. Even though Kollin had been there less than a year, Elijah couldn't quite remember what home felt like without him there. Clearly it had to be different for Kollin. Six months didn't erase the fifteen years he spent living with his parents, nor should they, but he'd hoped Kollin considered this place home.

Adam and Kollin spoke so quietly Elijah couldn't hear what they were saying. It felt like forever before Adam backed away and Kollin turned his watery eyes to Elijah.

"I'm sorry," he began, but Elijah cut him off.

"Don't even apologize."

Kollin nodded. "I really appreciate the car and everything else you do for me. I know this is home. I just… they were my mom and dad, and I feel guilty for being happier here most of the time than I was with them. But I still miss them too. You know?"

"I'm glad you're happy here." Elijah hesitated. "I hope you don't think I'm trying to buy you or anything. You know I love you, and I'd do anything for you. You having a safe car is more for my benefit than yours."

Kollin shook his head. "It's not that. It's… hard to explain."

Elijah looked at Adam, whose face had clouded over. He was probably fighting his own demons after his conversation with Kollin. How the hell had Elijah ended up being the least fucked-up one of their family?

"Then you don't have to. Take all the time you need, and when both of you are ready, we can open gifts. Or screw the gifts. We can save them for another day, and I can just make breakfast."

"No," Kollin exclaimed. "I mean, I still want to do everything. I just didn't expect them to slam into my head right now."

"What about you?" Elijah asked Adam. "Are you okay?"

"Yep," Adam said, clearly ready to move on. "Are we gonna test drive this thing or open the rest of the gifts first?"

Elijah grinned. His giddy feeling slowly returned as Kollin stood and peeked out the window at his car. "Up to him, I guess."

"Oh, we are so driving this first. Last one to the car pays for my first tank of gas," he shouted as he opened the door and ran to the car in his bare feet. He danced over the frosty grass and shrieked from the cold. Adam looked at Elijah. A slow smile spread over Adam's face, and he grabbed his pajama bottoms and pulled them up. Then he took off after Kollin, hollering even louder than Kollin about the frigid temperature.

Laughing, Elijah shook his head and opened up the closet to slide his feet into a pair of slippers—no way his feet were touching that frost—and took off after his boys.

CHAPTER 18

"THERE HE is."

Adam glanced at up the sound of Elijah's voice to see Kollin and him walking into the multipurpose room. The week between Christmas and New Year's was always unpredictable at the center. Some days the place would be packed, and others he wouldn't have more than one or two kids show up. That day the latter held true, with only one person there at the moment—a nineteen-year-old who'd shown up for the first time two weeks earlier. Still firmly in the closet, she barely acknowledged the fact she liked girls. Adam hoped she'd find acceptance in herself through her visits.

"Hey, guys," Adam greeted them. "What're you up to today?"

Following the tradition of his father and grandfather, Elijah closed Langley L&C for the last week of the year, so he and Kollin had found different things to keep themselves busy while Adam worked. Most of them involved Kollin driving his new car, and they'd already made plans to take it on a trip to the Outer Banks on Adam's next day off.

"Not much, actually," Elijah said, standing behind Adam and Cynthia on the couch.

"Looks like about the same as you," Kollin said. He sat next to Adam and then leaned around him to talk to Cynthia. "Hi. I'm Kollin."

She offered him a small smile. "Cynthia. Nice to meet you."

"Mind if I cut in? They're probably gonna go hide out in Adam's office and do things I don't want to think about my dads doing."

Adam grinned as he shoved his shoulder against Kollin's. He'd started testing out the word "dads" occasionally, usually in a joking context. But he hadn't actually called either one of them Dad yet. Adam didn't care if he never did. He was just glad Kollin wanted to try.

"Shows what you know," Adam said. "You two can't be alone in here together, so we'll be in the back corner doing things you don't want to think about us doing."

Kollin scrunched up his face and grabbed the controller. "Whatever. As long as I can't see you."

Adam laughed and then addressed Cynthia. "Elijah and I will be back here talking. Let me know if he gets outta control," he said with a wink.

Adam grabbed Elijah's hand and started for the homework corner on the other side of the room. Before they got too far away, he heard Cynthia whisper, "They're your dads?"

"Yeah. I mean, not yet… I guess. But they're adopting me."

Elijah leaned into Adam. "You know, if he's going to tell people you're adopting him, you might as well do it."

Warmth flooded Adam's chest at the thought of being Kollin's legal guardian. Maybe it meant more to him than he realized. "It's possible I might've been thinking the same thing, especially after everything recently. I was wrapped up about it feeling awkward with the rest of the kids here, but if it's what's best for Kollin…."

"Who cares what everyone else thinks?"

Adam nodded. "Yeah. Pretty much."

"Think about it. Talk it over with your therapist, and we can bring it up to Kollin if you want. I'm supposed to start my background check next week. We can add you onto that or ask them to push it back until you decide."

"I'll do that." Adam peeked over his shoulder and saw both teens engrossed in *Mario Kart*, Kollin chattering away as he swayed his body in a vain attempt to make Yoshi turn left. Adam tilted his head up to peck Elijah quickly on the lips. He smiled. "Hi. I'm glad you stopped by."

"Me too. And even more so because it's not just a social visit." Elijah gestured to one of the seats at the table. "I have some good news for you."

They settled into their chairs, and Adam angled his so he could stretch his leg out to rest against Elijah's. "Lay it on me."

"After you told me about that teacher—the music teacher who helped you when you were a kid—I did a little digging. Well, I hired someone to do some digging, and I think I found the guy. The school wouldn't give me a list of the students he taught, but my guy contacted him and he said he remembered you."

"Oh my God. Are you serious?" A chill ran through Adam's body as goose bumps covered his arms, chest, and legs.

Elijah nodded. "He still lives in Elm City, and that's where your parents lived when you were growing up."

"This is insane. I never imagined this would actually happen. What's he doing? Do you know?"

"Still working. Still teaching piano lessons after school too. He's married and has three teenage boys. She's the head chef at a local private school. Real swanky shit."

"Damn, Elijah. Did you find out their social security numbers too?"

"Oh, relax. That's all information I found out through Google after my guy gave me his name."

"So he's married to a woman?"

Elijah nodded.

Adam always assumed the guy was gay as well. He didn't know why. There were plenty of straight people who supported LGBT individuals back then. Matthew and Amelia were prime examples. "What's his name?"

Elijah grinned. "Well, his first name is Elijah."

Adam snorted. "Of course it is."

"You probably knew him as Mr. Sanderson, though."

"Yes." Adam's eyes widened. "That's it. I can't believe I forgot, but then, I only had a few lessons with him before I went to live with Gramps. And then I attended a different school."

Elijah pulled a piece of paper out of his pocket. "Well, here's his number if you want to give him a call."

Adam swore. "This is so surreal. I can't even believe it. What am I gonna say to him?"

"I don't know, but like I said, he remembers you."

"Should I call him now?"

Elijah laughed, and Adam looked up from the phone number he'd been staring at.

"Shut up," Adam said, grinning. "This is the best news I've had in a long time. Thank you so much." Without caring about Cynthia catching them, Adam leaned over and hugged Elijah.

"You're welcome. I wanted to give it to you on Christmas, but I needed to make sure the guy hadn't turned into a grade-A asshole over the years before I handed the number over."

"And if he had?"

Elijah shook his head. "You never would've heard me utter a peep about it. I'm not that stupid."

"God, this is amazing. I've got to call him now." Adam pulled his phone out of his back pocket. "Do you want to meet him too? Maybe I can invite him over for dinner?"

"If you don't mind me intruding, I'd love to meet him. I owe him a thank-you as well. You sure you don't want to settle down first? You sound like a starstruck fanboy right now."

"I can't believe this. Do you know how many times I've thought of him over the years? How many times I lay in a bed at the group home or at a new foster home and heard his voice telling me that it was okay for me to be gay? That I was normal?" Adam shook his head, still in disbelief he was a simple phone call away from someone who had been his own personal hero.

"Maybe you should invite him to the center so he can see everything you've built and all the people you've helped. I can't imagine he ever thought saying something so simple would turn into all this." Elijah spread his arms to the side.

"Yeah. But I don't want to sound like I'm bragging or anything."

Elijah rolled his eyes. "Oh my fuck. You're impossible. Crediting him for helping you through your childhood so you could turn into the kind of person who would want to help others is not bragging. And even if it were, who gives a fuck? You need to learn to brag about yourself from time to time."

"Geez. Tell me how you really feel."

"Well, shit, man. You do." Elijah leaned closer to Adam. "Maybe one day you'll see it for yourself if you start recognizing your own accomplishments."

Adam's heart sank a little, but he pushed back the urge to self-loathe. Elijah's words made him feel worthy. But they also brought up feelings of guilt for putting his boyfriend through so much suffering because of his own insecurities. Reminding himself he'd gladly take on the same burden if their roles were reversed, Adam smiled at Elijah. "Thank you."

"Now that *that's* settled, I have an idea I want to run by you before you call him," Elijah said. Adam nodded. "I know you don't like me giving HOPE money outright, but I'd like to start some sort of scholarship in honor of Mr. Sanderson for you to give to one of your students each year. I don't know if we have enough interest here for it to be solely a music scholarship, but maybe we can somehow tie music in?"

"Elijah—"

"Nope," Elijah said. He crossed his arms over his chest and tucked his legs under his chair, breaking the contact at their ankles. "I want to do this. Not only does it help the kids, but it honors a man who gave you hope when you had none. That could've been the difference between life and death for you, Adam. Literally. And without you.... Well, it may be more figurative where I'm concerned, but you're the difference between life and death for me. So when you think about it, it's not even about you. It's about me, and I'm being selfish."

Adam hooked his foot around the leg of Elijah's chair to pull him closer, but Elijah was so big he ended up scooting his chair closer to Elijah's. Suited him either way.

"If you'd listen, I was going to say I think it's a fantastic idea. I'm honored you'd want to do that for me." Adam grinned. "I mean, for you, of course. Besides, there's a difference between accepting money for a scholarship program and using it to pay someone to paint a room when we have plenty of able hands and bodies to do it ourselves."

"Yeah, yeah. Whatever. We would have more time to relax if we paid someone."

Adam chuffed. "As if you enjoy relaxing. You're tenser on our days off than when we're running in four different directions. Taking a vacation with you is probably going to be a nightmare."

Elijah shrugged. "I'll bring a book."

"Okay, so can I call this guy now? I'll see if he can stop by here someday or if he'd even want to, and we can present him with the scholarship idea then."

"Go for it."

Adam sucked in a deep breath and tapped the numbers into his phone. He held his breath while the phone rang, two and then three times.

"Hello?" a deep, melodic voice answered, bringing Adam more than twenty years back in time. The sound nearly brought tears to his eyes.

"Mr. Sanderson?"

"This is he," he answered.

"I... uh... this is Adam Lancaster. I don't know if you remember me, but I took a few piano lessons from you when I was a kid."

"Ah, yes. Of course," Mr. Sanderson said, and Adam could nearly hear the smile in his voice. "The fellow who called the other day asked me about you. Is everything okay? He wouldn't comment on your well-being."

"Everything's fine, sir," Adam replied. "I'm so sorry to have bothered you."

"It's no bother. I've always enjoyed hearing from former students."

"I'm glad to hear that. I'm actually calling to see if we could meet in person sometime. I have a story I'd like to share with you, and it's a little extensive for a phone conversation. I know it's random. I was only your student for a few lessons, and it was over twenty years ago. I'm surprised you remember me, to be honest."

"I guess I can't claim to remember every single one of my students, but most of them stay with me. You certainly did. What'd you have in mind? Coffee somewhere?"

Adam winced. He hadn't thought about it before, but the drive to HOPE from Elm City was over an hour. It was too late to come up with another plan on the spot, so he plowed forward. "Uh, actually I run The Center for HOPE in Cary and wondered if you could stop by sometime. I know it's a bit of a drive, so if you'd rather, I'd be more than happy to meet you somewhere else."

"Nonsense. I'd love to come by. The wife and I can drop the boys in Raleigh for the day while we visit. They're starting to get stir-crazy and need to get out of the house, so this is the perfect excuse. Is tomorrow okay?"

"Oh, wow," Adam said, laughing. "Tomorrow's perfect. And yeah, bring your wife and kids too, if you want. There's plenty of stuff for them to do here, and we usually have teenagers in and out all day."

"Might just do that," Mr. Sanderson said.

Adam rattled off the address, and Mr. Sanderson said he'd see him around eleven the following day. After he hung up the phone, Adam grinned at Elijah.

"Well…."

"He sounds exactly the same," Adam said. "I always loved piano lessons because he really seemed to enjoy teaching. I never felt like I was just a job to him. He really wanted me to learn and to love learning how to play."

"That's really cool. He sounds a lot like you."

Adam waved off Elijah's comment. "He's coming by tomorrow around eleven with his wife. Can you and Kollin be here?"

"Wouldn't miss it for the world. But if he's coming tomorrow, I need to get going and figure out the logistics of setting up this scholarship."

Adam grabbed Elijah's hand and squeezed it. "Thank you for everything. You can work in my office if you want, so Kollin doesn't have to leave. Looks like he's having fun."

Kollin had pulled Cynthia out of her shell, and they were playing an exuberant game of *Wii Tennis*. Adam grinned when Cynthia high-fived Kollin for winning the match.

"Another one bites the dust," Elijah said, smiling. He grabbed Adam's hand and squeezed lightly. "I'll come find you if I have any questions."

When Adam ventured into his office several hours later, Elijah was working on the computer, his sleeves rolled up. Adam stopped short and admired him. He wished he could somehow preserve moments like this forever. Sitting behind a desk and buried in paperwork, Elijah looked far sexier than anyone had a right to.

"Hey," Adam said, drawing Elijah's attention away from the computer. "How's it going?"

Elijah looked up and stretched his arms over his head, leaning the chair back. The movement showed off his strong chest and lean waist, and Adam's eyes momentarily dropped lower to peek at Elijah's crotch. Then he popped back up to meet his eyes. Adam felt his face flush at being caught ogling.

Elijah grinned back. "Not bad. I should be able to get something set up soon. If you go ahead and open a new account at the bank, I'll transfer the starting funds and have my broker invest some for later years. I figured we could see if Mr. Sanderson wants to be involved in deciding exactly what it's used for—or how we select the winner."

Adam propped himself against the side of the desk and smiled. Elijah's presence and unwavering belief in Adam had pulled him through some of his darker days over the past weeks, and now he was single-handedly starting a scholarship fund in honor of the first man who ever made Adam feel normal.

"I love you," Adam said softly.

Elijah looked up, startled by Adam's out-of-place confession. He didn't scrunch up his face in confusion or ask why Adam suddenly felt the need to be so sentimental. With the same love and support he'd shown Adam over the past few months, Elijah took Adam's hand and kissed his knuckles. "Love you too."

ADAM PEERED out the front window for probably the tenth time in the past five minutes and finally saw an unfamiliar car pull into HOPE's parking lot. "They're here," he said as he backed away from the glass to stand casually next to Chloe's desk.

Elijah smiled up at Adam from Chloe's seat. She and Kollin had left to pick up lunch for everyone, so Elijah offered to cover the front desk to give Adam a few minutes alone with his former teacher.

The bell over the door dinged, but Adam was already smiling as he met them halfway. "Mr. Sanderson, it's good to see you again."

Mr. Sanderson shook Adam's hand as he looked Adam up and down. "I don't believe I would've recognized you if we passed on the street. I know I raised three boys since I last saw you, but it's hard to believe enough time has passed for you to be this grown."

Adam grinned. "Well, you look the same. Hair's a little shorter now."

Mr. Sanderson laughed. "Back then I thought I should've been born a hippie."

"Nothing wrong with that." Adam gestured toward Elijah. "I'd like you to meet my partner—in business and life—Elijah Langley. He helps out regularly here at HOPE. Our receptionist went out to get us some lunch. Elijah wanted to be here when you arrived."

Elijah stood and offered his hand. "It's a pleasure to meet you, sir."

Mr. Sanderson shook Elijah's hand and turned to his wife. "This is my Judith. She did some research on this place after we spoke yesterday. It's quite an impressive establishment you have going here, particularly with the Home for Hope."

"Nice to meet both of you," Mrs. Sanderson said. "I second my husband. I've been looking forward to visiting since he told me."

Oh God. The moment of meeting Mr. Sanderson again in person surpassed even the best scenarios Adam had conjured in his mind. Over the years he'd never allowed himself to consider that his old music teacher wasn't the hero he'd built him up to be. His status was paramount to Adam's mental and emotional stability some days. And Adam was finally meeting the man, shaking his hand, and showing him the person he'd become. Mr. Sanderson seemed even better than he'd imagined.

"Thank you so much," Adam said. His chest felt like it might burst with pride. "Why don't I give you two a quick tour? The food should be here soon, and over lunch I'll explain why I've invited you here. If you have time, we can head over to the inn this afternoon."

Twenty minutes later they returned to the front desk to find Chloe eating a sandwich.

"You must be Mr. Sanderson," she said, cleaning up with a napkin to shake his hand. "I'm Chloe. Welcome to HOPE."

"Thank you very much."

Chloe pointed down the hallway. "Kollin and Elijah are in the kitchen."

"Thanks, Chloe," Adam said and gestured for the Sandersons to follow him. "I hope everyone is hungry. Elijah ordered lunch for all of us, and he doesn't do anything small. He probably got enough to feed everyone here two times over—including the kids wandering around today."

"Sounds like you have quite the generous partner. Lucky man."

Adam's steps faltered at Mr. Sanderson's simple statement. The truth of his words echoed in his head as he turned back to smile. "I certainly am."

They entered the kitchen, and Adam saw Elijah really had gone overboard. There were three trays on the counter—one filled with at least twenty different sandwiches, one with a wide selection of sides, and one with several dessert selections.

"Hope you guys are hungry," Kollin said, mock-rolling his eyes toward Elijah.

Elijah shrugged. "It's not like they'll go to waste."

"Can we eat now?" Kollin asked. "I'm starving."

Adam nudged his elbow. "Hey there, Manners. Do you think you could take a moment to introduce yourself?"

"Oh, sorry. I'm Kollin. I'm his kid." He pointed his thumb over his shoulder at Elijah. "And sorta his kid too, since they're shacking up."

Adam shook his head and threw his arm around Kollin's shoulder, almost pulling him into a headlock. Kollin was the king of sarcasm, lightening any situation with a funny quip. But Adam suspected Kollin hid behind those jokes too often, and this one hit home. "We're going to have to work on that introduction, kiddo."

Kollin shrugged. "I'll add it to my therapy list."

Mr. Sanderson's eyebrows furrowed, but he didn't comment, and instead gestured for Kollin to get some food. "As I told Adam earlier, I have three teenage boys. I'd be the last one to keep you from eating."

Kollin grinned and grabbed a plate. "Thanks, man."

Once everyone sat down, a swarm of butterflies hit Adam's stomach. He'd thought all night about what to tell Mr. Sanderson, but nothing seemed right. Either he would be dumping too much personal information on a man who didn't care to hear it, or his appreciation would seem trivial and unimportant. He'd run out of time to perfect his speech, so he plunged ahead. "I guess you're probably wondering why I invited you here."

Mr. Sanderson had just taken a bite of his sandwich, so he simply tilted his head to the side in a slight nod of agreement.

"The fact that you remember who I am makes this a little easier. Maybe you remember the day I asked you about the word 'faggot'?"

Mr. Sanderson frowned but nodded. "I do. You were far too young to understand what that word actually meant. I hope I didn't get you in trouble with anyone."

Adam laughed humorlessly. "Not exactly." Pausing, Adam considered his words. "This is hard to explain without going into detail. I don't mind sharing my story, but it's not easy to hear, so please stop me if it bothers you.

"After talking to you that day, I came out to my mother—my birth mother. You see, you'd made being gay, being a 'faggot,' sound so normal, I didn't realize I had any reason to be concerned about telling her. She didn't take it quite as well as you, and my birth father was even less enthused. They sent me off to live with my grandparents, which was a blessing. But once they could no longer care for me, I went into the system. My time there, for the most part, was very unpleasant."

"He's lying," Kollin said, scowling. "It was a damn nightmare."

"Kollin, watch your mouth," Elijah said.

"What? I'm just saying it wasn't unpleasant. It was hell."

"I think he gets the picture," Adam said, raising his voice as the Sandersons watched the three of them with looks of sympathy and confusion on their faces.

"I ended up eventually being placed with a wonderful family, who are still a huge part of my life. They helped me start HOPE and still volunteer regularly. They're literally the best family I could've ever asked for. But before them, when I was being tossed from home to home, constantly told I was going to hell and that I deserved every bad thing happening to me, there were two things I clung to in order to stay sane. My grandparents… and you. I never forgot how quickly and effortlessly you accepted my declaration and moved on as if I'd told you pizza always had cheese on it. I can never thank you enough for what you said to me.

"Over the years all I could think of was that you'd never know the impact you had on my life. I had help from my family along the way. Yes. But you were practically a stranger, and you made me feel accepted. Without that I don't know if I would've made it through the bad years in the system. I never would've lived long enough to create HOPE. I'd like to offer my most sincere and heartfelt thanks."

Mr. Sanderson had stopped eating, and his wife covered his hand with her own. She hastily swiped away the tears that flowed from her eyes. Adam could see the pride in her face as she smiled at her husband.

Elijah cleared his throat. "I'd like to thank you as well. I'm one of the people Adam's helped through the center. I know this place is for kids, but meeting Adam, loving Adam, is the best thing I've ever done. He changed my life simply by being himself, living his life out loud and unashamed of who he is. Without Adam and Kollin, I wouldn't be anything more than a shell of a man. When he told me about you, I knew I had to help him find you. I owe you as many thanks as he does."

Mr. Sanderson pursed his lips and studied his food. To his right Kollin leaned over and offered Adam a shoulder bump. Adam bumped him right back.

"I'm sorry to have just laid it all out like that. Like I said, there's no good way to tell that story."

"No, no. Please," Mr. Sanderson said. "You have nothing to apologize for, but I don't feel I deserve any of this gratitude. I only did what everyone should do. Doesn't make me worthy of anything special."

"Oh, geez," Elijah said. "Are you sure you two aren't related?"

Mr. Sanderson scrunched up his face as he looked at Elijah in confusion.

Adam cleared his throat. "What he means is sometimes, a lot of the time, unfortunately, what everyone should do isn't what everyone actually does. I understand all too well not feeling like anything special simply because I've done right by someone. But please know, to me, to Elijah, and probably to hundreds of other kids you've taught over the years, you've done or said something to change their lives for the better. That makes you a hero in my book."

Obviously choked up, Mr. Sanderson nodded. "Thank you. Your words have humbled me more than you'll ever know."

Elijah grabbed a folder he'd placed at the end of the table. "Since we're already all overwhelmed, I may as well give this to you now. Adam and I would like to start a scholarship at HOPE in your honor. I have most of the logistics in here, but we'd love your input as well. We're thinking graduating seniors will be eligible, and anyone interested should submit an essay on what music means to them, but we're certainly open to other ideas."

This time Mr. Sanderson propped his forehead against the tips of his fingers and rested his elbows on the table. When he raised his head again, his eyes were red. "Thank you. I don't deserve such an honor. But I'd never even think of saying no to the kids, so I'll accept as gracefully as possible."

Kollin paused and set his sandwich on his plate. Looking Mr. Sanderson directly in the eye, he said, "No disrespect, sir, but you do deserve this. You have no idea what Adam means to each and every person who walks through those front doors. He didn't just found this place. He breathes his energy and spirit and hope into it, and he never asks for anything in return. Ever. If you had even the smallest part in helping Adam decide to open HOPE, you deserve much more than this."

Frowning and looking somewhat embarrassed, Kollin picked at his sandwich, completely avoiding everyone's gaze. His words touched Adam's soul. Kollin had never spoken that way about anything. He threw his arm around Kollin's shoulders and gave him a half hug, hoping to thank him but not embarrass him further. These were the moments he held on to during his dark days.

Adam turned back to Mr. Sanderson and smiled. "See? You do deserve it."

"Guess he told you," Mrs. Sanderson said, a bright smile on her face.

"Guess he did. Where do I sign?"

The rest of lunch passed on a much lighter note. The Sandersons told them about their three boys and agreed to bring them by one day. The idea excited Adam, knowing how beneficial straight LGBT allies could be for some of his youth who believed life was them against the straight world. He couldn't half blame them, considering what some of them lived through on a day-to-day basis. At the same time, the world was so much bigger than their small town. The youth here needed to see they had allies outside of the people within the walls of the center. By the time the Sandersons left, Adam knew he'd made a lifelong friend.

CHAPTER 19

ADAM HAULED the last of the boxes from his old garage into the trunk of his car. Lucinda had been storing them, and he'd finally found time to clear everything out and officially say good-bye to his first house. It looked the same—yet different. Not his. Lucinda didn't have much. She'd left most of their belongings with her husband when she left. But she'd hung several pictures on the walls and bought new throws and pillows for Adam's old couch. He left most of his furniture since he didn't need it at Elijah's, and he was glad to see Lucinda was able to add her personal touch to make the house her home.

"Sorry it took me so long to pick this stuff up."

Lucinda waved her hand at him. "Don't even. We both know you're doing me a huge favor by letting us move in here."

"I'm just glad you could use it. How's Corrie doing at the inn?"

"Pretty good. She's smart and she doesn't take shit from anyone. Some of those kids can be a handful, but I've seen her put them in their place more than once."

Adam grinned. "Perfect."

"Oh yeah. She'll fit in fine."

Months earlier Adam had applied for the proper permits to allow underage youth to live at Home for Hope. Unfortunately red tape and unforeseen obstacles slowed up the certifications, which were finally coming through. Adam hated turning away the youth who weren't old enough to stay at H4H, but the trial period of allowing eighteen and up had given their whole team time to acclimate to running the safe house. Lucinda fell effortlessly into her caregiver role, and she genuinely cared about every youth who stayed at H4H. But she didn't have the professional qualifications to be in charge of and care for underage at-risk runaways.

Corrie's resume was a diamond in the rough when they filtered through the applicants. Even though Adam knew looks could be deceiving, he was somewhat let down when they met for the interview and she didn't even reach his shoulder. Some of the residents at the inn were twice her size. Adam couldn't discount the fact that at-risk youth were often untrustworthy and volatile—even to the people trying to help them. Aside from her stature, she was perfect for the job. So when Adam offered her the position, he relayed his concerns. She waved them off with a sly smile and told him she had a brown belt in jujitsu.

"Well, I need to get out of here. I'm supposed to be in court at three."

"With Chad and Jessica, or for one of the youth?" Lucinda asked.

"Chad and Jessica, thankfully. I'll be glad to put the whole thing behind us."

Lucinda held her arms out and wrapped Adam into a big hug. "Well, good luck, then. Kick some ass."

Two hours later Adam walked up the courthouse steps and greeted Elijah with a quick kiss on his cheek. "You look nice," he said.

Adam wore a suit and Elijah eyed him up and down. "Likewise. We need to find more reasons for you to wear this."

Adam smiled. "Deal, but preferably not occasions like this."

"Definitely not. You ready?"

"Sure. I don't have to do anything. It's all up to Mr. Beuford now."

Elijah trailed the back of his index finger down the length of Adam's tie, worry evident in his eyes. "They'll be in there. You gonna be okay?"

"I don't have a choice if I want to honor Gramps's wishes. But I think I'll be fine. Might need some time after."

"That's easy enough." Elijah grinned and leaned in to whisper in Adam's ear. "But can you keep the suit on until you're done moping… 'cause damn, son."

Adam laughed and shoved Elijah away. "You're so evil."

"What? I'm just sayin'…."

"You're utterly ridiculous," Adam said, smiling. "And I love you for it."

Elijah held out his hand and weaved his fingers through Adam's. "Let's go face the monster."

Chad and Jessica stood in the hallway when they approached, but neither party made any attempt to acknowledge the other. Several minutes later Mr. Beuford waltzed in with a smile on his face.

"Afternoon, gentlemen. Ready to put this whole thing behind us?"

"You sound pretty confident," Elijah said.

"I am." Mr. Beuford lowered his voice. "Not only did I secure two witnesses who can attest to your grandfather's state of mind, but I also found a fatal flaw in the evidence presented by Jessica's lawyer. The birthday card with the Ty Cobb collectible your grandfather supposedly gave your mother for her sweet sixteen wasn't even made until she was in her twenties. That should be enough to lock up the case, but if it's not, I can go with our original plan and push for a handwriting analysis."

"Shit. Seriously?" Adam asked.

Mr. Beauford nodded.

"How much of a dumbass is their lawyer for trying to pull this over on you?"

"Who knows? He may not be aware it's a fake. If the card were real, she'd have a decent case—given the mental stability of most Alzheimer's patients. My guess is Jessica scrounged up an old card, scribbled the message herself, and conveniently forgot to mention that part to her lawyer."

"He's still an idiot," Elijah mumbled.

"You won't hear me arguing," Mr. Beuford replied.

Moments later the clerk summoned everyone into the courtroom, and Elijah filed into the front row of the seating area while Adam and Mr. Beuford sat in the defendant's section.

Jessica's lawyer gave his statement first, weaving a tale of a loving daughter who wanted to cling to the last remaining pieces of her beloved father. Adam had to fight not to roll his eyes as he spoke of how Jessica doted on her father, and how her favorite childhood memories all involved her dad—either attending baseball games or hunting for new baseball cards.

Mr. Beuford followed, detailing the exact wishes of Adam's grandfather and the lengths he took to ensure Adam—and only Adam—received the cards. To show Jessica's character, he didn't hold back when he detailed how she dropped Adam off to live first with his grandparents and then at a group home, because she and her husband didn't want the responsibility of their gay child. Adam worried Mr. Beuford's attempt to draw sympathy would backfire. America had come a long way over the past few years, but North Carolina was still a red state with very conservative views. He couldn't get a read on the judge, though, so he stayed quiet and trusted his lawyer to do his job.

Mr. Beuford got out his smoking gun after Jessica's lawyer produced the supposed birthday card for evidence. He pulled out several sheets of paper from his file, proving the birthday card was first printed six years after she supposedly received it. A jolt of triumph shot through Adam when Jessica's lawyer looked at her with shock written all over his face and Jessica sank down in her seat.

The judge turned to them. "Do you have anything to refute his evidence?"

"Not at this time, sir. We'd like to request a short recess."

"Granted. Fifteen minutes."

The judge banged his gavel and swiftly left the room, and Elijah leaned over the railing to grab Adam around the shoulders. "You did it."

Adam couldn't help the huge smile on his face. They had. But no way would he voice that thought aloud. "I guess we'll know in fifteen minutes."

Elijah laughed and pointed toward Jessica, Chad, and her lawyer, who were arguing right there in the courtroom, their voices growing louder by the second. "I think that's all the answer you need."

Sure enough, when the judge returned, Jessica's lawyer moved to dismiss the case. Ten minutes later Adam found himself outside on the courthouse steps, once again finally, totally, and officially free of Jessica and Chad Lancaster.

"I can never thank you enough, Mr. Beuford. You've saved me once again." Adam shook his hand for the fourth time.

"Glad I could help, son."

"I say this calls for a celebration," Elijah said after they finished saying their good-byes to Mr. Beuford. "What do you say we play hooky tomorrow? Let's go get Kollin and head to the beach tonight."

Adam's eyes lit up. "Really?"

"Yeah. It'll be fun, and all three of us need a break. Kollin will only miss one day of school, and it's not like he's struggling or anything. He hasn't missed even a single day this year."

"Let's do it." Adam felt like jumping up and down. "Wait. We don't have anywhere to stay. I doubt we'll be able to book something this late."

"Yeah," Elijah said, drawing the word out. "About that. I might've bought a house in Emerald Isle."

Adam's jaw dropped. "You did what?"

Elijah held his hands up. "Before you get all screechy on me—it's a wise investment. Beachfront property always is. I know you prefer the Outer Banks, but Emerald Isle is a shorter drive. So I figured we'd get more use out of one there. I can find something in OBX too, if you want. And if you're going to get your panties in a twist about it, we can always rent it out whenever we aren't there. But I really hope you don't make me because I hate the idea of someone else sleeping in my bed."

"Your bed?" Adam spluttered. "You've already furnished it?" He couldn't wrap his head around the fact that, not only had Elijah bought an entire house without him having a clue, but he'd also furnished the damn thing and was now offering to buy another house.

"Well, yeah. What good is a house without furniture?"

"Shit, Elijah. You bought a house, and I had no fucking clue."

"Okay, okay." Elijah held his hands up and took a step back. "Don't make a big deal about this. We don't have to stay there if you don't want. I'm sure I can find somewhere else for us to stay."

Guilt swept through Adam as he took in Elijah's crestfallen face. He wasn't angry with Elijah. He was free to do with his money whatever he pleased. And though Elijah had no qualms about spending his money, he rarely made impulsive purchases on anything that wouldn't give him a promising return on investment—his car notwithstanding. Elijah had tried to do something nice for him—nice for their family—and Adam was ruining it.

"I'm sorry," he said. "I'm just surprised. I didn't expect any of those words to come out of your mouth."

Elijah grinned. "So I can keep it?"

Laughing, Adam nodded. "Of course. It's not up to me, anyway. Thank you for thinking of us. I can't wait to see it."

"Me either. My realtor said we'd be able to walk right out of the master bedroom onto the balcony and see the ocean. And it has two heated Jacuzzis. So whenever Kollin brings his friends, we can retire to our own private one."

Adam grabbed the jacket of Elijah's suit and pulled him close. "Now that sounds like my idea of a relaxing vacation. Maybe we can even sneak away and leave the kid here one weekend." Heedless of the people milling about on the steps, Elijah wrapped his arms around Adam's waist. Adam's heart speed up. He bit his bottom lip, trying to hold back his smile. "Mmm…. You know, in a couple years, Kollin will be away at college. We'll have plenty of alone time."

Elijah nuzzled Adam's neck. "Yeah. But we'll probably have one or two more by then."

Adam closed his eyes and saw his life unfold before him. Two more kids wreaking havoc around their house. But not babies—everyone wanted babies. They'd adopt older children who were starting to think their chance was over. And just as Elijah and Kollin and Mr. Sanderson and everyone else in his family had restored his faith in a life full of promise and love, Adam and Elijah would love that child and resurrect his or her hope.

He knew he shouldn't care about gender, but one of them had to be a girl. He couldn't wait to see Elijah dote all over their daughter. He'd buy her the world and scare away anyone who tried to touch her, double standard be damned. He could see Kollin, head bent close to his younger brother, whispering secrets to help get him through the first few nights in a new place. His heart practically burst with love.

Adam grabbed Elijah and cradled his face in his hands. As his lips met Elijah's, he poured the dream into the kiss. Elijah sighed and returned the gesture with the same fervency Adam gave him.

KOLLIN LOOKED up from his homework when he heard the tap on the door. Eli and Adam hovered in the doorway. Adam had the anxious forehead crinkle that appeared every time something bad happened. Kollin groaned under his breath as he saved his work and turned around.

"What happened now?" They'd just spent the best family vacation ever in Eli's new house at the beach, and he wasn't ready to ruin that high with whatever bad shit they were about to lay on him. Uncharacteristically Adam seemed more nervous than Eli.

"Nothing bad," Eli assured him. "You got a second?"

"If nothing bad happened, then why does Adam look like he's gonna vom any minute?"

Elijah cut his eyes toward Adam and sneered at him. Kollin grinned. Guess it wasn't too bad, after all.

"I wanted to talk to you about something," Adam said as he sat on the bed.

"Okaaaay." Kollin drew the word out when Adam didn't continue, and he saw Eli bump Adam's knee with his own.

"Right. I've been talking with Elijah and my therapist for a couple of weeks about an idea I have, and I'm ready to run it by you," Adam said. "I hope you already know this, but whatever I say next, I want your honest feedback on what you think is best for you. Please don't make any decisions because you think it's what I want or just to make me happy."

Kollin scrunched up his face but nodded for Adam to continue.

"We told you there was a glitch in the paperwork, and that's why Elijah's background check was delayed a couple of weeks. But that wasn't exactly the truth. We asked CPS to hold off for a bit. See, I heard you tell Cynthia that Elijah and I were your dads and that we're adopting you. I was so damn happy to hear you say those words, and they confirmed something I'd been feeling since I came back from my little mental vacation." Adam took a deep breath and looked Kollin directly in the eye. "If, and only if, it's something you want too, I'd be honored to formally adopt you with Elijah—to officially and legally be your dad."

Kollin's eyes widened. "But what about the rest of the kids at the center?"

Adam winced, and Kollin's heart sank, fearful he'd just kiboshed the entire plan by blurting out the first thing that popped into his head.

"Honestly right now I can't figure out why I was more worried about them than you in the first place," Adam said. "Of course I wish I could help every single one as much as we're helping you. But that's not how it worked out, and I wouldn't change what we have here for anything. I've told you all along that you come first, but my actions never matched my words. If this is what's best for you—if me signing that piece of paper makes your life any easier or less stressful or proves I love you more than my not signing it—then that's what I want to do. I'll deal with the rest of it."

More than anything, Kollin wanted to jump at Adam's offer, but he couldn't help the heavy weight surrounding his heart. "Do you want to do this because it's best for me, or because it's what you want to do?"

"Both." Adam answered so quickly and with so much conviction that Kollin believed him. "This is what I want for me. I wouldn't have brought it up if that weren't the case, but nothing changes as far as how I feel if you don't want to do this."

Kollin closed his eyes as he felt the tears mounting. The thought of having two real parents again—two parents who understood him and would go to bat for him time after time—was overwhelming. "Are you sure you don't want to do this just because you feel guilty?"

Adam slid off the bed to kneel at Kollin's feet. "Completely. I waited to talk to you until I hashed through all of those feelings with my therapist. The mess with Jessica might have given me the kick in the ass I needed to see what I wanted, but that's it. I want this, Kollin, because the idea of being your parent makes me feel complete."

Kollin clenched his fists in a pitiful effort to control his emotions. He nodded, unable to speak. He hoped Adam understood.

"I don't expect an answer right now. Take all the time you need to think about it, or maybe talk to Riley." Adam shook Kollin's knee. "I know this is a big decision."

Kollin choked back a sob and shook his head. He was frustrated he couldn't find the right words to tell Adam. But he knew that no matter what he said, they wouldn't be enough to convey how he felt. Besides, after weeks of daily phone calls and texts, he hadn't heard from Riley in over a week and a half. Apparently his second semester of college was going much better than his first. Well enough he'd dropped Kollin like a bad habit, anyway.

His voice wavering, Kollin said, "I don't need time. I'd love for both of you to be my real dads." Kollin broke down and cried into his hands. Adam and Eli comforted him, wrapping their arms around him while Kollin laughed through his tears. "I don't even know why I'm crying this time. This is a good thing. Like the best thing."

"Yeah," Eli said. "The very best thing, but also a very big thing. Cry all you want."

Kollin thought back to the day he heard the court declare his parents guilty of child abuse—of physically harming him. He sat on the bench, grappling with the guilt of being responsible for sending his parents to jail. Though he loved Eli and Adam even back then, he felt desolate and alone, like an orphan. This time, though their position was a mirror image, Kollin couldn't have felt more loved or more at home. His blood family may have abandoned him, but the family that found him was pretty damn epic.

Chapter 20

ADAM SMOOTHED down the flap of Elijah's jacket where the whipping wind had flipped it over. Smiling up at his almost-husband, he said, "You sure you want to hitch your horse to my wagon?"

Elijah frowned and ran his left thumb over the inside of his ring finger. "I think it's too late to back out, even if I wanted to."

Adam bit back a laugh. "You know that's like the smallest tattoo in the world, right?"

"Shut up," Elijah groused. "It's on a sensitive spot."

"Keep telling yourself that."

"What do you know? You're clearly a masochist, covering yourself in these things."

"Maybe my threshold for pain is just higher than yours. Ever think of that?"

Elijah grumbled, and Adam grabbed his hips and tugged their bodies together.

"I really appreciate the gesture," Adam said. "No one's ever tattooed my name on himself before."

"In case you've forgotten, that's still the case."

Adam nuzzled his nose into Elijah's neck and tasted the salty sea air on his skin. "As good as. Everyone who sees it will know the A stands for me. Stop beating yourself up over it."

"I played rugby, for fuck's sake. I should be able to handle four letters." Elijah sank into Adam's embrace and wrapped his arms around Adam's back as he pouted.

"You wanna go back and let them finish it?"

Elijah froze. "Fuck no. I'm not letting that demon needle near my skin again."

Adam ran the tip of his tongue along Elijah's collar. "Then stop—" He kissed the tender spot on Elijah's neck. "—griping about it." Punctuating his point, Adam dug his teeth into Elijah's flesh.

Elijah jumped back and huffed. "Fine. Besides, I think the real question is, are you sure you want to hitch your wagon to *my* sissy ass?"

Adam forced back his smile, cupped the sides of Elijah's face, and looked deeply into his eyes. "I think we both know how I feel about your ass by now."

Elijah's lips broke into a beautiful smile that lit up his face. His laughter could probably be heard over the crashing waves down by the shore, where the rest of their family waited for them.

"I think we do too," he said softly, and leaned in to kiss Adam.

"Aren't y'all supposed to wait until after for that?" Kollin shouted as he walked toward them.

"I'm pretty sure that's just a rumor," Adam said. "Is everyone ready?"

Kollin nodded. "Just waiting on you two."

Adam grabbed Elijah's hand. "Let's do this, then."

Kollin turned and waved to Kirsten, who was standing on the beach. He waited until she waved back. When Kollin's adoption finalized, Adam tentatively mentioned marriage to Elijah. Relief coursed through him when Elijah immediately pounced on the idea. He suggested a small ceremony that mishmashed the most meaningful parts of the traditional wedding ceremony. He wanted to have it outside their new beach home—immediate family only. They planned a reception later on and invited everyone from the center and Elijah's work colleagues. Elijah wanted to marry as soon as possible, and the best way to do that was to keep the whole thing simple and short.

Kirsten became a bona fide, ordained-over-the-Internet minister just for the event. She stood in front of her parents, Elijah's parents, and Derek while she waited for the three of them to walk down the beach. Kollin walked between Adam and Elijah and fell a step behind when they reached Kirsten. He didn't want to give either of them away, but they refused to leave him out of the ceremony.

Kirsten's smile could've cracked her face open, and tears were already pooling in her eyes.

"Hi," she whispered.

Adam laughed. "Hey, Kris."

"Would it be totally inappropriate of me to hug you before we start this?" she asked.

"Yes," Elijah hissed while keeping a smile on his face. "Can you please get on with it, woman?"

Trying to look angry but failing miserably, Kirsten stuck her tongue out at him and then smiled primly.

"Adam and Elijah asked us to be here today to help celebrate their marriage. I want to thank them before I start. This may be my first wedding, but I know I could perform a million more, and none will ever hold more significance to me than theirs. I love all three of you more than I could ever say, and it's an honor and a privilege to stand up here with you today."

"Aw, geez," Elijah muttered. "Give him a hug already."

Kirsten gave Elijah a grateful look and threw one arm around Adam's neck. "I'm so happy for you," she whispered. Adam didn't even have a chance to hug her back before she stepped away again. "Now let's get you two married."

"Yes, please," Elijah said.

"Adam and Elijah have written their own vows. Go ahead, Elijah."

Elijah grabbed Adam's hand and ran his thumb back and forth over Adam's fingertips while he spoke. "I didn't know how much I was missing from life until I met you and Kollin. I still can't pinpoint what it is about you that ties my heart so tightly to yours, but I feel it binding me closer to you every day. You saved me from a life of solitude and loneliness by being insufferably stubborn, kind, and compassionate, all at the same time. Simply by being Adam, you reminded me how to love with an open heart. I vow to always try my best to be worthy of your love. I vow to work hard in our life and our marriage. To provide the best life possible for us and our children. And I vow to love you first. Always."

Adam squeezed Elijah's hands, grinning through the overwhelming urge to tackle hug him. "Adam?" Kirsten said, prompting him to start.

"Elijah, there's no one else on this earth who sees me quite like you do, who sees the very best in me all the time… things I don't even see in myself. Your patience and confidence in me are overwhelming, and I vow to always be worthy of that. I vow to give you the absolute best version of myself and to always remain open to you, to let you see all of me, even the dark and ugly things I want to hide from the world. I vow to love you first. Completely and forever."

"Kollin asked me if he could say a few words, as well," Kirsten said. "Go ahead, Koll."

His cheeks flushed, Kollin looked over both of his shoulders, first at Adam's family and then at Elijah's parents, and then turned back to the two of them.

"Yeah. I'm not quite as mushy or proper as you guys, and I know this day isn't really about me, but I wanted to tell you how happy I am for you two. As your kid it's awesome to see you doing something that makes you so happy, and as a gay kid, well…." Kollin ran a hand down his face. "Not that I'm ready to think about marriage or anything, but knowing it's a possibility and seeing it happen in real life are two different things. It's pretty cool. So, yeah. I vow to try not to be a pain in the ass all of the time. That's it. Congrats."

Almost as one, Adam and Elijah pulled Kollin into a three-way hug. When they separated, Kirsten held out identical rings in the palm of her hand, and they each took one.

"The wedding ring is an outward symbol of Adam and Elijah's love for one another and serves to remind them of the vows they've just taken. I pray the Lord blesses these rings and the men who wear them. May they live in unity and love with one another until their dying day. Amen."

Elijah grabbed Adam's hand and slid the ring on his fourth finger, covering the small tattoo of Elijah's name. "With all that I have and all that I am, I honor you."

The band felt heavy and unfamiliar on Adam's finger. It made him smile. He fumbled with Elijah's ring until he eventually slid it onto Elijah's finger. He thought his smile would split in two when he covered the small A and repeated the same words Elijah had just spoken.

"That's it, guys. I'm over-the-moon excited to pronounce you two married. You may now share your first kiss as husbands."

Elijah tugged Adam closer. Whispering so quietly Adam didn't think Kirsten could've even heard him, Elijah said, "I love you, husband," and gently kissed Adam's lips. Adam held tight and kissed him again, harder, and then pulled away. He grabbed Kollin and tugged him into another hug. Adam felt Kirsten wrap her arms around them, and moments later the rest of their family had joined the group hug.

The moment felt… complete, and for once, instead of questioning why he deserved people who cared about him so fully, Adam reveled in their love and support and silently vowed to never again abuse their confidence in him.

"So," Kollin said, his voice muffled from the center of the pile, "who's ready for cake?"

Stay tuned for an excerpt from

Redeeming Hope

Home for Hope: Book One

By Shell Taylor

Fifteen years ago Elijah Langley's world came to an abrupt halt with the death of his high school boyfriend. He keeps his past—and his sexual orientation—hidden until he attends a fundraiser for The Center for HOPE, an LGBT youth center, where he meets Adam Lancaster, HOPE's infuriatingly stubborn and sexy founder.

A survivor of a turbulent childhood, Adam understands better than most the challenges his youth face. He's drawn to Elijah's baby blues and devilish smile but refuses to compromise his values and climb back into the closet for anyone—not even the man showering time and money on HOPE. Months of constant flirting wear down Adam's resolve until he surrenders to his desires, but Elijah can't shake his demons.

When a youth from the center is brutally assaulted, Elijah must find a way to confront the fears and memories that are starting to ruin his life, so he can stand strong for those he loves.

Prologue

ELI CLUTCHED the glossy eight-by-ten as tears welled in his eyes. He could hardly believe the emaciated, washed-out figure in the picture was the same person he'd centered his entire world around just a few weeks earlier. Eli would recognize that face anywhere. God knows, he'd spent enough time staring at it—running his fingers over those soft lips, sucking on the kidney-shaped birthmark just below the ear. He never imagined he'd see those eyes so lifeless.

"It's him," Eli whispered, dropping the picture on the officer's desk.

His mother rested a hand on his shoulder. "E.J.—"

"Don't pretend to care, now that he's dead." Eli shrugged out of her grasp and clenched his jaw to hold in the gut-wrenching sobs brewing in his chest. "Will I need to identify the body in person too?"

The officer avoided Eli's eyes, but his voice was kind. "If you're certain, this is good enough for us. He'll be released in the next thirty-six hours. Will you be claiming him, or will the city keep him?"

Eli's eyes widened, and panic ripped through his heart. He'd never expected the search to end with a dead body, and there was no way he'd be able to give his boyfriend the funeral he deserved—the one Eli owed him for his own part in Brian's death. Prepared to beg, he turned and met his father's eyes for the first time since Brian disappeared from their house almost three weeks earlier.

"We'll take care of his arrangements." Eli's mother spoke quietly but firmly, and his father dipped his chin in silent agreement.

Relief carried Eli back to his parents' car, but grief consumed him as soon as he slid into the back seat. Burying his head in his knees, he shut out the rest of the world. Eli didn't leave the quiet safety of the car until long after he arrived home, his cheeks crusted with salty tears from mourning the loss of the future he'd been so sure of.

CHAPTER 1

SOMETIMES LIFE just sucked.

There was no rhyme or reason for why good things happened to bad people—or why bad things happened to good people, for that matter. Karma was nothing more than a myth, made up to trick everyone into doing good deeds. Life consisted of a random series of events that would inevitably occur whether you were generous enough to hold doors open for complete strangers or selfish enough to jam the Close elevator button when your boss came running around the corner.

But on days like this, Elijah couldn't help but wonder what the fuck he'd done to deserve the shitfest that had been dumped on him.

It started on his morning commute when the moron in front of him slammed on the brakes to avoid hitting a squirrel—a fucking *squirrel*—forcing Elijah to swerve off the road and spill hot coffee all over his Dior slacks. Fortunately Elijah kept a spare suit in his office, but as soon as he sat down at his desk, he was assaulted with a list of ten "friendly" reminders from the "former but not quite ready to give it up" CEO of Langley Lumber and Construction—also known as his father. Then the head of his accounting department—the man he'd been training to officially take over the role of CFO so Elijah could cease wearing both hats—put in his two weeks' notice.

When a conference call ran over, Elijah missed lunch. By the time some environmentalist freak who didn't think Langley Lumber was doing enough to save the planet showed up in his reception area, he wasn't even surprised that she'd demanded an audience with "whoever's in charge."

Elijah was tired. His nerves were shot, and for the first time in… well, ever… he wanted to cut out of work early, go home, and do absolutely nothing. But it was Wednesday, which meant dinner with his parents, and they always ended the same way—a lecture from his father about everything Elijah needed to do for the business and apologetic looks from his mother while she sipped her wine.

Shoving the cuff of his shirt back to check the time, Elijah saw he still had twenty minutes before his next appointment, and he needed a break to survive his last meeting as much as he needed a quick bite to eat. Shrugging on his suit jacket, he walked down the short hall to reception.

Elijah rapped one finger on his secretary's desk. "Sherri, I'm heading to Etman's to get a sandwich. I should be back in time for the four-thirty meeting. If I'm not, tell them to start without me."

Oblivious to his sour mood, Sherri offered her tight, patented almost-smile and nodded.

Elijah dipped his chin once, a habit he'd only grudgingly acquired from his father, and started toward the door. He stopped in his tracks when the front doors opened and laughter ushered two strangers inside. A young woman, maybe midtwenties, with a pretty, oval face and choppy, shoulder-length blondish-brown hair nudged the kid beside her as if reprimanding him for whatever he'd just said. When she turned her smile toward Elijah, her entire face lit up, making her even prettier than Elijah had first thought. But once he got a good look at the kid beside her, she could've been J. Lo and Elijah wouldn't have noticed. The kid's hair was different—darker, shorter, and artfully swept to the side—but Elijah would have sworn he was staring at a younger version of the guy he once thought he'd spend his life with.

"Hi," the woman chirped to Sherri. "I'm Kirsten and this is Kollin. We're making rounds in the neighborhood, dropping off some information about The Center for HOPE. It's the LGBT center over on Leftwich. HOPE stands for Healing, Opportunity, Protection, and Equality, and we're committed to providing a safe place for queer youth to feel accepted and help prepare them for their futures. We're having a fundraiser in a few weeks to purchase the old Tarboro Inn just down the street from us. We thought it would also be a great opportunity to bring awareness to the community about what HOPE is and what we do."

She spoke quickly, but Elijah didn't get the impression it was out of nervousness. He couldn't say for sure. His eyes stayed glued on the boy she introduced as Kollin.

Kollin shrugged off his book bag and pulled out several information pamphlets. He handed one to Sherri and then turned to Elijah and gave him a curious once-over.

"Nice suit. Dior?"

Elijah nodded once and offered a rare, small smile. "Impressive."

Kollin raised his shoulder and gestured toward his own outfit—burnt orange pants, a white hippie shirt, and black suspenders he somehow managed to make look good. "I'm into fashion."

"Ah, I see that," Elijah replied.

He held out another pamphlet. "You want one of these too?"

Elijah took the paper and glanced at the front page. "You look a little young to work for a place like this."

"I'm just helping Kirsten out today. She can't go anywhere by herself apparently." Kollin raised his voice enough to catch Kirsten's attention, making her hip-check him in the middle of her conversation with Sherri but not slowing her down at all. "But I'm also one of the impressionable young minds who benefits from everything HOPE has to offer." He rolled his eyes, but the warmth of his smile told Elijah the kid was grateful for the center.

"You are, huh?" Elijah waved the pamphlet around. "So, what's the plan for the Tarboro Inn?"

"Adam wants to renovate all the rooms and set up some kind of system so homeless youth can have a safe place to stay. He wants to help them find work and all that. Give 'em a chance to get back on their feet."

Elijah nodded, once again impressed. What Kollin described was no small undertaking, but if successful… well, his life would've been a lot different if something like that had been around seventeen years earlier. He had no business asking something so personal, but as he glanced back at Kollin's too-familiar face, he couldn't help himself. "And will you be needing the inn?"

Flashing him a bright smile, Kollin shook his head. When he spoke, the sarcastic lilt was back in his voice. "My parents tolerate me well enough, as long as I don't wear the suspenders in the house."

Elijah huffed out a laugh.

"Ready, kiddo?" Kirsten asked, grabbing the back of his shirt.

"Yes, ma'am. Nice meeting you, sir."

Elijah shook Kollin's hand and thanked him, purposely not introducing himself. Even if Kollin hadn't reminded him of Brian, Elijah would have found him to be a breath of fresh air—once he got over the initial shock of staring his past in the face, that is. Kollin was comfortable in his own skin and didn't seem to give two shits what anyone else thought of him. Elijah didn't want the kid to know he'd just made one of the most influential men in Cary nearly speechless.

"Mr. Langley, sir?" Sherri stared at him, a questioning look on her face as Kollin and Kirsten left his building. "Would you like me to run down to Etman's and get you that sandwich? Your meeting starts soon."

Elijah's gaze strayed to the clock on the wall. He'd spent over half of his break talking to Kollin. "No thank you. I'll find something in my office."

Elijah tapped the pamphlet on Sherri's desk and went back to his office to review its contents. He showed up at his final meeting of the day almost ten minutes late and still hungry.

IF ELIJAH'S parents noticed how distracted he was at dinner that night, they didn't mention it. They also didn't question why he wanted to go through his old room when he excused himself after dinner. His parents had redecorated immediately after he moved out of the house, so it looked nothing like the room he'd grown up in. He found the box he was looking for shoved into the very back corner of his old closet, and briefly considered grabbing the other two as well, but he childishly decided he liked the idea of inconveniencing his parents.

Elijah placed a kiss on his mother's cheek and assured his father he'd prepared for the quarterly board meeting the following day. He dropped the box in the passenger seat of his Lexus and spent the short drive home wondering what in the hell he was doing. He'd quickly learned that the only way to move past Brian's death was to pretend he'd never existed. It had been over fifteen years since Elijah locked his past away in his childhood bedroom closet and metaphorically thrown away the key. He knew leaving his past in the past was the smartest thing he could do, but he couldn't stop himself from plowing forward when he had that old box within arm's reach.

At home, Elijah poured himself two fingers of scotch from his fully stocked bar and stared at the black and red Air Jordan shoebox on his coffee table. He took a healthy swig of his drink, topped it off again, and sank into the couch. Steepling his fingers, Elijah eyed the top warily and wondered what fresh hell awaited him. As he gently removed the lid, he immediately regretted his decision to take a trip down memory lane.

Staring up at him was the seventeen-year-old version of himself. His smile was huge, and he had a basketball tucked under one arm, but all Elijah could see was the boy tucked under his other arm. Instead of looking at the camera, Brian was grinning up at Elijah, the smile on his face betraying how utterly smitten he'd been. Elijah had always loved that picture. While he'd never considered himself closeted—more like careful—that particular picture told the truth about what he and Brian really were to one another.

The alcohol in Elijah's stomach swirled around, and he shoved the top back on the box, unable to look into those trusting blue eyes any longer. He pushed it farther away, stood, and ran his hands through his hair. What the fuck was he thinking when he grabbed that box? He hadn't been able to deal with Brian's death when he was seventeen, and he sure as hell hadn't done anything since to change that.

Clearly time didn't heal all wounds.

Elijah stripped off his suit as he climbed the stairs to his bedroom and carelessly tossed the discarded clothes into a pile outside his closet door. Kollin's flippant comment about his parents merely tolerating him popped into his mind. Elijah didn't know the kid from Joe Blow on the street, but he couldn't help wondering how much truth lurked behind his facetious words. His heart twisted at the thought of Kollin ending up like Brian. Had anything improved? Were there more places like The Center for HOPE? Was it easier to be a gay teenager today than it was fifteen years before? Elijah had no idea, but he was damn sure going to find out.